# Out of Body Universe

Martin Chu Shui

Out of Body Universe

Copyright © 2016 Martin Chu Shui

Author: Chu Shui, Martin, 1962 –
Title: Out of Body Universe
ISBN:  9798696056067

# Chapter 1

"What's his name?"

"Nathan, Nathan Jenkins."

"Are you sure he's an OBU virgin?"

"Yes, he is."

"Okay, keep a close eye on him. Let's hope he is the one the prophecy predicted; if he is, we hope to finish this soon."

"Let's hope so."

\*\*\*

Nathan sat there alone, pretending to watch the girls' show, but his attention was really on the guy that he thought was a girl, a very attractive one that he just couldn't get his mind off. Nathan was sure that he had seen her real face, together with all the people around her; surely if he did it once, he should be able to do it again. Nathan concentrated and focused his mind's eye once more but saw nothing different when he opened his eyes. Anyway, he kept watching her, and he noticed that she was glancing at him as well; each time Nathan looked at her, she quickly moved her gaze somewhere else. It intrigued him: why would a girl, disguised in a man's mask, be interested in him, a stranger? Nathan really wanted to confirm that he had seen that she wore a guy's mask; otherwise, he would have a series problem on his hands.

A group of around six young men walked into the bar, talking loudly, and headed towards the girl's table; there was nothing unusual in such a group moving in and out of bars, but the unusual thing was that Nathan could sense their hostility; he somehow knew that they were going to hurt or kill someone. He had no idea how he could know such a thing, but looking at their bulging

1

clothes, he guessed they had weapons concealed underneath.

Soon the girl and her group also noticed the upcoming group; from their reaction, Nathan immediately realized something was going to happen and sure enough, at the same time as the newcomers withdrew their concealed weapons, the girl and her friends also jumped to their feet, lifting up their chairs and bottles; a mass fight was about to burst out in the crowded bar.

The people sitting near the girl's table were screaming and trying desperately to get away. The sounds of shouting, screaming, swearing, and glasses and bottles smashing filled the bar. Nathan never took his eyes off the girl who was in the centre of the struggle. It was apparent that the girl and her mates knew how to fight, but their enemies were better trained and equipped, armed with knives, daggers and short swords. Before long the girl and her friends were all sporting stab wounds or slashes, and there was blood everywhere; it would not be long before they were all killed.

Nathan looked around and noticed the wall of people watching the fighting from a distance, but nobody was willing to get involved. The police were nowhere to be seen, although he had seen people ringing the authorities on their mobile phones, and they'd be too late to save the girl if they didn't turn up soon.

The girl was thrown to the ground not far from Nathan, and for a split second she looked up and her eyes met with his. He could see her plea for help in her piercing blue eyes; she was looking right at him, so there was absolutely no doubt. Nathan didn't know how he managed it and would not be able to figure it out afterwards, but in that moment, he launched into action.

It was almost like his body knew what to do without any assistance from his mind; one attacker leaped forward with his short sword out, trying to stab the girl, who was in the process of getting to her feet. Nathan's arm flashed out, gripping the attacker's wrist, and he pulled, twisting the man's arm; from the pained scream coming out of the attacker's mouth, Nathan was confident that he had just dislocated the attacker's shoulder, elbow and wrist joints, but he had never done that move before and hadn't known how to do it. He heard a sound burst out of his own mouth: "Tai!"

Nathan's body lurched forward at high speed; he twisted his body, just in time to allow the next dagger to miss him narrowly. Still in the turning motion, his elbow jutted out, cracking the guy's rib cage. He lowered his body, landing gracefully on the floor, and kicked at the next attacker; the unmistakeable sound of bones cracking indicated the attacker's leg would be out of action for a long time.

He almost felt like he was watching himself carry out all these amazing stunts, like an out of body experience. In less than sixty seconds, Nathan had beaten every one of the attackers to the ground, leaving them painfully screaming about broken bones and dislocated joints.

"Don't move! Put your hands over your head! Otherwise, we will shoot!"

Nathan looked up; a group of police officers arrived, and all of them had their guns pointed at him. Glancing around, he saw that the girl and her friends were nowhere to be seen. Nathan slowly put his hands up.

The police officers moved forward, handcuffing Nathan.

"Nathan, what happened?" Gary shouted. He walked towards Nathan, but a police officer pushed him back.

"This must be a mistake, Officer."

"Back off." The police officer put his gun up, forcing Gary to step backwards. And then Nathan was pushed out of the bar, into a police van, and driven away.

In no time at all the van pulled into a high walled yard, but Nathan wasn't surprised; he had to remind himself that this was still OBU. Wordlessly, he was dragged out of the van and pushed into the building, along a long corridor, and then into a room.

Nathan was forced into a metal chair, and his hands were cuffed behind his back; from the restriction he felt, Nathan assumed that the cuffs were attached to the chair as well. He tried to move the chair but realized that it was fixed to the concrete floor.

Without a word, the escorting police officers walked out of the room; with a clunk the heavy metal door closed, leaving Nathan inside the isolated, cold, and highly secure cell. He scanned the room and deduced that he was inside an interrogation room, where a few people would presumably be watching him from behind the large one-way glass window on the opposite wall.

Nathan could not believe what had happened in his life recently. As he stared vacantly at the glass window, his mind went back to only yesterday, according to his memory, but fifteen years ago according to everyone else.

\*\*\*

Nathan walked into the bakery and said nothing; he didn't even look at Amy. In the back room, he changed into his uniform in silence, and then came out and stood beside Amy behind the counter.

4

"What's the matter, Nathan?" Amy asked carefully.

Nathan stared outside, past the door, not focusing on any particular object. He didn't turn to look at Amy whilst speaking. "Sorry for being rude to you, Amy…Cathy sent me a text this morning saying she's breaking up with me…"

"What? Cathy broke up with you by text?" Amy realized her voice had risen and quickly apologized.

"Yeah, Cathy is very tech savvy, even with a breakup." Nathan laughed bitterly.

Amy thought for a while. "Nathan, did she give you any particular reason, if you don't mind me asking?"

Nathan turned around and looked at Amy's chubby face for the first time. "Well, this is the best part: Cathy said in the text that I am too polite and too gentle for her, so I've become boring; she wants to be treated rough, to be with a 'real' man. I never would have thought that being 'too gentle' would be the cause of our breakup."

Amy pushed a strand of her short brown hair away from her sparkling brown eyes, and then patted Nathan's arm. "Nathan, not every girl is like Cathy, and many like a gentle-mannered man, and that's why they are called gentlemen."

Nathan forced a bitter smile. "Thanks, Amy, I do appreciate it…"

He broke off as two guys rushed through the door.

"Hi, Amy." Dave turned to Nathan. "Is it true that Cathy broke up with you?"

"Yeah, but how did you find out about it so quickly?" asked Nathan.

Gary leaned his slender six-foot-two body against the counter to steady himself. "It's all over Facebook; everyone already knows about it."

Nathan nodded, but said nothing.

Dave glanced at Amy, and then turned to Nathan. "We all knew that Cathy has been online dating for a while, so it's not really a surprise to me."

"What? Did you all know she has been seeing other guys all this time? Why didn't you tell me? I thought you were my friends."

Gary shook his head, speaking slowly, his words accompanied by alcohol fumes from last night's party, and maybe some from this morning as well. "We didn't want to damage your relationship..." he started, but Dave interrupted him.

"Nathan, forget about Cathy; she's just another slut. You know what, tonight I'll take you to a party and introduce you to a few new girls. You know, there are plenty of lovely girls out there and it's time for you to get some fresh meat anyway..."

Nathan shook his head; he didn't know what to think, and all he wanted to do was get away, away from everyone.

"Amy, I can't stand it anymore...I have to get out of here." He turned to Dave and Gary.

"Get out of my way; I thought you were my friends." Without another word, he walked to the back room.

As he left, he heard Amy calling after him, "No problem, Nathan, leave everything to me, just go. I am so sorry about what happened to you today..."

## Chapter 2

Nathan tried to walk in a straight line. It was getting late, but the crowded streets were still packed. He couldn't remember the last time he was drunk. Cathy's face flashed in and out of his spinning brain, and he was unable to push the images of her pretty eyes out of his mind. His stomach felt hollow, despite the fact he had just filled it with vast quantities of alcohol.

Since entering the dating world when he was fifteen, he had experienced a few breakups with a few girls, but never like this. Cathy was his first serious relationship ever, and he had been with her since starting university two years ago. Everyone, including himself, believed that he and Cathy were a perfect match and completely happy. Hundreds and thousands of questions kept popping up in his not very clear head. Why would she do this to him? Why…

Turning around the street corner, Nathan saw an unusually dressed man sitting beside his board game. During the last week while passing by, Nathan had seen him lay the board game out in the same spot each day. He was dressed in a long blue robe, a bit strange in the hot weather, and his long hair was tied up in a ponytail at the back of his head. Beside him, there was a note, written in both Chinese and English: it only cost ten dollars to play, and the prize was one thousand dollars if anyone beat him at the game; the challenger could choose to play with either the black or white pieces.

As the Taoist was about to pack the game board up, Nathan croaked, "Wait a moment, Taoist Master…I want to challenge you."

"Oh, I see." The Taoist looked at Nathan in a calm manner for a second. "It is very late; why don't you come back tomorrow?"

"I don't want to come back tomorrow; here is my money." Nathan took out a twenty-dollar note.

"I don't think it's fair to play the game with you tonight." the Taoist refused to accept Nathan's money.

Nathan shook the bill in the Taoist's face. "Are you afraid of me? You know I will beat you at your own game. We have to play tonight, right here."

"What's your name?"

"Nathan; my name is Nathan."

"Okay, Nathan, I will play with you, but not here. If you really want to play, you'll have to come with me to my place."

"That sounds okay to me," Nathan said in an even less clear voice.

"It's a long walk to my place. Are you sure you are up to it?"

"The further away from the city the better; please lead the way." Nathan staggered forward, following the Taoist and heading away from the city.

Nathan tried to walk in a straight line as he followed the Taoist; they had been walking for a very long time. They were basically following the waterfront, passing each bay. Occasionally looking back over his shoulder, Nathan could still see the Opera House and the Harbour Bridge, but his surroundings were very unfamiliar; he couldn't remember there being so many bushes and so much forestry close to the Rocks area, but his spinning head didn't let him focus too much at the moment.

Nathan had lost track of time; they could have walked for an hour, even three hours. He didn't really care and felt quite relieved to be this far away from his life, leaving the mess behind.

Finally, they stopped in front of a straw-roofed hut among the thick forest. Nathan didn't even question that there was no forest within walking distance of Sydney's city centre. The Taoist opened the simple wooden door, used a match to light a couple of candles, and then signalled Nathan to come in.

It was surprisingly spacious inside the humble hut, at least the size of a four-bedroom house. There were no internal walls or separate rooms; the whole interior was a large hall furnished with simple wooden tables and chairs. The Taoist put his bag down on the floor of packed clay and lit a log campfire in one corner of the hut. He hung a kettle over the fire and said,

"Nathan, I have to say it's a surprise to find a white kid like you who knows how to play Weiqi (Go in Chinese). How did you come across it?"

Nathan collapsed into a nearby chair. His legs were stiff and sore, as if he had been walking for weeks. After taking a deep breath, he said,

"I am studying ancient oriental philosophy at university and my major is Taoism, so it's not that peculiar for me to know something about Weiqi."

"Studying Taoism? Nathan, you surprise me even more. Why would a white kid like you choose to study Taoism?"

"Could you please stop the 'white kid' stuff; you should know that the majority of the students in my Taoism class are 'white kids'. The irony is that there is not a single Chinese student in the class."

The Taoist put two mugs on the table. "Would you like a cup of green tea? I should think you need it."

"Yes, please. Thanks."

After they settled down at the table with a cup of green tea each, the Taoist said slowly, "Nathan, you are right, nowadays, not many Chinese kids are interested in Taoism. It's the main reason why I am here, to find some non-Chinese persons who are seeking Tao, the way."

Nathan sipped a bit of the green tea. It helped to clear his mind.

"Master, are you telling me that you are seeking a student so you can teach him about Taoist magic?"

"Magic? There is no magic in Taoism. Is that what you have learnt in your classes?"

"Oh no, not in my classes, but I've read tales and legends about Taoist magic. You know, the stories about immortal Taoists, that kind of stuff."

"Glad to hear that. Nathan, tell me, what have you learnt about Taoism?"

Nathan put his mug down on the table. "Master, what's your name?"

The Taoist thought for a moment. "Wuwei. My name is Wuwei."

"Wuwei? Isn't that the fundamental Taoist principle of inaction, or doing nothing?" Nathan asked.

"Yes, it is, but Wuwei does not mean either inaction or doing nothing. It means following the natural laws, not fighting against them to find solutions; it means resolving conflicts without relying on violence; it means accepting people as what they are without judgment; it means accepting change as part of life. I could go on for the whole evening, but hopefully that will give you some idea as to what Wuwei is really about."

"Okay, Master Wuwei, I sort of know what you are talking about and I did learn something about Taoism. In

Tao Te Ching, Laozi (or the Old Master in English) said the greatest sages get things done effortlessly; is this the same thing you are talking about?"

"Yes, the greatest efforts seem effortless, but it would require ultimate knowledge and skill to make those efforts seemingly effortless; anyway, enough of that topic. Nathan, did you just break up with your girlfriend?"

"How could you tell?"

"Well, it's not that hard. The fact you were drunk was the first clue and I can tell it is an unusual event for you; you are not the type to be getting drunk regularly. Based on your age and your education, it's most likely related to relationship issues."

"Yes, my girlfriend texted me this morning to break up with me, because I am too gentle and too polite and she wants to be treated rough and wants to experience a 'real man'. What's wrong with this world?" Nathan tried very hard to control himself and not swear or use the worst words he could think of to describe Cathy.

"There is always something wrong or right about the world. Nathan, tell me what you think is wrong about this world."

"To start with, I believe I behaved like a real gentleman, but she wants to be treated rudely and roughly. Don't tell me you think there is nothing wrong with her."

Wuwei didn't respond immediately. He sipped his green tea and then said slowly, "Nathan, to be treated gently may not be what she wants, and there is nothing wrong about that. You can't judge her based on your own point of view."

"All right, let's talk about her being a slut." Nathan didn't feel guilty about using the word to describe Cathy now. "I have been faithful during our two-year-long relationship, but she slept with others behind my back, finding guys online."

"Nathan, to be faithful to her was your choice and you can't force her to do the same; she has the right to decide what she wants to do."

"Let's forget about my relationship problem and focus on her being a slut."

"Do you mean she's had sex with many men?"

"Yes. There is a reason that slut is a negative word. Women generally are more careful about choosing whom to have sex with, because they are genetically designed to ensure their offspring have the best genes; therefore, women don't normally sleep around. In other words, slutty behaviour is against her nature and that's why she is wrong."

"What you said may be the case, but there is nothing wrong with her behaviour if she doesn't want to have children."

"Okay, what about the risk of disease associated with sleeping around? She is abusing her body, don't tell me that's right."

"Nathan, she is an adult and has the right to use her body any way she wishes. Tell me if there is a huge difference between her using her body to sleep with others and you using your body to get drunk. From a Taoist point of view, there is nothing absolutely right or wrong."

"That is the concept I just can't grasp about Taoism. We all know that something must be right, and something must be wrong; you can't make that statement."

"Nathan, it's also common knowledge that one person's angel could be another's evil; one's terrorist

12

could be the other's freedom fighter. Right or wrong all depends on where you are standing. People regard others who don't agree with their views as enemies. For example, the reason you think your girlfriend is wrong is because you feel hurt that she broke up with you to sleep with others. It's wrong from your point of view but it's right for her to break up with you to avoid you getting hurt more."

Nathan was usually quite good at debating in classes, but not tonight; it had to be because of the alcohol he had consumed earlier. Nathan decided to change the angle.

"All right, let's talk about what's wrong with modern females. There are very few real women left in this world. The girls in the West are more and more like men; they don't know how to cook, sew, or retain any of those feminine skills and qualities; they swear, drink, smoke, and try to be equal to men in as many ways as possible. This is wrong."

Wuwei nodded at Nathan, smiling.

"Nathan, I don't want to debate with you about feminist movements, but all of your comments are from a man's point of view. A girl would say she really wants to meet a traditional man who knows how to hunt, fish, and build huts with his hands, who does not care to tell everyone about his feelings, and wants to drag a woman by her hair to his cave; so, from a girl's point of view, there are also very few real men left in the modern world. Nathan, the only thing that remains unchanged is change. We have to change ourselves to adapt to the changes."

"I don't want to discuss this anymore. Should we start the game?" Nathan decided to call off the debate. It was not his best day.

"Do you still want to play the game?"

## Chapter 3

After the green tea, Nathan found his head was much clearer. "Maybe another time. Master Wuwei, I've always fancied learning how to fight, the Kung Fu stuff, you know. Could you please teach me?"

Wuwei stared at Nathan for a second. "Is that all you white kids think about Chinese people; that everyone knows how to fight?"

"Oh, no, of course not, and I know much better than other 'white kids' because I actually know something about the Chinese. Master Wuwei, I know Taoists are generally good at Tai Chi; it's part of your meditation and training to gain Tao, so please teach me something about Tai Chi."

"If you have learnt anything about Taoism, you must know that Tai Chi is not designed to fight against others, but only as a meditation exercise."

"But I also heard that some kinds of Tai Chi can be used in combat, right?"

"Yes, some forms of Tai Chi can be used in combat, but it would take years of meditation to train one's mind, it's not a quick learning experience that can be done overnight."

Nathan knelt down the way a Chinese student saluting his master would; he had learnt the move through his studies. "Please, Master Wuwei, please just teach me something about combat Tai Chi, and I can practice it in my lifetime."

Wuwei thought for a while, and then said, "In that case, I would need to test to see if you have the talent to learn Tai Chi. Although everyone is able to learn Tai Chi, someone with natural ability would be able to learn it much faster; the key is your ability to understand Tao, the way. Okay, put your elbows on the table, and put your two palms facing each other at shoulder width."

Nathan did as instructed.

"Now imagine that your palms are two magnets, and they are attracted towards each other. Can you feel it?"

Nathan concentrated, imagining there was a magnet attached to the back of each of his hands; slowly he felt his palms moving towards each other, without him intentionally moving his muscles.

Wuwei smiled. "Okay, now imagine that the magnets are rejecting each other, and then alternate them between attracting and rejecting."

Nathan was amazed that his two palms were moving towards and away from each other, without his muscles controlling them at all.

After a while, Wuwei asked Nathan to stop. "That's a very simple exercise to give you an idea about meditation and mind control. Okay, let's start with the basic steps of a Tai Chi lesson."

In the following hours, Nathan couldn't remember how many, he learnt how to concentrate and use his mind, not his muscles, to move his body. Just as Nathan felt hungry, as if knowing his mind, Wuwei gave him some dry fruit to eat, with some rice wine to wash it down; after that, he felt neither thirsty nor hungry anymore.

Finally, Wuwei said, "That's enough for today. I am going to cook rice porridge; would you like some? I am quite hungry, and you must be too."

Just then, Nathan did feel a bit hungry. "All right, I will have some. Thanks."

Nathan watched Wuwei hang a pot over the log fire and put some rice and water into it. It wasn't long before the fragrant smell of rice porridge filled the air. Nathan felt very tired, hardly able to keep his eyes open and his head got lower and lower to the table…

"Nathan, wake up, the rice porridge is ready."

Nathan opened his eyes, and noticed the sunlight shining in through the windows. He must have been asleep for a long time. Feeling embarrassed, Nathan said, "Sorry for falling asleep." He glanced at his watch.

"Master Wuwei, I have to leave right now; otherwise, I'll be late for work. I do appreciate your hospitality, particularly teaching me about Tai Chi. Will I be able to meet you again?"

"Unfortunately, I am leaving this city today."

"Will you be back? Or will I ever see you again?"

"Nathan, I am not sure; but you have learnt the basics of Tai Chi meditation, so you can practice in your own time. If you're persistent with it, you will achieve something in the end."

"I will, and thanks again." Nathan put his left palm over his right fist, saluting Master Wuwei in Chinese Kung Fu fashion, and walked out of the hut.

Nathan walked through the bush, which consisted of a few trees. It surprised him what alcohol could do to one's mind; last night he thought he had walked through a forest. As he reached the edge of the bush, he realized that he was not far from the waterfront. A question slipped through his mind: how could Master Wuwei build a hut inside such a small patch of bush? But he didn't have time to think about it, because he needed to hurry to get back to the bakery in time.

Again, it wasn't that far from the city centre, quite different from his memory based on last night's experience; he remembered having walked for ages, but he had been drunk then so his memory wasn't very reliable. However, Nathan noticed one thing that was unusual: the Rocks area, which was normally crowded with thousands of local residents and overseas tourists around the famous Opera House and Harbor Bridge, was now like a ghost town. Apart from a few road-cleaning motor cars, and a few gardeners working, there was not a single tourist in sight. Nathan glanced around but couldn't figure out what had happened; however, he didn't waste too much time wondering about it, instead quickly walking towards the bakery.

It was Sunday morning, normally the busiest time for the bakery, but there were no customers and the girl behind the counter was not Amy.

"Excuse me, you must be new. Where is Amy?" Nathan asked.

"I am not that new; I've worked here almost a year now. Who is Amy?" the girl said.

Nathan stepped back a few steps to double check the shop front, making sure he had arrived at the right place. He was afraid the alcohol had affected his mind. It was Croissant Classic, the bakery he had been working in for over two years. After confirming that he had come to the correct place, Nathan said, "I am Nathan and I have been working here for the last two years, how come I haven't ever seen you?"

"Nathan? Hang on, don't tell me you are *the* Nathan."

"*The* Nathan? What are you talking about?"

The girl stared at Nathan intensely for a few seconds, and then said,

"The first day I started working here, I was told about a guy called Nathan, who used to work here but he just disappeared one day, and that was fifteen years ago. His body was never found. Everyone, including the police, believe he died; so, are you telling me you are Nathan, *the* Nathan, who worked here and disappeared fifteen years ago?"

"What are you talking about? I never disappeared; I was working here only yesterday." Then Nathan noticed the calendar hanging on the wall. The thick letters stated that the girl had told the truth: it was now the year 2028. Fifteen years had indeed passed since the last time he had worked here.

## Chapter 4

Nathan didn't know what to think. How was it possible? He even wondered if he was in a dream, or still suffering the residual effects from last night's alcohol consumption. Looking at the girl's suspicious expression, Nathan knew it was impossible to explain anything at the moment.

"Sorry, I think I made a mistake and came to the wrong address." Nathan quickly walked away but could still hear the girl's voice as if she was talking to herself. "He'd be lucky to still remember his own name."

Nathan almost ran the whole way to where he had stayed last night. Walking into the patch of bush, among the thin group of trees, he saw there was no hut; in fact there was nothing except a picnic table with two benches attached to it.

Did he hallucinate last night under the influence of alcohol? Did his mind trick him by inventing the Taoist character? Nathan sat on the bench for a while, thinking really hard; of course, nobody would believe his story.

After careful consideration, he decided it would be better to tell people that he'd had an accident and lost all of his memories about where he was during the last fifteen years. And it was almost close to the truth. With some more thought, Nathan decided to go home first. After being missing for so long, his parents must be worried about him.

Nathan took the buses back home. His SmartRider didn't work, naturally, so he paid for the bus ticket with cash. It was lucky the bus routes hadn't changed that much, but again it surprised him that there were so few people around. He couldn't wait to find out why, however he didn't ask the bus driver or any of his fellow passengers at the back of the bus, because he was still unsure about what had happened to him.

Looking through the bus windows, Nathan noticed another fact about the city: the streets looked much cleaner than he remembered. *It may be related to there being so few people around*, thought Nathan. The city landscape hadn't changed much; the old buildings he knew were still there and there wasn't really anything noticeably new. It was much the same as fifteen years ago.

Nathan pushed the doorbell and waited but got no response, so he walked past the side fence and went into the backyard through the side gate. The overgrown backyard, however, was different from his memory. His mother always kept the garden tidy. Walking through the overgrown weeds, Nathan saw his mother sitting at a table under the pergola, staring at the backyard motionlessly.

Her hair was totally white. She was an old mother and had given birth to Nathan when she was forty, so adding the missing fifteen years to her age, she should be in her mid-seventies by now, Nathan calculated. Looking at her fragile body and aged face, Nathan felt sorry for not visiting her more often before.

"Mom, how have you been?" Nathan spoke softly as he walked towards his mother.

As if she had been hit by lightning, his mother's body shook, and turned. "Nathan, is it really you? My Nathan has finally come home."

"Yes, it's me, Nathan." Nathan bent down and hugged his mother's thin and fragile body.

"Oh, it really is my Nathan." Tears filled her eyes as she clung onto Nathan tightly, as if he would disappear if she let him go. "Where have you been for so many years, Nathan?"

"Mom, it's hard to explain. I will tell you later. Where is Dad?"

"Nathan, we all believed you were dead; your father died five years ago…" his mother sobbed.

"What? Dad died?" Nathan couldn't believe his ears. He hadn't really had a good relationship with his father then; he thought he was a total idiot and said the most stupid things all the time, but now he was gone, Nathan felt like he really didn't know much about him at all.

"Nathan, have you had lunch yet? Would you like me to make you a sandwich?" His mother walked to the house.

"Yes, please, I am really hungry." Nathan sat on the high stool next to the kitchen bench, watching his mother making him a lettuce, tomato, cheese and ham sandwich, a super large one.

"Nathan, where have you been all these years? Why didn't you contact us at all?" His mother passed Nathan a large glass of milk.

"To be honest, I don't know myself," Nathan said in between bites of his sandwich. "I literally woke up this morning and found fifteen years has passed. I have no memory at all about where I was or what I did during all of that time." Nathan was telling the truth, but he would not mention the Taoist, because nobody would believe his story.

His mother looked concerned but at the same time so happy to see her son home. "Nathan, you could have had an accident and it may have caused your memory loss, but I am so glad you're now home safely."

"Me too, Mom, I am so glad I came home. I should have visited you more often before."

Nathan cleaned up after lunch and made a cup of tea for each of them. Sitting in the living room, Nathan asked, "Mom, how did Dad die?"

"Lung cancer, smoking too much for too long," Nathan's mother said.

"Did he suffer in the end?" asked Nathan.

"No, he didn't." His mother sipped her tea. "Five years ago, he went to see the doctor for something else and they discovered the cancer by chance. Nathan, he was so sad at losing you that he lost his will to live. He refused to have any treatments, and died a few months later…"

Nathan felt a heaviness in his chest; he hadn't got on well with his father since high school, and it had gotten worse in university, because his father wanted him to study medicine, but he had chosen to study philosophy, a subject that his father regarded as a useless degree. Nathan moved out soon after graduating from high school and had rarely visited his parents during the two years he had been in university, before his 'disappearance'.

Nathan's father was from one of the original settlements in Australia; despite working as a manual labourer his whole life, Nathan's father hadn't spoken a single swear word in front of Nathan and had also taught him to be gentle and respectful to women, because he and his mother (Nathan's grandmother) were badly abused by Nathan's alcoholic grandfather. Nathan's father really wanted Nathan to become a medical doctor; he spent his life savings putting Nathan through private school. Now for the first time, Nathan actually started to understand his father's feeling of disappointment when Nathan told his father that he didn't want to study medicine at university. Before today, Nathan only thought of him as an uneducated, unsophisticated, know-nothing idiot.

Nathan felt tears fill his eyes; he sobbed quietly. "I am so sorry for disappointing Dad…I should have studied medicine as he wished…"

His mother said, "Nathan, before your father died, he said to me that, if he could see you again, he would want to tell you that he was very proud of you for studying at one of the best universities in Australia; he wanted to tell you that he was happy whatever your choice was. So Nathan, please stop blaming yourself; your father had forgiven you. He loved you very much."

Nathan cooked dinner and also washed the dishes afterwards. His mother stared at him, full of happiness. Nathan did all of this because he still felt guilty.

"Nathan, will you stay with me for a while before you move out again?" his mother asked hopefully.

"Mom, yes, I will stay home for a while. I need to figure things out for myself before I can leave; are you sure it's all right to stay with you?"

"Nathan, this is your home, and I am your mother; of course, you can stay home as long as you wish."

Someone knocked on the front door. Nathan went and opened the door. Standing there were Dave and Gary.

"It really is you, Nathan," Dave shouted. He hugged Nathan. "We heard the news about someone turning up at the bakery, claiming to be Nathan, so I told Gary we needed to check it out."

"Hi, mate, where have you been all these years?" Gary patted Nathan's back.

Nathan didn't smell alcohol fumes on Gary's breath and that was new to him. Nathan told them the same story as he had told his mother about his lost memory.

"Man, that sucks." Dave thought for a moment. "Nathan, you haven't changed one bit, you've still got the look of a twenty-year-old second-year university student. How did you manage that?"

"It may have something to do with your lost memory." Gary offered his opinion.

Nathan looked at them both, and said, "You both look pretty good for thirty-five years old."

Dave patted his stomach. "Well, we are looking more and more like potatoes each day."

"Nathan, why don't you come and stay with us?" Gary asked.

"You guys are still sharing the same old house? I thought you must have got good jobs and be married by now," Nathan said.

"Oh, no. Who would bother to get married nowadays?" Dave glanced at Nathan's mother, and then spoke in a quieter voice. "Nathan, you have no idea what has happened in the last fifteen years. Come with us, and we will educate you about the new world."

"Thanks, mate, but I think I will stay home for a while before figuring out what to do with myself," Nathan said.

"All right, that's fine with us, but you should at least go out with us to celebrate your arrival home," Dave said.

"All right." Nathan turned to his mother. "Mom, I'm going to go out with Dave and Gary tonight; please don't wait up for me."

"Nathan, don't worry about me. Go and talk to your mates," his mother said happily.

## Chapter 5

Outside, the Sydney summer night was much cooler than it had been during the daytime.

"Where is your car?" asked Nathan.

"Car? Nobody drives cars anymore. I ordered us a taxi," Gary said. Then Nathan saw a taxi pull over and stop beside them.

"I noticed there are hardly any people on the streets, and no tourists at all. So, what happened?" Nathan asked after they got inside the taxi.

"It's because they are all in OBU," Dave said mysteriously.

"OBU? What is that?" asked Nathan.

Gary spoke over Dave. "Nathan, is it for real that you have never heard of OBU, O, B, U, OBU?"

Nathan shook his head firmly. "No, mate; never heard about it."

Gary looked at Dave and laughed. "In that case we will have a hell of a lot to tell you."

"And lots to show you." Dave spoke with enthusiasm.

"What's all this about?" Nathan felt more frustrated by the minute.

"Be patient, Nathan; when we get to our place, you will know."


The taxi stopped in front of a high-rise residential apartment building. Gary led the way through double glass doors, while nodding to the two-armed guards standing at each side. Nathan couldn't believe that Gary and Dave would live in a building that had armed security guards, but he didn't ask because everything would make sense to him soon enough, at least he hoped so.

They walked into a lift. Gary inserted a plastic card into the slot, and then pushed their floor number. Their apartment was on the thirty-third floor.

The heavy, framed security door on their apartment surprised Nathan again. Maybe this was the standard arrangement in the future, Nathan thought.

After everyone was inside the apartment, Gary made sure all the locks on the doors were latched, both inside and outside of the two-layer security doors.

"You guys seem really big on the security," said Nathan.

'You will know why soon," Dave said. "Anything to drink?"

"No drinking here; it's far better to drink in OBU," Gary said.

"What hell is this OBU?" asked Nathan. He couldn't wait any longer to find out.

"Sit here, make yourself comfortable; it'll be a long night." Gary sat on the sofa in the living area.

Nathan looked around; it was just like any other apartment he had been to fifteen years ago. But he did notice the heavy, framed security windows. Security seemed like the priority in the future; maybe the crime rates were very high.

"Nathan, have you ever heard about OBE, out of body experience?" asked Gary.

"Of course, I've heard about OBE." Nathan wondered where the conversation was going.

"Do you know exactly what OBE is?" Dave asked.

Nathan thought about it for a few seconds. "Isn't that when someone experiences their mind leaving their physical body, so they can see their own bodies from above or from a distance?"

"Yes, it is," Gary said. "People have been obsessed with OBE throughout history in all cultures and religions around the world. There were so many documents and reports about people's OBEs. Religious people thought they got calls from their gods; dying people thought they were flying to heaven; but in fact, OBE is quite simple in scientific terms."

"Come on, Gary, we don't have the whole night to go through these boring theories," Dave said.

Gary put his hand up to silence Dave, and then turned to Nathan. "It is very important for you to understand OBE. People may experience their mind or soul floating out of their bodies and watching themselves from somewhere else, but the truth is that it is just a trick of the mind."

"What do you mean?" asked Nathan.

"Well, your mind hasn't left your body and isn't watching you from outside of your body. It's your mind creating this illusion that, in an imaginary world in your mind, you are observing your own body from the ceiling or the corner of the room…" Gary said.

"Stop it, Gary; just let Nathan see it for himself." Dave went through one of the bedroom doors and came back with a helmet in his hand.

It looked almost like a normal construction site safety helmet to Nathan, except there was a socket at the back and an eye-shield at the front of it. Dave pulled out a cable from behind the sofa and plugged it into the socket on the helmet. He put the helmet on his own head and flapped the eye-shield up and down a few times. "After you flap the eye-shield down, you'll be in the Out of Body Universe, OBU, right away."

"But first make sure you are sitting comfortably; in fact, it's better to lie down on the carpet, because you don't want to find out that you have strained your muscles while you are away from your body." Gary watched as Nathan lay in a comfortable position.

"Here you go, enjoy the ride, my dear OBU virgin." Dave mounted the helmet on top of Nathan's head.

Apart from wearing the helmet, Nathan hadn't felt anything special until Dave flapped the eye-shield down and plunged him into complete darkness, until a tiny light appeared in the centre of his eyes. The light spot was enlarging fast, and soon flooded the room with bright light, so bright that Nathan had to put his hand in front of his eyes to shield the blinding light. Just as he was doing so, he saw his body lying right on the carpet beside the sofa, and he was watching himself from the corner of the room. Nathan turned around, scanning the room; he saw Dave and Gary standing where they were before his helmet was on.

"This is fantastic, guys. Look, I can see my own hands, legs, arms, everything; I am walking around outside of my body…" Nathan suddenly stopped talking; from Dave and Gary's blank expressions, they could neither see nor hear him at all, as if he was a ghost, but then Nathan heard Gary's voice.

"Nathan, Dave and I will join you right away."

Nathan knew that Gary was unable to see him because he was looking in the wrong direction while speaking to him. He saw Gary and Dave go into their bedrooms, and then come out with a helmet each. After dragging two more cables from behind the sofa and plugging them into their helmets, they both lay on the carpet beside Nathan, and then flapped their eye-shields closed.

In no time, Gary and Dave stood in front of Nathan.

"How is this possible?" Nathan rubbed his hands together. "I can feel my own hands touching each other; I can feel the cool air from the air-conditioner; I can feel my feet touching the carpet, while my body is lying right in front of me. Is this my soul that's left my own body?"

Gary walked over and sat on the sofa, right beside the three bodies that belonged to the three of them. "Come here and touch your own body."

The concept was just too strange for Nathan to contemplate; staring at his own body only a few inches away, Nathan couldn't believe that's where he had been residing for his whole life. At that exact moment, he suddenly understood people's belief in the separation of soul and body; for many religions, bodies are just temporary hosts for people's souls.

Nathan put his hand out slowly and poked at the cheek of his own face; he didn't feel anything himself, just like touching someone else's skin. The best and closest experience Nathan could come up with was when, after he had his tooth extracted, half of his face was under local anaesthetic, he had poked his face and couldn't feel anything, as if it was just a piece of rubber sticking to his face. That was exactly what he felt right now: the body in front of him, although he knew it belonged to him, was just like a corpse.

"I would have believed in heaven and hell if I'd had this experience without your explanations," Nathan said to Gary.

"Tell me about it," Dave said. "We were all astonished when entering OBU the first time."

"Nathan, the body you are in now is not your soul, but your self-projection; the image of you as you perceive yourself…" said Gary.

"Come on, Gary, I am getting bored with all this talking; let's take Nathan out and show him around OBU for real," said Dave.

Nathan walked towards the door, but Dave stopped him. "Where are you going, mate?"

"Aren't you going to show me around in OBU?" said Nathan.

"Yeah, but we are not going to walk through that door to OBU," said Gary. "I suppose you could if you really wanted to." Gary waved his arm and a large screen appeared in front of them. A transparent screen that hung in mid-air, displaying something like the Internet Nathan was familiar with, that's the best he could describe it.

Gary moved his hand and brought a few different screens up, like navigating the web, and then the globe of the world was floating in mid-air. "Nathan, where would you like to go?"

"Nathan wouldn't have any ideas; let's just go to Little Amsterdam," said Dave.

"Amsterdam? Are we going to visit the Netherlands?" asked Nathan.

"What's the big deal with visiting the Netherlands? It's OBU age, and we can go anywhere in the world, it's all just a click away," said Dave.

"Dave is not entirely correct; we are not going to Amsterdam, but 'Little Amsterdam'. In other words, we are not going to visit the real Netherlands," said Gary.

"I am confused; what's the difference between Amsterdam and this 'Little Amsterdam'?" asked Nathan.

"It's all to do with costs. You see, it'd cost a lot to maintain the giant databases and also refresh them regularly, so they are exactly like it is in the real world. As a result, we would have to pay quite a bit to visit the real Netherlands in OBU, but on the other hand, 'Little Amsterdam' is only a replica of the real Amsterdam, a snapshot of the city, and does not need the expensive refreshing and updating all the time; maybe twice a year, so it's much cheaper to visit there," said Gary.

"I see, like a theme park, rather than the real thing," said Nathan.

"Well, better than a theme park because it's a snapshot of the real thing, just not updated as regularly as the real city in OBU," said Dave. "But who cares about the city; it's the people we are going there for."

"Okay, it's fine with me; I am happy to go wherever you guys want to go," said Nathan.

"Before we go, you had better put this mask on." Gary took a mask from his jeans pocket. It was a skin-coloured face mask. "Quite simple, you just put it over your face and it's done."

Nathan watched Dave as he also took a mask out of his pocket and put it on his face; in the blink of an eye, not only had Dave's face changed to a much younger and more handsome face, but also his body. The large midriff was gone and replaced with a well –developed, muscular, athletic body. He was now wearing a black suit like secret agent James Bond; it must have been Dave's secret inner desire, being an ultra-sexy, famous spy. Turning around, Gary was now a longhaired hippie with tattoos and sunglasses; maybe a rock star from the last fifteen years Nathan had no idea about.

Nathan put his own mask on. He didn't feel anything on his face, as if the mask had melted into his skin; he quickly went to the large mirror in the living room that must have been put there for this exact purpose. In the mirror, Nathan saw a stranger staring back at him: a blond beach surfer boy. It seemed the mask had left his body untouched, only changed his face and hair colour.

"Well, a spy, a rock star and a surfer boy. Let's go and have some real fun." Gary spun the floating globe in mid-air, zooming in on Amsterdam, and then touched the dot of the city gently. Like switching scenes in a movie, Nathan found he was no longer in the high-security apartment in Sydney. Now he stood in a large field, like a giant car park, except there were no cars, only countless shiny metal poles as far as Nathan's eyes were able to see, sticking out of the ground like a forest.

"Where is this place?" asked Nathan.

"It's nowhere; just like the place you go before you get to heaven or hell," Gary chuckled.

"It's the entry point, like in the olden days when you had to log in for the paid websites." Dave put his left wrist close to the metal pole. A green light beam came out and scanned his wrist. Before Nathan could blink Dave had disappeared from their sight.

Nathan turned, looking at Gary who said, "All masks have their own unique ID, and you load money into its account, and then you can spend it in OBU, including the entry fee."

"Like the multi-riders for the bus, or rail passes for the train," said Nathan.

"Yes, just like the passes, mate." Gary was about to put his wrist against a pole, but Nathan stopped him.

"One last question: why are there so many poles for only three of us to log in?"

"Well, it's the privacy law requirement. Because we could randomly log in from any of these poles, it's impossible for anyone to trace our login origin. See you there." Gary also disappeared.

Nathan stared at his own wrist; there was nothing on his skin as far as he could see, so there must be some invisible barcode or imbedded chip of some sort. Anyway, he decided there was not much point wondering about it at the moment, so he put his wrist against a pole next to him; the transition was similar to how he had been transferred from the apartment to the login area. In no time, Nathan found he was on a street among millions of people walking around him.

## Chapter 6

Nathan had never been to Amsterdam, so he was not sure if he was in the famous city; the buildings around did look very European, but, based on the conversations around him, most people nearby seemed like tourists from the USA. Well, that was not too surprising to Nathan, as the Americans were everywhere even before OBU.

Dave led the charge, Gary and Nathan followed. Looking at the tree-lined canal in the middle of street, the typical Amsterdam postcard scenery, Nathan felt quite excited that he finally had the chance to enjoy the exotic city he had always wanted to visit. Then, after noticing the red-light-illuminated buildings and the half-naked girls in the window displays, he realized that they were right in the middle of the famous red-light district; he now understood why Dave was so keen to get here.

The bakery Nathan used to work in fifteen years ago was not far from Kings Cross in Sydney, supposedly Australia's equivalent of the red-light district in Amsterdam, but it had no resemblance to the real thing. "Gary, is the real Amsterdam exactly like this?"

Before Gary had opened his mouth, Dave said, "This is actually much better than the real city; if you were walking on the real streets in Amsterdam right now, it'd be like a ghost town because everyone is here, in OBU."

"I thought people would prefer the real Amsterdam in OBU, rather than a cheaper version of 'Little Amsterdam'," said Nathan.

"For tourists, it's true, but for what most people are looking for, this is better; in fact, 'Little Amsterdam' is much more popular than the real city, so the Netherlands' government has been increasing the entry tax to visitors here each year," said Gary.

Dave waved his arm to indicate the countless windows of girls. "You know that what we are looking at now is not the exact same dimensions as the physical city area, but the digital extension, easily a hundred times bigger; and the girls are from all over the world, a true global red-light district." Dave stopped beside a large window; inside there was a blonde girl who smiled at them. "Nathan, would you like to have fun with this girl? It'd be my shout for your homecoming."

"Thanks, mate, but I'll give it a miss today," Nathan said. "Do you guys do this quite regularly?"

"Oh no, for a charming guy like me, why would I need to pay to get girls?" Dave said. "This is just giving you a tour, a sightseeing; the real action is at the bars if you want to catch girls, the real girls you don't have to pay."

"Yeah, let's get to our favourite bar; I am tired of this boring window shopping, and I also need my fix," Gary said.

"Nathan, do you know Gary has a secret lover in OBU?"

"Really, a secret lover, Gary?"

Gary waved his arm to dismiss the question. "Dave is joking."

Dave turned, looking at Nathan. "Mate, are you done with the red-light district?"

"Sure, I am easy," Nathan said.

The bar was right in the thick of the red-light district, so it was no surprise that the waitresses were in extremely short skirts and tank tops. Inside, patrons were speaking all different languages, a true global gathering place of drinking, dope smoking and meat-swapping.

35

The biggest difference to Nathan between this place and the normal bars he was familiar with, apart from the near-naked waitresses and girls around, was that all the patrons looked beautiful, handsome, elegant, young and fit; if he didn't know about the secret of the masks, Nathan would have believed these people were actually themselves.

They sat down at a corner table; the waitress spoke English with a British accent—a part-time job during her university studies, Nathan guessed. She took their orders. Dave gave her a very generous tip after she brought their drinks, and dope for Gary. It seemed that they visited this place quite regularly.

Nathan swallowed some of the Dutch beer; it was pretty good, just like drinking the real thing. He watched as Gary lit up his dope, and blue smoke filled the air around them. Nathan turned around, seeing many were doing exactly the same thing as Gary. "Gary, I know this sounds silly, but does smoking dope in OBU feel the same as in the real world?"

"Better, much better." Gary closed his eyes, keeping the smoke in his lungs as long as possible, and then blew it out.

"How so?" said Nathan.

Gary said after blowing more blue smoke into the air. "Normally when you smoke dope, the chemicals would have to be in your lungs, absorbing into your bloodstream and then flooding into your brain, and only then can you feel high, but this shit cuts all the middlemen out, and jumps straight to the final stop. Nathan, you should try it, pure heaven."

"No thanks," said Nathan. "I suppose that, smoking in OBU, you at least don't get lung cancer; getting high without the negatives."

"Not always." Dave pulled his eyes from the girls and waitress and back to their table. "Some dope is better than others, but if you smoke the dodgy stuff, you could get a brain tumour or memory loss."

"Really, do people get brain tumours from smoking a piece of software?" asked Nathan.

"Unfortunately, it has happened, more and more actually," Gary said. "Although your brain only accepts signals, the repeat stimulation sometimes causes damage to the brain, particularly the cheap and illegal dope in OBU."

"Well, it seems nothing is totally positive after all." Nathan swallowed more beer.

"That's why I don't smoke dope, and don't drink much alcohol either," said Dave. "But girls are the must. There haven't been any reports about brain damage related to orgasms, so sex is the way to go, mate. Gary, what do you think about the girl on the left, four tables down?"

"I would have to put my sunglasses on." Gary took a pair of sunglasses out and put them on. Dave did the same.

Nathan turned around, looking at the girl Dave was referring to. She looked like she was in her middle twenties and in Nathan's opinion was quite plain, not really to Dave's taste.

"She is definitely pretty and attractive, but seems a bit shy, that's why she chose the mask she is wearing," said Gary.

"I agree with your assessment; I love a shy girl. You know, she could be a virgin," said Dave. "I'll see you guys later then." Dave stood up and went over to the girl.

Nathan looked at the girl again; to be politically correct, he wouldn't say she was ugly as such, he would say she was average at the most, but definitely nowhere near pretty or attractive. Nathan couldn't imagine that any girl in the world would choose a mask that made her look less attractive than her real body. "Excuse me, Gary, have I missed something about this girl?"

"Yes, you have indeed." Gary took his sunglasses off, shaking them in his hand. "What do you think this is?"

"A pair of sunglasses."

"No, it's more than just a pair of sunglasses." He lowered his voice. "They enable you to peel off people's masks and see their real faces and bodies."

"Really? You are able to see people's real faces?"

"Ssh," Gary said in a low voice. "It's illegal to possess these types of sunglasses theoretically. Only law enforcement officers have the privileges; they're called 'seekers.'"

"Theoretically?"

"Well, it's against the privacy law, but it's not enforced; still, you don't want to tell everyone in public that you have seekers."

"How do they peel off one's mask?"

Gary drank a mouthful of whisky in between dragging on his dope. "Whatever you see here is just computer data, so seekers strip off the extra data to show people's real bodies; having said that, it's not as easy as it seems, as there are always new versions of masks coming out, so there are also new seekers."

"Like computer virus and anti-virus software?"

"Yes, it's the same principle; both masks and seekers are software after all."

"Where do you get the seekers?"

"You can't buy them in normal shops the same way you would buy your masks, for obvious reasons, but you can get them if you know where to look; anyway, this is the latest version, so they'll be able to see through most people's masks."

"Gary, can I have a look through your seekers?"

"Of course, you can." Gary passed the sunglasses to Nathan.

They looked just like a pair of ordinary sunglasses to Nathan. Apart from everything getting darker, all the people around him looked just the same. He gave them back to Gary. "I don't see anything different."

"It's because they've been set up for my eyes only, just in case the police by chance want to check on them. Don't worry; I can help you to get a pair later."

"Thanks, mate."

"No worries, that's what friends are for."

"Gary, what's the point in knowing what someone's real body is like? I mean, as long as you don't wear seekers, you would only see their masks anyway."

"Masks are good for looking at, but when you have sex, it's better to take them off."

"Do you mean the mask desensitizes one's physical sensations, like wearing condoms?"

"Not like wearing condoms, more like having sex through a pair of winter pyjamas," Gary said. "Believe it or not, people do keep their masks on just because they don't want the other person to see their real bodies."

"That wouldn't work, as the other one would know, just because he or she wouldn't take their mask off."

"Not if he or she wears two sets of masks."

## Chapter 7

While Gary closed his eyes and enjoyed each deep drag of his dope, Nathan scanned the people around them. A couple of girls climbed up on top of the counter, crawling and twisting their bodies, obviously part of the attraction of the bar. Men, and some women, were cheering and whistling.

Nathan was not used to this kind of situation; although he had been to skimpy bars before, he had never been comfortable. He lowered his gaze and concentrated on his beer; suddenly he had a feeling that someone was watching him.

Nathan turned around, scanning the crowd. He could see nothing unusual, but he was certain a pair of keen eyes were observing him somewhere in the crowd. Nathan looked up, pretending to stare at the girls crawling on the bench top, but really busily scanning the crowds: still nothing.

Nathan closed his eyes, concentrating and focusing his mind's eye, the technique he had learnt from Master Wuwei. After feeling his heartbeat slow down, the noises around him seemed to disappear from his ears; he opened his eyes and what he saw took his breath away: the patrons were not what they appeared at all. Instead of the glamorous, young and fit-looking people, there were men with bald heads and protruding midriffs, aged and overweight women, and obviously under-aged teenagers.

Nathan turned to Gary and saw him in his real body, rather than in the rock star mask. Then Nathan's eyes caught the person who was watching him: a very attractive woman in her early twenties. The pair of blue eyes under her red hair were electrifying; Nathan felt his heart skip a few beats. He could feel the chemical attraction he had towards this girl.

Nathan blinked his eyes, and everything went back to normal. He didn't know what had happened; maybe it was just a delusion. However, he did locate the person who was watching him, except she was not the attractive girl he had seen a moment ago, but an ordinary guy, holding a beer bottle and sitting among a group of young guys. There were six of them in the group, cheering and whistling at the show girls. Nathan closed his eyes and tried to concentrate, hoping to reproduce the same effect, but without much luck: the young guy remained a man.

"Gary." Nathan patted Gary, who opened his eyes, blowing out a large cloud of blue smoke.

"What's the matter, mate?"

"Gary," Nathan whispered. "Look at the guy, at the third table to the left, the one with the checked short-sleeve shirt and jeans."

"What about him?"

"I don't know how but for a moment I saw him as a very attractive girl."

"Let me have a look." Gary put his sunglasses on. "Well, although his real body is quite young and fit, he is definitely a man, not a girl." Gary looked at Nathan, very concerned. "Nathan, have you turned gay, maybe as a result of your lost memory?"

Nathan shook his head. "I am not gay, mate. I swear that I saw him as a girl, red hair and blue eyes… Never mind."

"Yeah, enjoy the show." Gary stood up. "I need to go to the bathroom."

"What? How can you go to the bathroom in OBU? And why do you need to go to the bathroom anyway, because you haven't eaten or drunk anything real."

Gary sat down again. "Mate, people's bodies in the real world still need to go to the bathroom. Instead of peeing your pants there is a specially designed software in OBU that synchronizes your projected body in OBU and your real body, so you can relieve yourself in the real world; of course, you would need to have a toilet to go to in your home first."

Nathan though for a moment. "In that case, one could synchronize other activities, such as drinking real water and eating real food, so you could actually live in OBU for a very long time."

"Indeed, you can, and most people are doing exactly that; so now you understand why we live in a high-security apartment building. See you later, mate." Gary left.

***

The sound of the metal door opening dragged Nathan back to the present, the OBU. A beefy police officer walked in; he pulled the chair out from underneath the desk and sat opposite Nathan. He lit up a cigarette and blew a large cloud of blue smoke at Nathan's face. Well, it seemed everyone was smoking dope in Amsterdam, including the police interrogator, thought Nathan.

"What's your name?" He spoke English but with a strong Dutch accent.

"Nathan. Nathan Jenkins."

'Okay, Nathan, my name is Bart; Bart Vos, your interrogator." He blew another cloud of blue smoke. "Nathan, who are you really?"

"Mr. Vos, I'm only a tourist from Sydney, Australia. You know Sydney, don't you?"

"Of course, I know Sydney, the place with the seashell Opera House. But Nathan, you are not an ordinary tourist. Please tell us your real identity; it will save us all the trouble of having to find out."

"I don't know what you are talking about; I am just a normal tourist, and this is my very first-time visiting Amsterdam."

"Well, let's talk about what happened in the bar today." He dragged on his cigarette a couple of times in quick succession, and then pushed a button on the desk. "Watch it yourself. Quite an astonishing performance, I have to admit."

On the large one-way glass window, a video began playing: a recording of Nathan fighting against the attackers in the bar.

"They were trying to kill the tourists. I merely did my duty as a citizen; I stopped the killing and saved the innocents."

"Innocents? We will get to that soon, but you are no ordinary tourist if you can beat up six armed guys with your bare hands; so, tell us, who are you really?"

"I have told you that I am just a normal guy from Sydney."

"Normal guy; where did you learn how to fight like that?"

"Today I saved a lot of lives; you should be giving me a medal, not interrogating me." In his mind, Nathan was also wondering if his newly discovered fighting skills were the result of his meeting with Master Wuwei.

"Okay, let's talk about the 'innocent' people you saved today." The interrogator pushed the button again. An enlarged photo of a young guy appeared on the one-way glass: the girl in the male's face mask. "Is this the guy you saved?"

"Yes, he is one of them."

"But he is not what you think he is." The interrogator pushed the button again; beside the guy's face, the girl's face appeared.

It was a high-resolution photo; Nathan could really see her long red hair and blue eyes clearly. Yes, it was her, exactly as he had seen her in the bar, so it was not him being delusional; he had seen her real face, but how could he see through people's masks? Besides, Gary didn't see the girl's real face with his seekers. While Nathan was wondering, the interrogator spoke again.

"You can see that he is in fact not a him, but a her. Her name is Mary O'Brian, an Irish woman and the most wanted terrorist in the world. You have heard about her, no?"

"No. Never."

"Nathan, normally we would think you were a member of Mary O'Brian's group, but because we haven't witnessed fighting skills like you demonstrated tonight before, we are giving you the benefit of the doubt that you didn't know who you were dealing with. Tell me, Nathan, where have you been during the last five years if you have never heard about her?" He used his cigarette to point at Mary's photo.

"Well…" This was actually the question that Nathan kept asking himself since he had found out he was fifteen years in the future. "Well, I woke up this morning and found that I had just gone fifteen years into the future. I suppose that I must have had an accident and lost my memories."

The interrogator thought about it for a few seconds, and then blew more smoke rings at Nathan. "I suppose that's possible." Just then, a light began to flash on the desk beside the button. He stood up and walked out of the room without a word.

Very soon he returned, followed by another police officer.

"Nathan, we believe that you didn't know who Mary O'Brian was and acted on good faith to save the innocents."

"Thanks. By the way, Mr. Vos, who were the attackers in the bar?"

"They were the special field agents of Interpol."

"Oh, I am so sorry I injured police officers."

"Don't worry about that too much; with some healing software, they will soon get over it, even forgetting about the pain altogether."

"Why didn't they use guns when they were hunting the most wanted terrorist in the world?" asked Nathan.

"We don't want to injure or kill bystanders, do we?"

"What happens if someone is killed in OBU? Would he die in the real world?" asked Nathan.

"So, you are really an OBU virgin; if you are killed in OBU, the violent signals would cause your brain permanent damage, so yes, you would die."

"It's very fortunate I didn't kill anyone in the bar."

"It's your lucky day, Nathan; if you had killed someone, you would be in big trouble. For now, you are free to go, but you need to inform us immediately if Mary O'Brian tries to contact you."

"Of course, Mr. Vos; I will do my best to assist the police in the fight against terrorists."

## Chapter 8

Nathan walked out of the police building and saw that Gary and Dave were waiting for him.

"Nathan, was it really you that beat up six armed guys with your bare hands?" Dave asked.

"I did, although I have no idea how I did it," Nathan said.

"Mate, we have lots to talk about when we get home," Gary said seriously.

"How do we get home?" asked Nathan.

Dave pointed at a flashing spot nearby. "There are exit points everywhere. Even though they are in different shapes, materials and colours, they are easily identified: by flashing lights in the night and by their shine during the day."

The spot Dave had pointed to was a shiny metal box mounted on the wall of the building along the street. Nathan guessed that they would just scan their wrists against it, the same way as when they logged in. Sure enough, that's exactly how Gary and Dave exited, so Nathan followed suit, and in no time he was back at the apartment again.

Nathan climbed up from the floor, then slumped on the sofa, feeling exhausted. All he wanted to do was go to sleep, a long, deep sleep; he felt like his brain was overloaded.

"Nathan, where did you learn to fight like that?" asked Gary.

"Yes, tell us, mate," said Dave.

Nathan thought for a while, and decided it'd be better not to tell them about Master Wuwei. He didn't know why but his instincts were telling him not to.

"I don't know. It may be part of my lost memories."

"Man, you are awesome; next time we go out I'll let you play the cool spy," Dave said. "But don't snatch my girls."

"Nathan, you told me that you saw through the girl's mask; was that also caused by your lost memories?" asked Gary.

"I did see her real face, but only once. Anyway, the police showed me the photo of her real face, and she is Mary O'Brian," said Nathan.

"What? Are you telling me you just saved the most wanted terrorist in the world, Mary O'Brian?" shouted Dave.

"Yes, at least that's what the police told me. Who is this Mary O'Brian anyway?"

"Oh man, you have missed so much." Dave looked extremely excited. "Mary O'Brian is one of the leaders of SOH, Salvation Of Humanity, and has been on the top of the most wanted list for the last five years, but the authorities never seem to be able to get her. But today you actually saved her from the government's secret agents, holy shit! My God, this is big!"

"Well, I didn't know who she was, and I didn't think to ask, I just acted when those agents tried to kill her."

"Was it because she was attractive?" said Gary calmly.

Nathan thought about it, and then said, "I suppose I am attracted to her. Very much so; I've never felt like that in my whole life."

"Man, way to go." Dave patted Nathan's shoulder. "Imagine that, having the most wanted terrorist as your girlfriend. By the way, how come the police let you go so easily? Considering that you not only let the most wanted terrorist slip away, but also beat the shit out of their agents?"

"I don't know; I suppose they knew that I didn't do it intentionally. Besides, I fortunately didn't kill any of the agents," Nathan said. "What exactly has she been doing to earn the most wanted title?" asked Nathan. For some reason he didn't use the word terrorist.

"You would have to ask Gary about her and SOH; I only know that SOH claims OBU is destroying everything about our civilization and eventually the human race, so they sabotage OBU utilities around the globe and vow to completely eliminate OBU altogether."

"Has she killed many innocent people by doing that?" asked Nathan.

"I don't know if she has been personally responsible for killing anyone, but SOH as an organization has definitely caused the deaths of many innocent people as collateral damage in their war against OBU," said Gary.

"How come you didn't see through her mask?" asked Nathan.

"I supposed that her mask must be a newer version than my seekers," said Gary.

"Tell me more about Mary and SOH; I want to know more about her," said Nathan.

"It's getting late, and you look exhausted. I suggest we continue this conversation another time," said Gary. "More importantly, what are you going to do? I mean, are you going to get a job?"

"I don't know; I need time to think this through. Don't forget I only woke up this morning."

Nathan went back to his mother's house. The next morning, he helped her to tidy up the backyard, getting rid of the overgrown weeds, cutting unruly tree branches off, trimming the climbers along the garden fences and repaving the footpaths. His mother watched Nathan with a big smile on her face.

Nathan went back inside and had a shower; meanwhile his mother made him lunch. As he came out of the bathroom, someone rang the doorbell. Nathan opened the front door and to his surprise, the person standing in front of him was Cathy, his ex-girlfriend.

Cathy, with her slender, six-foot, model-like body, looked as striking and sharp as Nathan remembered. The last fifteen years had left traces on her face, but she was still absolutely stunning.

"Hi, Nathan, it's so exciting that you finally came home. We all missed you so much."

"Hi, Cathy." Nathan was surprised by his own reaction. He thought he would feel angry and demand explanations as to why she dumped him for no apparent reason. He should even shout at her and tell her to get lost as revenge, as many people would do in his situation, but he didn't feel angry. Nor did he desire any explanations. He supposed that the conversations and Tai Chi training with Master Wuwei had helped him get over the breakup, and he was very pleased with himself.

"You are looking as beautiful as ever," Nathan said in a very relaxed manner.

"Thanks, Nathan." Cathy pushed her blonde hair away from her eyes. "I have to say you look exactly the same as you were fifteen years ago; you haven't aged one bit."

"That's what they tell me."

"Are you going to invite me inside, or are we just going to talk in the doorway?"

"Of course, please come in."

"Nathan, could you please help me carry this box inside?"

Nathan then noticed a large box lying on the ground behind Cathy, so he carried it inside.

"Oh, it's Cathy; I haven't seen you for a very long time," Nathan's mother greeted Cathy.

"Yes, Betty, it's been a very long time. I'm sure you are happy that Nathan is finally home."

"Yes, I am so happy…Cathy, I was just about to make lunch for Nathan and myself, would you like to join us?"

"I knew that I was coming at the right time, and I am more than happy to have lunch with you, but today I'll cook," Cathy said.

"I don't…I mean I didn't know you could cook," said Nathan.

"Nathan, that was fifteen years ago, people can change a lot." Cathy opened the large box that Nathan had just carried inside, taking three helmets out.

These helmets looked identical to the helmet he had worn to go to OBU in Gary and Dave's apartment. Before Nathan could open his mouth, his mother asked first, "What are these for?"

"Betty, please be patient for a moment, and I will show you a few tricks," Cathy said as she took some vegetables, bread, and fruit out of the box.

Nathan watched Cathy in awe; she prepared the food in a very sleek style, as if she was in a TV show. Cathy washed the vegetables, peeled and boiled potatoes, and in a very short time she had got the food organized.

"Now comes the fun part."

Cathy asked Nathan and his mother to sit at the dining table. She then put a helmet on each of their heads and put the last one on herself. "Now flap your eye-shields down; right, just like this."

Nathan was expecting the same out of body experience as he had just yesterday with Gary and Dave, but, instead of observing himself from outside his body, Nathan was still looking at the same dining table, or rather, to be exact, the same table covered with different things.

Nathan turned his head around; in front of his eyes the room had transformed. It was no longer his mother's humble kitchen and small dining table, but a splendid modern kitchen with a snow-white tablecloth set up with silver knives and forks. Nathan heard his mother's voice.

"Cathy, what happened? Where is my kitchen? Where are we?"

"Betty, please don't panic. We are still in your kitchen. It's only a mind trick this helmet is doing to you."

Nathan didn't see helmets on either Cathy or his mother's head. He used his own hand to touch his head. Yes, the helmet was still there but he no longer felt it, just like the paper hats people wore during Christmas dinners.

Cathy stood in front of the sparkling new kitchen counter. "Betty, would you like to have a roast for lunch?"

"Roast beef? Oh, I would love to have some right now but where did you cook…"

Even before his mother finished her sentence, Cathy opened the stove and brought out a tray of steaming roast beef; the wonderful smell of the roast immediately filled the air around them.

The lunch was wonderful, a five-course meal ending with an exotic desert, in true French style. During the whole meal, Nathan's mother kept commenting on how lovely the silver knives and forks were; how tender the roast beef was; how fresh and delicious the fruit salad was; and how wonderful the real French champagne was. Although not sure exactly how Cathy was pulling off the tricks, Nathan knew it had something to do with OBU, but he didn't say anything, deciding to just play along.

After lunch, Cathy suggested they all remove their helmets.

"Cathy, where are the roast beef and the champagne?" Nathan's mother asked.

Cathy grinned.

"Betty, it was the helmet playing tricks on your mind; it created an illusion that we were eating a five-course lunch."

"So, what was the roast beef we just ate?" asked Nathan's mother.

"Boiled potatoes."

"The champagne?"

"Tap water."

"The dessert?"

"Mashed potatoes and fruit salad."

"Oh, Cathy, this is just wonderful. You have to teach me how to use this helmet."

While Cathy patiently explained how to use the helmet to his mother, Nathan couldn't stop admiring this magic technology. With the help of this helmet, people could indulge themselves with whatever they liked, but still only eat simple, basic and healthy food; the potential applications were endless, and so joyful and healthy.

During the lunch Nathan had looked out through the back door and found that the backyard still looked the same as it always had, so the illusion was limited to the kitchen area only. Besides, he also remembered hearing bird sounds; he felt better about the application because his mother was still able to see and hear what was happening outside of her illusion.

After everything was cleaned up, Cathy said to Nathan's mother, "Betty, this afternoon I would like to show Nathan around since he hasn't been home for so long."

"Cathy, thank you so much for looking after Nathan."

"No problem at all. Before we leave, I would like to show you another function of this magic helmet."

Nathan watched as Cathy talked to his mother and showed her how to access the main menu and navigate to the next; it took a while for his mother to become familiar with the system, but she eventually got there.

"Betty, now I would like you to go to the travel program. Yes, you are doing great; right, click that, and now you are in London."

Nathan heard his mother's excited voice.

"I can't believe I am walking along the Thames; I can see Big Ben…"

Nathan dragged Cathy away from his mother and whispered, "We can't leave her alone; there is no security around this house."

"Betty is not in OBU; she is just experiencing a high-definition 3D video and surround sound. She is still able to hear what is happening around her; not much different from watching a normal TV in the olden days."

"What happens if the sound is too loud and she's unable to hear the doorbell?"

"This helmet is quite intelligent; when it senses a sudden noise, it pauses the video. Let me demonstrate for you." Cathy walked towards the front door and rang the doorbell.

Sure enough, Nathan's mother flipped her eye-shield up and looked at them.

Cathy said. "Betty, Nathan and I are leaving now. Enjoy your tour of London."

# Chapter 9

Cathy told the taxi driver to go straight to the Rocks, where the Opera House and Harbour Bridge were.

As the car cruised leisurely along the main streets, Nathan was still amazed to see that there were so few cars around; apart from the occasional bus, taxi, or delivery vehicle passing by, he hadn't seen a single passenger car, or any pedestrians.

Cathy looked at Nathan's expression and seemed amused. "You must be wondering where all the people are on a Monday afternoon."

"Yes, I am, indeed. I know people are crazy about visiting places all over the world in OBU, but surely one has to work in order to make a living?"

"They do, and they are doing exactly that right now."

Nathan looked at the ghost town through the car's window, and then turned back to Cathy. "Oh, don't tell me they are all working in OBU?"

"Nathan, that's exactly what is going on." She pointed at the buildings that had been occupied by large businesses and corporations, as Nathan recalled.

"Almost every single building is empty, and they may be converted to apartments later; we have driven past a few that still have corporate logos and business names, but they are shop fronts only. In fact, apart from the few activities that have to happen in the real world, most business activities are conducted in OBU."

Watching the familiar streets and buildings pass by, Nathan felt sad; everything was so familiar but still so alien at the same time. He was a total stranger in his own hometown, the place he had spent the first twenty years of his life. Soon they arrived at the Rocks; the normally crowded, must-see location for all tourists was now still and empty, like a no-man's land.

"It's such a strange feeling to see nobody around," Nathan said, getting out of the taxi.

Cathy smiled but didn't say anything. She led the way to a nearby high-rise apartment building. Nathan followed. It seemed that she had done quite well to be able to afford to live on the prime real estate in one of the world's most expensive cities; at least it was before OBU.

The armed security guards at the foyer and heavy security doors and window frames in Cathy's apartment were much the same as Gary and Dave's.

"I suppose that we should get the ball rolling." Cathy gave Nathan a helmet that had a cable connected already. "Shall we?"

Nathan put it on his head and flipped the eye-shield down and soon he was looking at his own body sitting on the coach a few feet away. In no time, Cathy was standing beside the window. She signalled for him to get closer to her.

"Look down there."

Nathan looked through the window; although he had anticipated what it might look like, what he saw still took his breath away: twenty stories down on the ground, millions of tourists were jammed into almost every inch of ground between the seashell-like Opera House and Harbour Bridge. In the air there were cars flying at different levels over the city, a picture from a true futuristic science fiction movie.

"Flying cars?" said Nathan.

"Nathan, it's OBU age," Cathy said. "Flying cars are just a piece of software to intrigue your mind, there's nothing strange about it." She paused, and then said, "I suggest we take a ride in my helicopter so I can show you around."

*Your helicopter?* But Nathan managed to swallow the sentence before it came out of his mouth, because Cathy would tell him it was just another piece of software.

He kept quiet while Cathy pushed a button on the wall, and a panel of the wall slid open; inside there was a lift. He said nothing and just stepped inside it after Cathy.

The lift took them straight to the building's rooftop. Nathan followed Cathy out of the lift and walked towards a helicopter parked not far from them.

"Why don't you just drive a flying car?" asked Nathan as he climbed into the co-pilot's seat.

"Put those on." Cathy indicated the headphones in front of Nathan. She started the flying machine efficiently and professionally; it seemed that she had done this quite regularly. "We all know that cars can't fly in the real world, at least not yet, so driving a flying car is just a joy ride on a piece of software, but flying this helicopter is the real thing."

"The real thing? Are you telling me this is like a flight simulation?"

"Yes, Nathan, but it's much better than a simulation because I am actually flying the real helicopter. Even though it's in OBU, the altitude, air temperature, wind speed, weather conditions and the machine's mechanical performance all match the flight in real time; in other words, there is no difference between me flying it in the real world or in OBU."

"This is fantastic!" exclaimed Nathan. "It means that people can do all sorts of real training in OBU without the costs or dangers in the real world. There'd be no danger of them killing themselves in training accidents."

Cathy flew over the Harbour Bridge, towards the zoo, which was on the slope of a hill, a fair distance by boat but a short ride in a helicopter.

"The standard businesses that were already heavily represented on the Internet even before OBU, such as media, education, fashion, finance, and entertainment, have all naturally moved to OBU; the other businesses, such as heavy industry and military training, travelling and sightseeing, and hospitality, including hotels and restaurants, are also now thriving in OBU as well."

"I can't believe this." Nathan just couldn't stop mumbling the same words over and over. He looked down as they flew over the zoo, seeing the elephants and other animals. "Are they real or just digitally generated?"

"Some are real and some aren't."

"Cathy, I know I have been saying this ever since I got into this helicopter, but I just can't believe this is really happening. Look, that's the bakery I used to work in."

"Yes, it is. I intentionally flew over it for you."

"Thanks, Cathy."

"Nathan, do you still remember in our uni days when we protested and fought against mining corporations?" Cathy said softly.

"How could I forget? I remember clearly when we went to the north of western Australia, to stop the building of that oil refinery that would destroy the rocks with old aboriginal paintings from tens of thousands of years ago, and million-year-old dinosaur footprints. We fought shoulder to shoulder with environmental activists from all over the world, and aboriginal youths and elders..." Nathan's memories flooded back to his life

59

fifteen years ago, but he stopped when his breakup with Cathy came to his mind.

Cathy turned, patting Nathan's arm gently.

"Nathan, we don't need to protest and fight anymore; we won. Forests won; animals won; everyone won, all thanks to OBU."

"Right." Nathan was thinking and digesting Cathy's words.

"Nathan, you see, because of OBU, people don't need to cut down forests, or kill cows so that they can produce burgers; orangutans can finally survive because we no longer need to use palm tree oil; the Americans no longer need drugs from golden triangles and Mexicans; the Japanese no longer need to harm whales for their meat; the Chinese no longer need the ivory; people no longer need to breathe in polluted air, and Earth's temperature is no longer rising. Nathan, OBU has saved us, saved the environment, saved us from global warming…" Cathy said this with tears shining in her eyes.

"That's wonderful!" Nathan said. "But how could OBU help with reducing pollution? Don't we still need to burn fossil fuel to drive cars and generate electricity?"

"Yes, the world is still dependant on fossil fuel, but at a much-reduced scale." Cathy waved her hand at the city below.

"You have seen with your own eyes that there are hardly any cars on the streets because almost every possible business and private activity that can be conducted in OBU is being conducted in OBU. Air travel, luxury goods, hotels and resorts, fast food, you name them, all disappeared from the real world; as a result, the usage of fossil fuel is now only a fraction of what it was before OBU, and so is the pollution."

Cathy pushed a button on the instrument panel; in the blink of an eye, underneath, the endless red desert in the middle of Australia replaced the scenery of Sydney.

"How did we fly so quickly from Sydney to the middle of the desert?"

Cathy made the helicopter turn and they were soon close to the most famous landmark, the Uluru Rock.

"It's just a matter of changing the data set, so it takes no time at all. By the way, I don't think you have been to Uluru Rock before. Would you like to climb it now?"

"I thought it wasn't allowed anymore," said Nathan.

"Nathan, we are in OBU, and therefore won't be able to damage the real Uluru Rock." Cathy landed the helicopter beside the giant red rock.

Nathan was completely lost in admiration of the beauty and magnificence of the natural wonder.

Cathy was agile whilst walking on the rock. The weather was quite hot, which was understandable for being in the middle of the Australian desert.

Cathy took two pairs of sunglasses out of her pocket and passed one pair to Nathan.

"You had better put them on."

After going full circle around the giant red rock, Cathy turned around and walked back towards the helicopter.

"Nathan, I am a bit hungry, let's go back and have some afternoon tea. What about getting something to eat in your little bakery?"

"What a good idea." Nathan was looking forward to seeing what the old bakery was like in OBU.

## Chapter 10

Cathy landed the helicopter right outside of the little bakery, Croissant Classic. After they had climbed out of the machine Cathy waved her arm and the helicopter disappeared into thin air. Nathan neither showed any surprise nor asked any questions.

It was the same humble bakery Nathan knew so well, but at the same time it wasn't; there were some changes in this digital version of it. The street outside was nice and quiet, lined with trees, and had a spectacular bay view looking right at the Opera House and Harbour Bridge. With its proximity to the neighbourhood of Kings Cross, the little bakery was a tourist hot spot in OBU.

They walked inside the door of the bakery; the bakery's exterior was merely fifteen feet wide, but the inside of it went back as far as one's eye could see. It seemed that the contents of the business were far beyond the basic croissants and cakes; one could find every possible French delicacy that had ever existed.

"What would you like?" asked Cathy.

"Cathy, you should know exactly what I like."

"Well, that was fifteen years ago, people change. Anyway, let's order the lot and spoil ourselves."

Nathan watched as Cathy made the order.

"Nathan, why don't we sit outside? I've always liked the bay view under the trees, just like the good old days."

"Sounds good to me."

They walked out and found a table right in front of the store. No sooner had they sat down than a waitress brought their order out on a trolley. Nathan looked at the dozens of different kinds of delicious cakes, wondering how it'd be possible for them to eat them all.

"This is a bit overwhelming," Nathan said after the waitress left.

Cathy picked up a piece of cake and put it onto her plate. "Although these cakes are just software, they still cost money to create, so nothing is free in OBU but the price is just a fraction of what it would be in the real world, and a hundred times more delicious. The biggest benefit of all is that you can eat as much as you like, but never gain weight." Cathy started eating her piece of cake.

In no time, Nathan had tried dozens of the French delicacies; it was a wonderful experience, a true treat to one's taste buds without needing to worry about either your weight or stomach complications; he could keep eating for the whole day. Of course, one had to have the money to pay for the luxury.

Cathy put another piece of cake on her plate. "One of the biggest benefits of OBU is food revolution."

"Like you demonstrated at lunch time that we could taste whatever fancy flavour we wanted while only eating basic food in the real world."

"Exactly." Cathy finished eating the piece of cake and then continued. "Fast food and junk food are completely gone, and slow, local and organic food dominates today. Nathan, you see, because most foods are produced locally, they are not only healthier, but also reduce the carbon footprint dramatically, and all of this is again thanks to OBU."

More and more people came and joined them sitting along the riverfront, so it got noisier. Even before Nathan suggested that they went somewhere quieter, Cathy signalled to the waitress. They exchanged a few words, the waitress nodded, waved her arm, and Nathan found the nearby tables, together with the people, had simply disappeared, leaving Cathy and him alone.

'Wow, this is much better, but how did you do it?" asked Nathan.

"It's quite easily done in OBU, digital compartments, but it costs a bit more money; it's their marketing trick to get people to pay more for the privilege."

"Well, no matter where you are, making profit is still the goal for businesses," said Nathan.

Cathy pushed her plate away, her taste buds finally satisfied.

"Nathan, I heard Dave and Gary took you to Amsterdam, how was it?"

"Well, we only walked along the streets in the red-light district and visited a skimpy bar there," said Nathan uncomfortably.

"Trust Dave and Gary to do that for you on your first OBU visit," Cathy laughed. "But there's no need to feel embarrassed about it, everyone is doing it. OBU brought true sexual liberation for women, men and the world."

"I can see that" mumbled Nathan.

"Nathan, you have no idea how much OBU has done for all women around the world. They don't need to worry about sexual abuse, diseases, violence and they can use their bodies in whatever way they like. They don't need to worry about how society views their behaviour; they have finally been liberated from the male-dominated society in OBU."

Nathan didn't want to contradict Cathy; while agreeing with her points, he could still see that there were still a lot of body image issues and that's why everyone wore masks. He wasn't quite sure about the violence issue either because he had experienced one such issue himself. Nevertheless, women did have more sexual freedom in OBU.

"I agree that people have more sexual freedom than any other time in human history, but at the same time, doesn't all this causal sex destroy relationships, family and even turn love into a meaningless act?"

Cathy stared at Nathan, smiling.

"Nathan, it's not a surprise that you would reach that conclusion, but you are still inexperienced with OBU. Casual sex has always been there throughout human history; however, the majority of men and women in OBU are still looking for affection and relationships despite their casual sexual encounters from time to time."

"Cathy." Nathan felt the words were getting harder to force out of his mouth; he paused a bit, and then decided to proceed with it. "I suppose that you have found your real man by now."

'Oh, Nathan, over all of these years, you still haven't got over it?" sighed Cathy.

It had been fifteen years for the rest of the world, but only a couple of days for Nathan. He had been asking himself the same question since coming to the OBU age. Looking at Cathy's striking face, Nathan felt relief. He had got over their breakup, thanks to the conversations and Tai Chi training with Master Wuwei. He could look straight into Cathy's eyes in peace, and not feel the hollowness and pain in his heart and stomach.

"Yes, I have got over it; maybe I didn't realize that I had, but I have. Anyway, I was just wondering how you are getting on with your life."

"Well, I think I am doing quite alright; I work for the international environmental protection agency (IEPA), the kind of job I am passionate about and love. I get to

65

travel all over the world in OBU, and I also get quite well paid, so I can't complain too much."

"That sounds great. What exactly are you doing? I mean since almost everything is conducted in OBU, how much can you do to protect the environment?"

"You would be surprised to know that there is plenty more to do, even more in OBU than in the real world." Cathy drank some coffee. "For example, to inspect the impact of OBU cameras on the environment and wildlife. Apart from monitoring the old industries in the real world, like mining, construction, agriculture and the others, we also run educational campaigns in OBU as well."

"Obviously you guys have done a fantastic job in protecting the environment," Nathan said. "What about your private life? Are you married and have you got any kids?"

"Married and kids? Oh Nathan, I haven't had either the time or energy for that. Times have changed; the concept of family has changed radically in the last fifteen years. We are in OBU age after all, Nathan."

"Changed? Are you telling me that people are no longer getting married and having kids anymore in OBU age?"

"No, people are still getting married and having kids. You know what, Nathan? I don't think I am designed for monogamy, and that's why we broke up." After a brief awkward silence, Cathy said again, "Anyway, I am in a polygamy relationship, and am much happier."

"Polygamy? Are you living with multiple partners?"

"Why so surprised? Yes, I am living in a commune, consisting of a few guys and girls; we all love each other and are in quite good and stable relationships."

"I am really glad that you have found your happiness," said Nathan genuinely. He was even surprised by how much he really meant it; he no longer felt jealous or judged Cathy for her choice of lifestyle.

"Nathan, you are a decent man, and I still like you very much. You know, despite the ultimate sexual freedom in OBU, it's really hard to find real relationships. A genuinely good and reliable guy is very rare. Nathan, why don't you join our little commune? I know you would like and feel comfortable with the guys and girls; they are from all over the world and all work for IEPA. Join us and we can work together to protect the environment, like the olden days. Please, Nathan."

Cathy's soft voice triggered Nathan's memories; he had so many fond memories and experiences with her. Looking at her pretty eyes, Nathan really wished he could simply say yes to her, embracing her again.

A chilly breeze rippled the water's surface, distracting him; although it was still summer, Sydney's weather could be very unpredictable. The cool breeze dragged him back to reality, or OBU to be more accurate. Nathan blinked his eyes and focused on Cathy's face again.

"Thanks for the invitation, but I need time to think about what I am going to do; I only got back yesterday."

"Of course, you need time to settle down. Nathan, can I ask where you learnt all those martial arts skills?"

"How do you know? Oh, it was Dave, wasn't it?"

"You should have known he would tell everyone. I believe every single person who knew you fifteen years ago knows about the fight in the bar by now. So, where and when did you learn fighting skills like that?"

Nathan shook his head. He didn't want to mention Master Wuwei to anyone, because not only would nobody believe his story, but he also had an instinct that it'd be wise to keep it a secret; even he had no idea why. "As I said, I woke up yesterday morning and found that I had gone fifteen years into the future, so I may have learnt the skills during the past fifteen years sometime, somewhere, but I have no memories of it."

"I'd go and see a doctor if I were you."

"I will once I've settled down a bit first. Thanks for the lovely afternoon, Cathy. I think I'd better get going."

"No problem, Nathan. Please do let me know if there is anything I can do to help you at all. We are still good friends, aren't we?"

"Of course, you will always be my good friend."

# Chapter 11

Nathan asked the taxi driver to drop him at the park, a short walking distance from his mother's house; he felt like he needed some fresh air. It was fantastic to enjoy the spectacular stuff OBU could offer but Nathan still preferred the natural beauty, even the basic freedom to breathe fresh air. However, there was one point Cathy had made that did make sense: if pollution hadn't been reduced dramatically, there wouldn't be much fresh air for everyone to breathe.

On one hand, OBU was great for reducing pollution, getting rid of global warming and protecting the environment; but on the other hand, people had built an invisible cage to pack everyone inside. Nathan wasn't sure the approach of using one technology to solve the problems that were created by other technologies was the ultimate solution. He didn't have the answer; therefore, Nathan kept walking in the large park.

The park, like Nathan's mother's house, was far away from the oceanfront, the rich eastern suburbs of Sydney. Nathan had grown up in a sprawled out, flat, ordinary western suburban neighbourhood, and he had enjoyed this park throughout his life until he moved out of his parents' house when studying at university. Nathan had very fond memories of this park, with the large grassy oval where he had played cricket for many of his teenage years.

Nathan wasn't a fan of Australian football as he found it too aggressive for his taste. He was not a confrontational guy, and maybe that was the reason Cathy had broken up with him, because he lacked the male aggressiveness and roughness. While other male teenagers and university students were punching each other to fight for the girls they pursued, Nathan had never bother to get involved with that kind of stuff. It was fortunate he found Cathy, who loved him for what he was, but she eventually drifted away from him.

Through Nathan's life, until meeting Master Wuwei, he had never had a single fight with another guy. He knew it was quite unusual for a young white male like him in the highly sport-orientated, binge-drinking and aggressive Australian society. The night he had met the Taoist master was the first time he had ever gotten drunk in his life. He told Master Wuwei about his problems with Cathy and his wish to learn how to fight, and the next morning, not only he was fifteen years in future, but he also had this fantastic super fighting skill. He had beaten six big guys who were armed with daggers and short swords singlehandedly, without inflicting even a cut on himself. How did he know those graceful moves and how to break or dislocate a guy's joints without thinking, as if it was part of his second nature?

One thing was sure, that Mater Wuwei had some kind of power, so if he had the ability to send him into the future, it'd be no big surprise if he had also implanted these wonderful fighting skills in him. Nathan supposed that the ability to see through people's masks in OBU could also be the by-product of his mind training, although it had only given him a brief glance of Mary's pretty face and he hadn't been able to replicate the ability ever again since being in OBU. However, Nathan believed, for some unknown reason, that his ability to see through the masks would return to him one day.

As soon as thoughts about Mary entered his head, her piercing blue eyes immediately burst into his mind. Even with his eyes open, he could still remember meeting her eyes vividly. He was sure that her eyes were pleading for his help; somehow she knew that he was able to help her. Mary and her people were in danger; if he hadn't defeated all of the attackers, apparently government field agents, as he was told later, Mary and her group would have been killed.

Nathan understood the environmental benefits OBU had brought to the world, particularly after Cathy's tour and their conversation this afternoon, and knew he should feel disgusted and angry towards Mary, who wanted to destroy OBU and bring pollution and global warming back, but he didn't.

Nathan had always been a good boy. He had never broken any school rules, or put one foot wrong in his entire life, but now he just couldn't get Mary, the most wanted terrorist, out of his mind. Nathan shook his head in disbelief; what was wrong with him?

Nathan was in such deep thought that he almost bumped into another person.

"Sorry," he apologized but then shouted out immediately, "Amy, is it really you?"


It was Amy, his co-worker at the little bakery before his 'disappearance'. Amy had changed; the fifteen years had sculptured her into a stunning woman. Her chubby teenage appearance was replaced with a sharp and absolutely beautiful face.

However, Amy didn't seem surprised at all.

"Hi, Nathan. How have you been? I heard that you came back yesterday, and I thought about visiting you, but here we are, bumping into each other right on my doorstep."

"Your doorstep? Amy, I didn't know you were living around here."

"I only moved here a few years ago; that flat over there." She pointed at a greyish building right on the edge of the park. It must have been built recently because Nathan couldn't remember ever seeing it before.

"What a surprise! Amy, we are neighbours now."

"Do you live nearby as well?"

"Oh, I grew up in this area; my parents' house is only a five-minute walk that way."

"What a coincidence," Amy laughed.

"Amy, how did you know I was back so quickly? I haven't had time to talk to or meet anyone yet."

"Nathan, it's OBU age. Any local news can be spread out instantly the second it's on OBUK."

"What's OBUK? I assume it has something to do with OBU, right?"

"Yeah, the equivalent of Facebook in OBU; it's really called OBU book, but for short most people just say OBUK," Amy said. "Talking of Facebook, it's ancient history. I still can't believe fifteen years have passed since your disappearance. Nathan, what happened to you?"

Nathan offered the same explanation to her as to all the others.

"Memory loss," Amy said thoughtfully. She looked at Nathan, gazing into his eyes for a long time. It almost felt like an eternity to Nathan, but in reality, it'd been only a second or so. Although they had worked together in the bakery for almost two years, this was the first time Nathan had looked into her eyes. He sensed that there was something else behind the brown eyes; he wasn't sure what it was and didn't want to guess either.

Amy put a strand of her long brown hair behind her ear, and then said, "Nathan, I am so glad that you finally came back. We all thought that we had lost you…you know, you treated me so well, like a real gentleman in the bakery, and I was really sad after you disappeared…"

Nathan didn't know what to say; he patted Amy's arm. "Thanks, Amy. It was you who looked after me in the bakery."

A moment of awkward silence fell.

"Amy, what do you do now? I assume that you are working in OBU, right? It seems like almost everyone is working in OBU nowadays."

"Yeah, I am working in OBU." Amy regained her posture. She looked at Nathan again, back to the way she had looked at him in the olden days. "I work for an international charity organization, OBUarity that stands for OBU Charity. It was founded by the OBU Corporation, the largest corporation in human history. I suppose that OBU has made so much money that they decided to share some with the poor countries."

"Wow, that sounds great. So, what exactly are you doing for OBUarity?" Nathan found it much easier for their conversation to flow now.

"Well, we do move around a fair bit, but during the last few months I have been working at a school in Africa to help the poor kids from local tribes. Nathan, what are you going to do?"

"I don't know yet; remember I only came back yesterday morning, so I have to settle down first and think about it."

"Nathan, there are lots of perks to working for OBU, like visiting all of the places around the world for free."

"I thought one could do that in OBU anyway."

"Yes, but only in theory. Although it's much cheaper to travel and visit other countries in OBU compared with travelling in the real world, it still costs a lot if one wants to travel frequently. For an average person, it'd still be a struggle to have more than a couple of holidays each year; but if you are working for OBUarity, you'd have an unlimited permit to visit any place in the world."

"When do you have time to travel whilst you are working in African schools?"

"Nathan, it's OBU age; I could have a lunch break in Paris and be back at work in the African school afterwards. Travelling in OBU is just a data set switching, requiring no time at all. Of course, one would have to be able to pay for them, but in my case, it's free."

"It does sound really good, but I am not sure if I would be qualified to be a teacher because I haven't finished my uni studies."

"Nathan, you have done two years of uni, and I am quite sure that's enough to get you a position as a teacher in OBUarity; they need more hands than they have at the moment so anyone putting their hands up would have quite a good chance. Plus, you had quite good marks at uni."

"It's really tempting."

"Nathan, leave it to me, I'll make some inquiries and I'll get back to you very soon. You can always decline the offer or try it for a short time to see if it suits you. You have nothing to lose."

Nathan thought about it for a moment and then said, "Thank you very much, Amy; I do appreciate your help. You know I have been worrying about whether I'll be able to get a job in the OBU age at all."

"So, it's settled then. Nathan, I am so glad you came back, and it's so exciting to think we might work together again," Amy said after they exchanged contact details.

Looking at Amy's back as she walked away, Nathan felt quite good about the opportunity, but at the same time, he felt a bit uneasy with Amy. He sensed that there was something more than just friendship and the anticipation of being co-workers in Amy's tone. They had started working at the bakery almost at the same time but back then the three-year age gap had been huge for Nathan. Amy was basically a kid to him, therefore, during the two years they had been working together, he had rarely paid much attention to her. Amy could have had a typical high school girl's crush on him, an older brother type crush, thought Nathan, but that was fifteen years ago, and now Amy would be thirty-two years old. Even though he hadn't asked her if she was married or had any children, he knew by instinct that she was single and had no kids, just from the way she talked, her clothing and the way she walked. He didn't know why or how, but he found he had an increased ability to observe others, like how he had known the attackers in the bar in Little Amsterdam were hostile as soon as they had arrived. Maybe it was the violent energy around them.

Turning his thoughts back to Amy, Nathan thought it was ridiculous to think that she could still fancy him now even if she had had a high school crush on him all that time ago. After another moment, Nathan chuckled to himself and dismissed the thoughts. He remembered reading an article stating that in work situations, male colleagues always overestimated their attractiveness to their female counterparts, and it was exactly his situation right now. Who did he think he was, Prince Charming? Nathan laughed at himself; Amy was just genuinely concerned about him as a colleague, a friend, and nothing more than that. Nathan looked back at the grey building one more time, and then turned, walking towards home.

**Chapter 12**

After dinner, while his mother was watching some TV (yes there were still TV programs for those outside OBU), Nathan sat in front of the computer and logged on to the Internet. It was a double surprise to Nathan that the seventeen-year-old desktop PC was still functioning, and the old Internet was also still in service. He typed 'Mary O'Brian' into the search box, and then hit the return key.

He selected the images page and hundreds of Mary's photos appeared on the screen. Gazing at Mary's blue eyes, Nathan felt his heart beat faster; he felt as if he had fallen in love with this young beauty. Blinking rapidly, he just couldn't link this pretty face to the ruthless terrorist the police had described to him in Little Amsterdam. Maybe her dazzling beauty had deceived him. Nathan clicked another link and started reading details about Mary.

Mary O'Brian was born in Northern Ireland twenty years ago, a whole fifteen years younger than him, but Nathan didn't feel his age at all. In fact, he really hadn't aged over the missing fifteen years. He was still twenty years old, even though to everyone who knew him he was actually thirty-five. Anyway, the thought made him feel a step closer to her; he was the same age as her, thanks to Master Wuwei's magic.

Mary's grandfather had been an active member of the IRA in the seventies, and the authorities believed her father was also heavily involved with SOH; some even guessed he was quite high-ranking in the terrorist organization but there was no proof because nobody had seen him for years.

SOH had emerged about ten years ago as the major entity carrying out terrorist activities aimed at sabotaging OBU. They claimed that OBU had destroyed society's morality by making casual sex so readily available, stating that it had made marriages and family a concept of the past. As a result, civilization and most importantly the human race itself was in danger. As simple as it sounded, nobody wanted to have a family or children anymore.

Some articles stated that over the years, SOH had bombed many OBU data centres and regional hubs. As a result, many OBU staff and innocent civilians had been killed as collateral damage. Despite SOH constantly expressing their regrets and sympathies about the loss of lives, they blamed the deaths on the government and OBU Corporation.

Nathan refined his search criteria, focusing on Mary's track record. Mary had joined SOH five years ago at the age of fifteen. Unlike the hard line of old-fashioned SOH members, she and her young comrades were much more techno savvy and started targeting the software rather than the hardware. Mary's main activities involved introducing viruses to the OBU systems. Even less violent in the real world, her group had caused a few major OBU regional hubs to melt down and had caused a large amount of financial loss to the relevant governments and OBU Corporation. Mary and her comrades had inflicted much more damage to the government and OBU Corporation than the old-fashioned bomb attacks in the real world, and that was why she was at the top of the most wanted list. The rumours said that what the government and OBU Corporation feared most was that, if Mary and her comrades could gain access to OBU's HQ and release the virus there, it would destroy

77

OBU entirely. The consequence would be the largest global financial crisis the world had ever seen, making the great depression in the thirties and the GFC in the noughties look like mild hiccups; uncontrollable inflation, global bankruptcies, world poverty, regional and even world wars could follow.

Nathan turned the computer off. He felt too tired to think anymore. He had only been back less then forty-eight hours, and needed time to adjust himself to the future time he was in. He decided to go to sleep and deal with tomorrow when it came.

\*\*\*

In a room at an unknown location, an image of Nathan and Amy standing face to face in the park was frozen in mid-air.

One voice asked, "Has anyone got any idea as to why Mary O'Brian took such a risk to turn up in Little Amsterdam?"

"The only plausible possibility is that she wanted to meet an extremely important person there."

"Do you mean Nathan Jenkins?"

"Yes, and we believe that she might intend to recruit him."

"But he is nobody. Although he's shown some extraordinary Kung Fu fighting skills, she wouldn't have known that beforehand. I doubt even Nathan himself knew of his fighting ability, based on the interview he had with our Dutch police officer. So, the question is why she risked her life to meet some guy, a nobody."

"Don't know. One theory is that she believed the prophecy that an OBU virgin would help her to bring OBU down."

"OBU virgin? An interesting theory. Anyway, how could we only have placed six agents without firearms on site when attempting to arrest Mary O'Brian? It was a once-in-a-lifetime chance to get her."

"We had no idea she would be there. It was pure chance that our security program cracked her mask and the automatic facial recognition software spotted her."

"Why didn't you get the special forces onto it?"

"To tell you the truth, nobody believed it could be remotely possible that Mary O'Brian would be there, in a strip bar in Little Amsterdam. We have had too many of these kinds of computer errors before, so we just sent the unit nearby to check it out."

"Who is the woman Nathan met in the park?"

"Amy, his co-worker from the bakery he worked at before his disappearance."

"Is she clean?"

"We think so as she is working for OBUarity. It means that she passed the background check when she joined the company. She also promised to get him a position in OBUarity."

"Good, make sure she is successful with his application."

\*\*\*

In a room in another unknown location, a voice stated, "It seems that Nathan is going to work for OBUarity."

"Yes. Let's hope that OBU hasn't realized how important Nathan is to us, them and the whole world."

"If Nathan is the one the prophecy predicted, the struggle will come to an end soon."

"It won't be that easy, but let's keep our hopes up. Keep watching him closely."

## Chapter 13

"Good morning, Nathan," Amy greeted him as he walked out of his bedroom.

Things had happened quite rapidly in the last week. Amy had helped Nathan launch an application to work for OBUarity and he had gotten approval the next day; they needed extra hands, as Amy said. It was even better that two of Amy's roommates had moved out a couple of months ago, and she had been struggling to find someone to share the costs of renting the three-bedroom apartment, so Nathan moved in.

Amy commented that it'd be best if her roommates were working for the same company, so at least they would have some human interaction in the real world. Plus, the apartment was so close to Nathan's mother, he couldn't really get a better deal.

Nathan had initially felt a bit awkward when Amy suggested that he share the apartment with her. Though he tried to think that Amy must have got over her high school crush on him long ago, if she had ever had one, Nathan could still sense that Amy had feelings towards him. He might be completely off the mark, but if he were right, sharing a flat with Amy wouldn't do either of them any good. However, he couldn't really decline the offer either. Let's face it, for a guy like him with an unfinished tertiary education degree in oriental philosophy, what were the chances of him getting a job in the OBU age that he knew nothing about? The conclusion was quite simple and straightforward: if Nathan wanted to get employed, this was the only opportunity. Besides, Amy was quite open and frank towards him; she told him jokingly that, despite the fact she was supposedly three years younger than him, because of his much younger appearance, she should be his big sister. Nathan took it as a subtle hint to him not to worry about any complications in their relationship. So a decision was made and Nathan spent his first night in the apartment.

"Good morning, Amy," Nathan said. "It smells wonderful. Wow, bacon and eggs for breakfast. Why don't we just have some cereal, and enjoy it as bacon and eggs in OBU?"

"Well, we all need to spoil ourselves occasionally, don't we?" Amy put the bacon, eggs, fried mushrooms and tomatoes, and toasted bread onto Nathan's plate and her own. After sitting down, Amy said, "Little brother, tomorrow morning it's your turn to cook breakfast."

It seemed Amy was quite enjoying playing this elder sister role. Nathan smiled. "No problem, big sister; I'll do whatever you tell me to do." In fact, he didn't have much choice. He knew nothing about this new OBU age, and Amy would be the perfect guide. He fully appreciated her help.

After breakfast, Nathan did the washing up. When everything was done, Amy said, "See you in OBU," and walked into her bedroom.


It was OBUarity's standard policy that all employees wore masks during their working hours for security reasons; they supplied the latest version of anti-seeker masks. Of course, the employees were able to alter their masks to suit their individual needs. The adjustment and alteration of masks were in fact relatively easy, sort of like using Photoshop to change a photo in pre-OBU age, at least that was the best way Nathan could describe it.

Amy didn't bother about her look that much, she simply changed her hair to black and slightly altered the shape of her nose and eyes enough to make her look like a different person, but she left her body untouched. Amy was very fit and her body was in good shape so there was no need to change it at all.

Nathan, on the other hand, liked the blond surfer boy image Gary had created for him when he had visited little Amsterdam; he felt like he was watching the world from behind his mask, the way normal sunglasses would offer.

"Wow, a blond surfer boy. I didn't know you were a surfer, but I didn't really know you that well," said Amy.

"No, I wasn't a surfer. It's just a mask Gary created for me during my first visit to OBU; I'm just too lazy to change the design."

"Okay, let's go to Africa and start our adventure of the day." Amy brought the floating globe forward into mid-air and zoomed in to their destination. In no time at all they were in the login area. Following Amy's lead, Nathan scanned his wrist against the shiny pole.

The school was located in Africa, along the borders of Namibia, Botswana and Zimbabwe. The students attending the school were also from the tribes of those neighbouring countries. In theory there was no reason why these poor kids couldn't easily go to Europe, the USA and other western countries to get educated but in reality, it was still much easier to establish the schools where the students were due to financial, political, and cultural considerations, not to mention immigration reasons.

The digital version of the school campus was designed to follow local dwellings, the typical round mud walls and thatched dome-shaped huts, but inside they were very spacious, and contained modern computers and other educational facilities including libraries.

Nathan kicked the dirt on the ground, seeing the dust fly as the wind blew it away quickly. He knew that it was just a simulation of the real grassland. If one stood in this exact location in the real world, there would not be a single piece of evidence that there had been any human activities, just the vast grassland and wildlife.

It was still early for the students, so the campus was very quiet. Amy showed Nathan the classrooms. As they were walking into the library, Nathan saw two more European-looking people also stepping inside the door.

"Good morning, Amy," a brown-haired woman said with a strong French accent. "Is this Nathan, our new teacher you were talking about?"

"Good morning, Lucie and Pierre," said Amy. "Let me introduce you to each other. Nathan, this is Lucie, our science teacher, and Pierre, the geology teacher; they are both from France."

Nathan shook hands with both of them.

"What are you going to teach, Nathan?" asked Pierre.

Amy answered for Nathan. "Nathan is going to take English, philosophy and world history. I am so glad Nathan is here so I can concentrate on teaching math. To be honest, English is not my strength."

"We all know you have done a wonderful job teaching English," said Lucie.

Soon the students arrived. Nathan then understood why he had gotten the job so easily: there were at least three hundred kids ranging from eight to eighteen years old, so they did need any extra help they could get.

One of the advantages of a digital school was that you could expand the classroom to be as large as required. Looking at his class of over seventy kids, Nathan started his first English lesson. Amy had done a good job getting these kids started with basic English.

Even though Nathan hadn't got a teaching qualification, he did have some tutoring experience from his two years of studying at university. Of course, he had never tutored such a large group; nevertheless, he managed to get through the first class and he enjoyed himself very much. He loved the kids who were so eager to learn. He made fun games for them to play, sang simple English songs, and utilized any new technology OBU could offer. Combining a mix of visual and sound aids, Nathan was satisfied his students had learnt something from the class.

Time passed quickly when one was busy; it barely felt like he had blinked before it was time for all the students to go home at the end of the day. Only then, after saying goodbye to the last student, did Nathan feel exhausted. Soon the other three teachers stepped into his classroom.

"How did the first day go?" asked Amy.

"A bit of a struggle and quite stressful, but I'll manage," said Nathan.

"You seem to be doing great, much better than my first-time teaching," said Pierre.

"Nathan, why don't you come with us to Paris? We can have a few drinks together, and I can also introduce you to a few new friends," said Lucie.

Nathan thought about it and then said, "Thanks for the invitation but I'll give it a miss today. I feel exhausted so I think I'll have an early night."

"Well, too bad you'll be missing out on all of the fun." Pierre turned to Amy. "Amy, are you sure I can't persuade you to come to the party even once? I have failed for the last twelve months, but today may be my lucky day."

84

Lucie held Pierre's hand, dragging him towards the door. "Come on, Pierre, Amy is not interested in partying. Good night, we'll see you both tomorrow." They walked out of the door.

"Amy, why don't you like to go to their parties? It seems that Pierre was quite disappointed about it."

"Well, I am not into their ''all for one and one for all' French-style love party."

'Oh, do you mean that Lucie and Pierre have multiple sexual partners?"

"I think it's a bit beyond multiple sexual partners; they are basically large daily orgies for OBUarity volunteers from all over the world."

"Wow, I never imagined that. Amy, what do you normally do after work?" Nathan was going to ask if Amy ever went on dates but decided against it.

"Apart from attending fitness classes and taking a few recreational classes for fun, I have been travelling lots, making the most of the perks I get from OBUarity."

"It sounds great. What kind of fitness classes do you go to?"

"Why don't you come with me tonight and see for yourself?"

"Okay, let's do that."

## Chapter 14

The gym was in the basement of their building. According to Amy, all of these OBU-age apartment buildings had a gym like this one, usually in their basements. Unlike the kind of gym Nathan was familiar with, this style of gym was rather alien to him and he wouldn't have had any idea what it was if Amy hadn't told him beforehand. In the huge hall, there were rows and rows of glass cylinders.

Some cylinders were empty, and some had a person inside in his or her swimsuit. As Nathan passed an occupied one, he could see the cylinder was filled with some kind of clear liquid, and the person inside was totally immersed and wearing a helmet and a mask with a pipe attached, like a diver, so the pipe had to be used for breathing, Nathan guessed.

Looking further, Nathan could see more people inside cylinders, and they seemed to be doing all kinds of different activities. Some were walking, jogging, jumping on the invisible 'liquid treadmills', while others were boxing against non-existent punch bags; the strangest of all was one woman who was actually climbing up a set of invisible stairs.

Looking at Nathan's expression, Amy laughed. "Nathan, go and get changed into your swimming trunks; meet me back here and I will show you what to do."

"Push the button to open the cylinder," Amy said after they had both changed into their swimsuits. "When you are inside, put the helmet and mask on, like you would to enter OBU."

Nathan followed Amy's instructions.

The cylinder was about ten feet in diameter. He noticed there were holes, large and small ones, on the lower part of the cylinder. Nathan picked up the helmet and the mask from the floor and put them on his head; the mask changed and adjusted to seal his nose and mouth perfectly, and then he felt air flowing into the mask. The difference between this helmet and the other one he used to get into OBU was that here the eye-shield formed part of the mask.

As the mask sealed over his face, through the eye-shield, Nathan saw clear liquid springing out from the holes, filling up the cylinder quickly. He looked at Amy, who was inside the cylinder next to him, and she raised her thumb. Nathan also raised his, assuming it meant he was okay.

It didn't take long for the liquid to cover his head. It felt slightly cooler than his body temperature, quite pleasant, and then the eye-shield became dark, then completely black, and then he was in a room flooded with bright lights: he was in OBU.

Nathan looked at his body, now clothed in sporty shorts and a T-shirt, and then at Amy, who stood next to him. "Please explain, Amy."

"No need to explain very much; you are in OBU and can engage in any fitness activity you like."

Nathan looked around, seeing all the standard gym equipment he was familiar with spread out in the vast floor space: treadmills, weights machines, a boxing ring, punch bags and more. "I understand that all of these are software, simulations of real-world machines, but how do they simulate these activities in that cylinder?"

"Oh, that's the trick of the liquid you are immersed in now." Amy waved her arms around her in a circular movement. "The liquid has a very unique property: its density can be controlled by electrical voltage. It could be as liquid as water, or as hard as rock."

"So the software controls the hardness of the liquid so our bodies can feel and carry out all of the fitness programs?"

"Exactly." Amy turned and pointed outside of the glass door. "We don't have to do this boring gym stuff. What about climbing up mountains?"

"Climbing up mountains?"

"Why so surprised? Anything is possible in OBU, and just a click away. Which mountain would you like, the Swiss Alps, the Andes, or the Himalayas?"

"I don't think I am up to Mount Everest yet, so let's start with the Swiss Alps."

"Winter or summer?" asked Amy.

"Winter. I have never climbed up a mountain covered in snow."

Amy waved her arms and brought up a few screens in mid-air; after a few clicks and waves, Nathan found he was no longer inside a gym, but inside a room with many cubicles, like a changing room.

"It'd be too cold to climb in just sport shorts and T-shirts, obviously. Get some warm clothes from inside the cubicles and I'll see you outside." Amy disappeared into one of the cubicles.

Nathan found a warm jacket, pants and snow boots and put them on. After pushing the door open and walking outside, he found that he was standing on top of a mountain peak. He moved his legs, used his snow boots to stamp on the pure, powdery snow, and then took his thick gloves off and picked up a handful of snow. He put the snow into his mouth and enjoyed the cold, fresh taste.

Amy walked out from the cabin clad in a blue mountain-climbing suit. "I love the crisp, powdery snow so much." She threw herself backwards, so she was lying flat on top of the blanket of thick white snow. Amy moved both her arms up and down and her legs opened and closed. "I am making a snow angel." She laughed loudly and happily.

Amy's laughter was so contagious that Nathan couldn't help but also throw himself onto the snow. "I am making an even bigger snow angel." He had never felt so relaxed. He let go of all his worries, enjoying the pure air and cold, soft snow and all that nature could offer. He felt like he had gone back to his childhood and wished this moment could last forever.

Finally, they got up. Amy pointed at the next mountaintop on their left. "Ready to conquer that peak?"

"Sure, let's do it."


Nathan had settled into his new life at a relatively comfortable pace, thanks to Amy's help at each step. Each morning during the last week, he and Amy had taken turns to make their breakfast and then eaten it together in their apartment. Apart from the occasional special treat of bacon and eggs, they mostly ate cereal and enjoyed it as whatever they fancied in OBU. One morning they even made it into ice cream in the cyber space—yeah, ice cream for breakfast. Anything was possible in the computer world.

Nathan and Amy had developed quite an interesting schedule for their after-work hours, combining fitness activities with sightseeing: climbing all the way up to the top of the Eiffel Tower; hiking towards Monte Rosa in the Swiss Alps; tracing the crumpling ruins of the Great Wall of China. There was so much to experience and see, and they both enjoyed their adventures, and each other's accompany. Though Amy's face always wore friendly smiles, Nathan could tell her smiles these days were from genuine happiness; he felt happy for her and also for himself, too.

Meanwhile, teaching classes was also becoming easier each day. Nathan had got to know the kids quite well, particularly James, the eighteen-year-old son of the chief of a bushman tribe. James was slender and slightly shorter than Nathan. When Nathan asked him why he chose James as his English name, he said he liked watching 007 movies.

Based on his background reading about bushman tribes, Nathan was fascinated that the bushman tribes, although much less frequently now, still used the walking-hunt method to hunt, basically chasing their prey until the animals were exhausted to death. During one conversation, James told Nathan that their tribe's men gave up the practice long ago because the government had forced them to adapt to an agriculture-based lifestyle. Looking at James' face, Nathan couldn't help but sigh inside. More and more traditional customs and practices, together with many heritage sites, were disappearing around the world; he wondered how long it would take for everyone to speak English. Even though he agreed with Cathy about the food revolution in the OBU age that had ended hunger, junk food consumption and starvation and had instead moved towards slow, local, organic food, OBU had enforced and sped up the elimination of cultural diversity.

After all the students had gone home, and Lucie and Pierre had gone to one of their love parties, Amy came to Nathan's classroom. "Nathan, Vicky came to talk to me today in private; she has a serious problem."

"Who is Vicky?"

"She is sixteen years old, the daughter of the chief of a Zulu tribe; I mentioned her to you a couple of days ago."

'Oh yes, I remember her now. What's the problem?"

"Come on, Nathan, you can't remember anything I told you," Amy said. "Vicky had her eye on James; actually, the feeling is mutual."

"It's ringing a bell now; so, they fell in love with each other. Is that the problem?"

"Yes, it is. The Zulu and bushman tribes have been enemies for a while. If her father finds out, Vicky is afraid that there could be a tribe war. She asked for my advice. I told her that I'd think about it and talk to her tomorrow."

"It is a serious problem and quite a tricky one too. We all know Zulu tribes are very tough and good at fighting," Nathan said. "What about suggesting Vicky goes to study in the West?"

"No, it wouldn't work. I have talked about it with her. The problem is that her father has already made a promise to marry her to a chief's son from another Zulu tribe, and the wedding is at the end of this year so there is no way her father would allow Vicky to study overseas."

Nathan thought very hard for a while but still had no idea how to solve the problem. "Amy, there is no simple solution here. Why don't we both talk to Vicky and James tomorrow and find out more details about the arranged marriage and the hostility between the two tribes."

Amy nodded.

The next evening, back at their apartment, Nathan and Amy sat down to talk. "Amy, what did you found out about the arranged marriage?"

"Well, not surprisingly, considering how beautiful Vicky is, many chiefs' sons proposed marriage. I suspect, in addition to her beauty, it's also because Vicky's father's tribe is the most powerful one in this area. Anyway, it's little surprise that Vicky is to marry the chief's son of the second most powerful Zulu tribe."

"How many chiefs' sons of Zulu tribes proposed to Vicky?"

"Three in total."

"It means the chiefs of the other two tribes can't feel very happy about the result." Nathan thought deeply.

"What's James' story?"

"He told me his father was against the affair, too, because he is worried about a tribe war. There are never marriages between bushman and Zulu tribes. He also told me the details about the relationships among tribes in this area, which is quite interesting actually."

"Oh, I forgot to tell you one more thing. Vicky told me that she is six weeks pregnant."

"What? How could she get pregnant in OBU?"

"Not in OBU; they have met in the real world."

"Oh shit, this is now a real problem." Nathan thought about it for a long time. "The only solution I can think of is to get both James and Vicky to the West. If they are not there, the tribe chiefs may decide to forget about it."

"I wish it was that simple." Amy wasn't convinced.

"I know, but at least Vicky and James could escape any harm that might come from the potential tribe wars."

"How could we do that? I mean how could we get them to the West?"

Nathan thought about it for a few seconds. "Why don't we ask the OBUarity field staff to help us? I believe that there are quite a few of them in that region. If OBUarity could offer them scholarships to study in Europe or the

USA, James and Vicky could sneak out and escape. When they return with their newborn baby, Vicky's father might forgive her and James when he sees his own grandchild."

Just then, the phone rang. It was Dave and Gary inviting Nathan on an outing.

"I don't have time to visit the strip bar in Little Amsterdam right now." Nathan covered the phone with his hand, speaking to Amy.

Amy thought for a second. "Nathan, I think your idea of getting Vicky and James to the West is a possible solution, and I'll get on it right away. You wouldn't be able to help me arrange it, anyway, so why don't you just go ahead and have some time off."

"I don't feel comfortable leaving it all to you."

"Nathan, you have worked out the solution, so just go out and enjoy your time without me; you must be sick of being with me all the time by now."

"Amy, please don't say that. I really enjoy your company, and all of your help."

"I know that, little brother." Amy smiled; somehow Nathan sensed a slight bitterness behind her smile, but it disappeared immediately. "Nathan, you can't be with your elder sister all the time; you need to spend time with your mates. Go, enjoy your evening out."

"Thanks, Amy. But please keep me informed."

## Chapter 15

"Nathan, here are your seekers." Gary passed a pair of sunglasses to Nathan.

They were walking along a crowded street in Little Amsterdam. Sure enough, with the seekers, Nathan was able to see through most people's masks around him.

"Pretty good shit, eh?" Dave patted Nathan's shoulder.

"You had better put this on as well." Gary passed another item to Nathan.

It was a wristwatch, similar to a waterproof electronic watch, with a wide strap and many buttons. "Why do I need a watch?"

'Dude, it's not only a watch," said Dave. "It's called a jumper, the mobile phone of OBU."

"Jumper? But I saw people using mobile phones in OBU," said Nathan.

'You can call it whatever you like," Gary said. "They function as mobile phones in OBU, but much better. Because everything in OBU is already sending signals directly into your brain, a jumper enables you to both see and listen to others who are also using jumpers."

"Jumpers come in all different shapes; people wear them as hats, jewellery such as necklaces, rings, bangles, accessories like gloves, shoes; you name it," said Dave.

"Why don't they just combine seekers and jumpers together as a pair of sunglasses?" asked Nathan.

"Mine is just that but it's much more expensive, so I just got you a cheaper version of each one; I hope you don't mind," Gary said.

"I appreciate it, mate," said Nathan. "Why haven't I got a jumper from OBUarity? They provide us with the latest masks."

"God knows; maybe you don't need one whilst working in a remote village in Africa," said Dave.

"That's exactly why we need jumpers there. Gary, I have to get one for Amy," said Nathan.

"I am certain Amy has already got one," said Gary.

"How can you be so sure?" asked Nathan.

"Because I have talked to Amy with my jumper a couple of times," said Gary.

'I wonder why Amy didn't mention jumpers to me; anyway, Gary, can I talk to Amy's jumper? I mean right now?" Nathan was worrying about Vicky's problem.

Dave stopped walking and looked at Nathan. "Have you fallen for Amy?"

"Oh, no; we are just friends. The reason I need to ring her is because…" Gary interrupted Nathan. "You don't need to tell us the reason. Push that button on your jumper, and a screen should pop up in front of you."

Nathan did as instructed. A large screen popped up in mid-air, right in front of his face.

"Don't worry, you are the only one who is able to see the screen," Dave said.

The screen was much like the mobile screen Nathan was familiar with, so it was not difficult to navigate it to make a call. All he had to do was use his hand to pull one screen after another. He found Gary's number in the contacts, so he pushed the dial button.

As soon as Gary answered the call, Nathan saw live pictures appearing on his jumper's screen, like a video camera's stream feed. It was obviously from Gary's point of view. "You can see why I chose that particular jumper for you; it works like the old mobile phone."

"You can switch the visual signal off if you don't want others to see what you are doing," said Dave.

"Nathan, here is Amy's number," said Gary.

Nathan turned the visual signal off first, and then dialled Amy's jumper. He didn't feel comfortable letting Amy seeing the red-light district in the background.

"Hi, Amy, it's me, Nathan." It seemed Amy had also switched the visual signals off.

"Nathan?" He could hear Amy's surprise. "You've got a jumper."

"Yes, Gary just gave it to me. How come you didn't tell me about it before?"

"I suppose that we were together all the time so there was no need to have a jumper, so I completely forgot about it. I am so glad you have one now."

"How is it going with contacting OBUarity field staff?"

"I have talked to one of them already; since the situation is quite serious, OBUarity has agreed to help get Vicky and James out as soon as possible; nobody wants to have a blood bath of a tribe war."

"Great. Please keep me informed." Nathan hung up.

"All settled? Should we get to the bar? I desperately want a drink," said Dave.

"I thought you didn't drink much; it's the girls you are so desperate for," said Nathan.

'You know me well, mate," said Dave.


The bar was as noisy and crowded as Nathan remembered from their last visit. With his seeker sunglasses on, Nathan could see most people's real faces, but there were a few that still remained young and beautiful looking, so they were either wearing more advanced masks, or were genuinely young and good-looking people. Gary slouched into his chair, blowing

96

clouds of blue smoke, and Dave's eyes scanned the surroundings, looking for his prey.

Nathan sipped his beer and observed Dave; it would be interesting to see how long it would take him to find a girl. Once again, Dave didn't disappoint Nathan; he found his target in less than five minutes.

Gary's eyes were closed, deeply enjoying smoking his dope. Dave turned to Nathan. "Look at the girl at the fifth table on the left; yes, the one with the white jacket and short black skirt. What do you think about her?"

Nathan could see through her mask and was surprised that her mask hadn't changed her appearance much. She had a good body, full boobs, long legs and a flat stomach. The blonde hair was dyed—you could see that from the dark roots. Her face was quite attractive, obviously Dave's type. "I think you both suit each other."

"Wish me luck, mate." Dave stood up and walked over to the girl.

It was quite noisy so Nathan couldn't hear the exchange between Dave and the girl, but based on Dave's facial expression, Nathan was afraid the situation wasn't going as smoothly as Dave had hoped. After another few words, the girl stood up and walked to another table where two guys in suits sat. Dave came back seconds later and sat down beside Nathan angrily.

"What happened?" asked Nathan.

"What a bloody slut she is," Dave said.

"Isn't that what you are seeking here?" asked Nathan.

"Yeah, but she is particular slutty; she wanted to get two large guys together and have rough sex," Dave said, looking back at the girl.

Nathan looked at the girl more closely. She seemed to be about in her mid-twenties. The two guys she was talking with were quite large in their real bodies, easily a few inches taller and a fair bit thicker than Nathan and Dave; normally Nathan would think they were rugby players but from the way they dressed and talked, Nathan imaged they were lawyers or businessmen. He looked back at Dave. "There are plenty of other girls out there and you may have better luck later."

Dave looked up. Following his line of sight, Nathan saw the girl walking out of the bar with the two guys.

"There is no other girl I am interested in in this bar. Let's get out of here." Dave was not in a good mood.

"All right. I'm done with my fix." Gary stood up and they all walked out.

"Where are we going? Another bar?" asked Nathan.

"Not another bloody bar. To tell you the truth, I have been here so many times, but we always end up stuck inside the bloody bars. Why don't we walk around outside of the red-light district and have a good look at Amsterdam," said Dave.

"That'd be a first," Gary laughed.

"Good idea, let's go and have a walk," agreed Nathan.


They passed the crowds and walked towards the main street outside the red-light district. There were fewer people around the further they walked; soon they were the only people around. It was very quiet, and Nathan enjoyed the fresh air very much. Suddenly they heard a girl screaming; it was from the dark alley on their left.

"A girl's screaming," Dave shouted. "Come on, Nathan, let's rescue her."

Nathan didn't say anything but ran towards where the voice was coming from. It was a dark alley; Nathan could make out three figures in front of them. As his eyes adjusted to the dim light, he could see two large guys holding a girl up against the wall.

"Let her go," Nathan said calmly.

"It's none of your business; we are having consensual rough adult sex as she requested," one of the large guys said in a southern American accent.

"Please help me; I want to leave now," the girl screamed.

"Shut up." The other guy slapped her cheek. "You asked for rough sex but want to stop now. You can't do that, bitch. Bad luck, you have to stick with us until we are done with you."

"I said let her go." Nathan raised his voice a bit.

"Buddy, are you looking for a fight?" One of the guys walked towards Nathan, while the other still held the girl.

"I am not looking for a fight, but I am asking you to let her go," said Nathan.

"You forgot to say please." The large guy swung his huge fist at Nathan's head, the movement fast and powerful.

Nathan measured the angle and speed of the oncoming fist; he moved his body slightly, just missing the punch by half an inch. His own hand flashed out and grabbed the guy's wrist; with a twist and a jerk, he heard the man's pained scream as the bone cracked. Nathan knew the man wouldn't be able to use his arm for a while. But Nathan didn't stop there; he kicked at both the guy's knees to dislocate his joints so he wouldn't be able to walk either. "You son of a bitch…you broke my arms and legs…"

The second guy threw the girl to the ground, rushing towards Nathan like a raging bull. He made a noise like an animalistic roar.

Nathan didn't move but watched him calmly; in the split second before their bodies clashed, Nathan swiftly shifted his body sideways. As the guy's body passed him, he used the edge of his palm to chop at his neck. With a heavy thud, the large guy crashed face down onto the ground, unconscious.

The first guy writhed on the ground, screaming loudly. Nathan kicked at his arm and legs a couple of times to ease his pain, so he stopped screaming.

Nathan walked to the girl, who had put her clothes back on as best she could. "Are you all right?"

The girl held her torn clothes to cover her body, and cried, "These two bastards raped me, beat me…"

Dave stepped forward, recognizing the girl as the one who rejected him in the bar. "You are the slut from the bar. Isn't this what you were asking for?"

The girl whimpered. "Yes, I agreed to do it…with them initially, but soon I regretted it and asked them to stop, but they kept raping me and beating me and wouldn't stop even though I was begging them to let me go…"

Nathan stopped Dave before he could make another comment. "What's your name? Where are you from?"

"Ava; I am from LA, in the United States."

"Ava, could you please wait here for a moment." Nathan walked to the first guy, who was holding his arm, swearing and cursing. He looked up at Nathan, and then shouted in a fearful voice, "Who are you? What are you going to do to me?"

"I'm just doing a citizen's duty, stopping you from attacking an innocent victim," said Nathan.

"You broke my arm and legs…" the guy said.

"What's your name?" Nathan asked.

"My name is Jacob and he's Aiden. Is Aiden dead?" said Jacob.

"No, Aiden is alive, and your arm and legs haven't been broken, just dislocated," said Nathan. He then turned around and kicked the unconscious Aiden in the back a few times. With some groans, Aiden swore, then tried to climb up.

"You had better share the pain with your friend." Nathan kicked at Aiden's legs and arms; Aiden started screaming.

"Shut up. It's not that painful," Nathan said. "So now you know what your victim's suffering feels like."

Gary tugged Nathan's arm. "Can I have a word with you?"

Before Nathan could respond, Jacob said, "We are both lawyers and we will sue your ass off."

"Have you lost your mind?" said Nathan. "You are the bloody criminals here."

Jacob shouted, "We were having consensual adult sex, and you attacked us. Call the police and we will sue you and send you to jail…"

Aiden interrupted Jacob. "Mate, you are from Australia, right? If you fix our legs and arms and let us go, we are happy to forget all of this; what do you say?"

Dave dragged Nathan away from the two guys; Gary followed. After they were out of earshot, Dave said, "These guys are right: if it goes to court, they could sue you for bodily harm."

"What about their assault on the girl?" Nathan said.

"It'd be very difficult to prove the case because she willingly engaged with them in the first place; let them go and forget about this mess," said Dave.

"Dave is right, Nathan. We don't need the extra trouble," said Gary.

Nathan turned, looking at the whimpering girl against the wall, with her torn clothes wrapped around her naked body. "What about her rights? I can't let those two leave without any punishment."

"Nathan, you have punished them enough," said Gary.

"Not nearly as much as they deserve. They have to feel the suffering their victim felt." Nathan suddenly had a good idea. "Gary, can jumpers record people's voices?"

"Yes, they can. What's on your mind?" asked Gary.

"Leave it to me." Nathan walked back to the girl. He took her away from the two guys, and then said softly, "Ava, under the circumstances, it's unlikely we can prove the case easily in court, but I don't want to let them leave unpunished. I believe in the old laws, teeth for teeth and blood for blood. You have a jumper, right? Good, so connect it to my jumper. Now I want you to try to remember every detail of how they abused you and speak it out loud. I know it's a hard thing for you to do right now, but please do it for yourself and other possible victims in the future. I will record your words and force these two thugs to listen to it over and over; meanwhile I will dislocate more of their joints to make them suffer, so they will always remember the pain whenever they are thinking of abusing another woman in the future. Will you do it for me, Ava?"

Ava nodded. She thought for a moment and then started to tell him about her terrible ordeal. Nathan listened to her voice, feeling angry and enraged about how nasty and cruel these two animals were to her. For a moment, Nathan almost couldn't stand to listen to her words anymore, but he forced himself to finish recording her voice.

102

When it was done, Nathan took Ava close to the two guys who were sitting on the ground cursing and swearing. "Ava, look them right in the eyes; it's your turn to return their favour." With Gary's help, Nathan connected his jumper to Jacob and Aiden's; he then pushed the button to upload Ava's words to their jumpers. He pushed the repeat buttons on both their jumpers to play her voice in a loop; almost immediately, both guys started screaming again.

# Chapter 16

"Shut up." Nathan was about to dislocate their joints but stopped. Their screams were too real to be faked. Even Gary was concerned. "Did you accidently break some of their bones?"

"No. I planned to do it but haven't even started yet. It may have something to do with the jumper?" said Nathan. He walked over, put one foot on Jacob to stop him rolling around on the ground, and then pulled his jumper, a wristwatch, off him. His screaming stopped immediately. Jacob panted hard. "Mate, please stop torturing me like that; I'll go to the police and confess, I'll do anything you want but please stop…"

Nathan put the jumper back on Jacob's wrist and he started screaming again.

"What the hell is going on with these two?" Dave asked.

"It seemed that they are allergic to their victim's words." Nathan pulled the jumper off Aiden, and he stopped screaming. "Please, mate, I'll do anything you ask, just don't put it back on me again."

Nathan was puzzled. He passed the jumper to Gary. "You tell me what's going on with this jumper."

It only took a second or so for Gary to rip the jumper off him as quickly as he could. "Shit. It's painful."

"What are you talking about?" asked Nathan.

"I don't know how but the recorded voice is not only a voice, but a replay of the real encounter; in other words, whoever is on the receiving end of these jumpers is experiencing the victim's suffering in every detail, the raping, the humiliation and the violence," Gary said.

"Holy shit," Dave shouted. "So, these two can fuck themselves."

Nathan went over and put one of the jumpers back on Aiden and the other on Jacob; they both started to roll around on the ground and scream again. Nathan waited until they were screaming so much that they lost their voices and then took the jumpers off them; they both collapsed on the ground, panting heavily.

Nathan said to the girl, "I have dislocated both of their knees, so they are going nowhere. You can call the police and give them the jumpers with your recording on; I am sure they will go to jail for what they did to you."

Gary seemed worried but said nothing.

Ava thought for a while. "Thanks for all you have done for me, but I have decided not to get the police involved. I think they have suffered enough and will remember the pain enough not to abuse another woman in the future."

Gary let out a deep breath in relief.

"Well, it's your decision." Nathan turned around, kicking at their legs and arms to put their joints back in. They tried to climb up unsuccessfully. "Just stay where you are for another half hour, and your limbs will be back to normal," said Nathan.

Gary got the girl, Nathan and Dave away from the two guys, and then said, "Ava, I would really appreciate it if you never mentioned what happened tonight to anybody. We saved you tonight, so it is not such a big ask for you to return the favour."

"But why?" asked Ava.

"You don't need to know. Please promise us you won't mention this to anybody under any circumstances," said Gary.

"Okay, I promise," said Ava.

105

Gary turned to Nathan and Dave. "You had better escort Ava to an exit point so she can get home as soon as possible."

"What are you going to do?" asked Dave.

"I'm going to have a chat with those two guys," said Gary.

So Nathan and Dave walked with the girl towards the main street.

Ava asked Nathan, "I won't tell anyone but could you please tell me your name so I will at least know who saved my life tonight?"

Nathan smiled. "Never mind my name. Let's get you home first."

They walked along the main street and found an exit point. The girl thanked Nathan again; after swiping her wrist on the metal box, she vanished into thin air.

Soon Gary also came out of the dark alley and joined Nathan and Dave. "Dave and Nathan, particularly you, Dave, please don't mention what happened tonight to anybody. I am not joking; it's a matter of life and death."

"Dude, what are you talking about?" asked Dave.

"I can't explain it to you right now but trust me; if you tell anyone about it, it could cost you your life," Gary said very seriously.

"You must be crazy," said Dave. "All right, I will keep my mouth shut about it."

"Please try, Dave; I know it's hard for you to do," Gary said. "But remember it could save your life in the end."

"What happened to those two thugs?" Nathan tilted his head towards the alley.

"I talked to them and they both agreed not to contact the police about what happened; in fact, they'll be too embarrassed to mention it to anyone," said Gary. After that the three of them swiped their wrists against the metal exit box, and also disappeared into thin air.

They arrived back at Dave and Gary's flat, still in OBU. Nathan was going to ask Gary what happened to the jumpers, but received an urgent message from Amy, who wanted him to contact her immediately.

Nathan rang Amy on her jumper; soon he not only heard her voice, but also saw her face and her surroundings. He could see many people walking on the street and many stalls were jammed along the footpath. Amy seemed to be in a market.

"What's happened, Amy?" asked Nathan.

"Oh my God, Nathan; you had better come here immediately. All hell has broken loose." Amy looked so stressed that she was practically screaming.

"Calm down, Amy. Tell me where you are and I'll be with you in a second," Nathan said. So Amy did. "Mate, I have to go; it's an emergency call." Nathan brought the screen up in mid-air, selected his destination and logged in to the town in Africa.

Amy stood on the dirty road at the edge of the town, adjacent to a large food market, the one that Nathan had seen earlier. Beside her, a couple of European-looking guys were gathered. Nathan assumed that they were OBUarity field staffs.

"Nathan." Amy spoke breathlessly. "We organized a way of getting James and Vicky out, as by chance there is a fleet of trucks from OBUarity that are scheduled to leave the area today, so we thought it would be the perfect opportunity."

"Something went wrong?" asked Nathan.

"Yes, it couldn't be worse than this; it backfired. Vicky's father, somehow, found out what was happening. He interpreted this as the bushman tribes trying to kidnap his daughter, a premeditated plan to attack his tribe, so he collected all of his tribe's warriors and swore that they would kill every last man in James' father's tribe."

"That's bad." Nathan turned to the OBUarity field staff next to him. "Hi, I am Nathan, a colleague of Amy's." It was strange that they were neither looking at him nor responding.

"Nathan, they are not in OBU; you are looking at their images." Amy waved her arm, which went through the figures as if they were ghosts.

"So they are ghosts in OBU."

"No, we are more like ghosts to them, because we can see and hear them, not the other way around."

"Are we able to talk to them?"

"Yes, you can talk to them on their mobiles via your jumper; oh shit, here are the Zulu tribe warriors."

Nathan turned around, his jaw dropping as hundreds of Zulu warriors, carrying spears, clubs, and machetes, almost crashed into him. It was such a strange sensation, like watching an army of ghosts passing through his body; in fact, he was really the ghost, watching the real-world event unfolding in front of his eyes. The two OBUarity staff members were snatched by the Zulu warriors, taken with them to join their march to the battle. In the middle of the marching crowd, Nathan saw Vicky walking alongside a tribe elder, presumably her father, the Zulu tribe chief.

"Come on, we need to get to the front if we want to stop the blood bath." Amy and Nathan ran as fast as they could, bypassing the Zulu army. Soon they arrived at the square in the town centre. Opposite stood the bushman tribe; although they were not as well armed as the Zulu warriors, they did have the numbers to match. James and his father stood in front of their tribesmen.

"What are we going to do now?" asked Amy.

"I assumed that you had contacted the police and armed forces near the area," said Nathan.

'Yes, we did, but it would take at least a day for them to get ready, if by any chance anyone is interested enough to interfere with tribal conflicts."

"What did OBUarity say about this?"

"They promised that they'd provide whatever they could to be helpful, but in this situation that's the same as no help at all."

Nathan heard Vicky's father shout at James' father in their native language. As such, Nathan had no idea what they were saying, but from their expressions and angry tone, he had no doubt that they were accusing, insulting, and threatening each other; the blood bath was sure to begin any second.

# Chapter 17

There was not a moment to lose if he wanted to stop the fight, but he was thousands of miles away. Even if he was at the site, what could he do? Despite being good at hand-to-hand combat, confirmed by the two fights he was recently involved in, Nathan knew his skills were useless when trying to stop hundreds of armed tribal warriors attacking each other; therefore, he had to think of something else, and quickly.

Since using force to stop the fight was impossible, Nathan had to think outside of the box. His mind wandered back to his conversation with Master Wuwei. Wuwei, as the fundamental principle of Taoism, is to solve a conflict without force and that's exactly what he needed to do right now. As soon as the idea entered his brain and he started thinking, he turned to Amy. "I need to talk to Vicky's father right away. Can you organize it?"

"Yes, I can ring Vicky's mobile." Amy dialled the number and then passed her jumper, actually a mobile-like item, to Nathan.

"Vicky, it's Nathan, your English teacher. I need to talk to your father. Could you please translate for me?" said Nathan.

"No need to translate; he can speak English rather well," said Vicky.


"Most respected chief, my name is Nathan, your daughter's English teacher," Nathan said as he looked at the Zulu chief a couple of feet away from him, although the chief wouldn't be able to see Nathan.

"Okay, Nathan; what do you want?" said the chief in an impatient voice.

"Thanks for talking to me, sir. Could you please kindly advise me as to how I should address you? Please forgive me for not remembering your surname," said Nathan.

"No problem; just call me Paul," said the chief.

"I appreciate it, sir. Could I please ask what you are intending to do?" said Nathan.

"Nathan, I don't know if you knew about or were involved in this conspiracy to kidnap my daughter and use her as a hostage to attack my tribe, but it doesn't matter anymore because I am going to get them all to pay for it and get what they deserve, right here and right now."

"Sir, dare I ask if you have considered the consequences of doing so?" asked Nathan.

"If you mean that I should worry about the government's army and police, you are completely wrong. Do you know what, Nathan, my ancestors had wars with your British army and beat them? Our Zulu warriors are afraid of nobody; besides, this is self-defence," said the chief.

"Sir, I admire the bravery and fighting spirit of your Zulu warriors very much, and I also think you are right about your decision," said Nathan. He saw the confusions on the faces of the Zulu warriors. They must be wondering what was going on with the Zulu chief, who was talking to a mobile phone.

"So you agree that I should kill these bushman tribesmen?" Obviously, the Zulu chief was taken by surprise.

"Sir, it's not me, actually a Chinese sage said you were right about two and a half thousand years ago; his name was Laozi, or the Old Master in English," said Nathan.

"Nathan, you are bullshitting me; how could this old master know me that long ago?"

"Sir, it's true that the Old Master didn't know you in particular, but he said that there is no absolute right or wrong, it just depends on which side you are standing; therefore, from your point of view, you are absolutely right," said Nathan.

"I like this Chinese Old Master; Nathan, please stop calling me sir, just call me Old Paul," laughed the Zulu chief. "So, Nathan, you are not going to stop me attacking the bushman tribe?"

"Okay, Old Paul; the old master also said that, even if it's the right decision, you shouldn't do it if it's not the right time." Nathan could see the dubious expression on the Zulu chief's face.

"Nathan, what do you mean?"

"Old Paul, please excuse me for digging for a bit more information about your tribe; I understand that two other Zulu tribesmen proposed marriage to your daughter, but you refused them, and they were not happy about the result." Nathan saw the Zulu chief nod, so continued.

"I have no doubt that your Zulu warriors would be able to beat the bushman tribe today, but you would have losses on your side as well; the Zulu tribe your daughter was supposed to marry into would be likely to refuse the arrangement because of the fact Vicky and James have been boyfriend and girlfriend already. As a result, you would be very vulnerable; if the other Zulu tribes were to attack you right afterwards, you would be in a no-win situation. Besides, the government's police force and army would arrest you for the conflict too." Nathan stopped, watching the Zulu chief's expression.

"So what's your suggestion then?" asked the chief.

"Like the Old Master said, you can understand others better if you are in their shoes; Vicky and James love each other very much, so if you love your daughter, you should know what is best to do. By allowing a marriage with the bushman tribe, not only are you cementing your position as the strongest tribe around, but also thawing any threats from other Zulu tribes without one drop of blood. Old Paul, you are a wise Zulu chief, so you know your best option," Nathan said carefully.

The Zulu chief laughed loudly; just as Nathan started worrying whether his efforts had backfired, the chief passed the mobile to his daughter, and then spoke loudly to James' father, the chief of the bushman tribe, in their native language.

"My father said…" Vicky tried to translate her father's words, struggling with her limited English vocabulary. "He said…that he knew…agreed...with the Chinese Old Master…that one should wear others' shoes…to know them better…I am, no, he is happy that his daughter found her love with this handsome young man, the son of the chief of the bushman tribe…and he…with all of his Zulu warriors…are to send his daughter to marry James today. What? It's my wedding day today?" Vicky forgot to translate any more. She cried and hugged her father, thanking him, at least that's what Nathan guessed from their interactions.

Only then did Nathan collapse to the ground, feeling like he had just used all of his life energy.

Amy knelt down, holding Nathan up against her chest. "Thanks, Nathan; how did you pull it off like that?"

Nathan took a deep breath. "It's called Wuwei, one of Taoism's fundamental principles. Solve conflict without using force; follow the flow rather than fighting against it. It's a bit difficult to understand it at first but you will

113

eventually get it if you think about it all the time. As Taoists believe, there is no absolute right or wrong, it is all depending where you are standing."

"No absolute right or wrong, it all depends on where you are standing." Amy mumbled the words.

"Amy, please don't forget to say congratulations to Vicky and James."

Nathan and Amy jointed the tribe members from both the Zulu and bushman tribes, celebrating Vicky and James' wedding, although nobody could see them. There was plenty of food on the street for everyone to eat; people were dancing and singing in their native styles.

Nathan enjoyed every moment of it.

OBUarity sent Amy and him plenty of drinks and food in OBU, so Nathan could invite the chiefs and tribesmen to celebrate in OBU as well by using the mobile OBU helmets provided by the OBU field staff. Old Paul, the Zulu chief, loved OBU so much that he decided that he would attend Nathan's English classes sometimes, and wanted to know more about this Chinese Old Master.

After a long day of drinking, talking, singing, dancing, and wrestling, Nathan and Amy returned home, completely exhausted but extremely happy; they had really enjoyed themselves.


It was Nathan's turn to make breakfast. After he was all done, he called Amy and then turned the TV on, tuning it to a news channel.

"Nathan, I still can't believe what you did yesterday." Amy sat down at the table, picking up the teapot and pouring Nathan and herself a cup of tea each. "Just a matter of a few words and you completely averted a potential blood bath."

"Well, as the old say, wisdom is sharper than blades; I merely demonstrated the point."

"You are too humble about yourself, my little brother," Amy laughed.

Just then, Nathan's attention was caught by the news; the reporter said that two lawyers from the US were found dead in Little Amsterdam. The TV camera switched to the alleyway off the main street. Without waiting to finish watching the news, Nathan stood up and dashed to his bedroom.

He quickly put his OBU helmet on and used his jumper to dial Gary. Gary didn't enable the video signal.

"Gary, have you watched the news about what happened in Little Amsterdam? Yes, two American lawyers were found dead; do you know anything about it?"

"It was reported this morning actually," said Gary. "If you watched the whole news, you would know that the police found traces of drugs in their bodies. The deaths were initially suspected as drug related. Those two thugs well deserved their ends."

"Okay, thanks. Sorry to wake you up so early," mumbled Nathan.

"Early? Mate, it's two in the afternoon; I have just finished my lunch," said Gary.

Just then Nathan remembered he was living on African time, more than half a day behind Australian hours.

"Talk to you later." Nathan hung up.

"What happened?" asked Amy after Nathan reappeared from his bedroom.

"I just asked if Gary had heard the news about the two US lawyers' deaths; you know we were there yesterday." Nathan didn't know why he decided not to tell Amy the details of their involvement with the two lawyers.

"Nathan." Amy paused and then said, "After work today there will be a party for all OBUarity staff involved in the African regions. The party will be in London, on a river cruise boat along the Thames."

"Oh, one of these 'all for one and one for all' French-style orgy parties."

"Might be, but it's organized by OBUarity officially, so we have no choice but to attend."

Nathan had never been to London before in either OBU or the real world, so it was quite exciting to see the London Eye, Big Ben, the Houses of Parliament, and all the other old buildings along the Thames.

The cruise boat was quite spacious. Nathan and Amy stood on the upper viewing deck, enjoying the historically significant buildings along the way.

Beside them, since their journey started, Pierre had been persistently trying to persuade Amy to go to the lower deck so he could introduce a few new friends to her. Lucie was nowhere to be seen. Looking at Amy's expression, Nathan couldn't help but grin secretly; he could guess what happened on the lower deck—a sexual feast and large scale 'all for one and one for all' orgy for the hard-working colleagues from all over the world. He supposed that the people who remained on the upper viewing deck were the ones not into these comrade-sharing events.

It seemed that Pierre had finally run out of steam, giving up and walking away.

"He really tried; I have to give him credit for the effort," said Nathan. "Maybe you should give him a chance."

"He is so sweet, but I doubt that he and I actually want the same thing," laughed Amy.

116

"Excuse me, are you Nathan?"

Nathan turned around. The voice was from a blonde girl. She was very attractive, five foot ten, with long legs and full boobs; beside her stood a handsome young guy.

"Yes, I am Nathan. Do I know you?"

"Not yet, but you will soon, and that's why we are having this gathering," the blonde girl said. "Let me introduce everyone. My name is Eve, and this is my friend, Peter. Peter, this is Nathan, the famous old master who prevented the potential tribe war yesterday, and this is Amy, Nathan's co-worker."

"Oh, no, I am no old master," said Nathan.

"The young master then. It's an honour to meet you both." Peter shook Amy's hand, and then Nathan's.

"Amy, Peter is very knowledgeable about the Thames cruise; you know he has read the famous novel, *Three Men in a Boat*, many times over," said the blonde girl. "So Peter, why don't you show Amy the river you know best?"

"I'd be glad to. Shall we?" Peter offered his arm to Amy, like a gentleman from the age of *Three Men in a Boat*.

"Thanks; see you later, Nathan." Amy put her arm in Peter's, and they both walked towards the tail end of the viewing deck.

"Nathan," the girl who called herself Eve said, "I would like to have a few words with you in private. Why don't we go to the lower deck so we can have some privacy?"

"Well, Eve, you know, I am a bit old-fashioned; I am not into comrade love-sharing parties," said Nathan awkwardly.

The blonde girl stared at Nathan intensely; only then did he notice her piercing blue eyes. They were so familiar, but he couldn't remember where he had seen them before.

"Nathan, have you been to one of these love-sharing parties before?"

"No and I am not planning to."

"Nathan, in order to know the truth, you have to get firsthand experience, not judge based on what you've heard. Come on, let me show you the party, and you will find it's just another social occasion." She looped her arm through Nathan's and started walking downstairs.

Nathan had no choice but to follow her lead. From the corner of his eye, he could see Amy glancing in his direction.

## Chapter 18

Eve was right; the lower deck was nothing like Nathan had imagined and there was no orgy going on anywhere he could see, just a normal social party.

"Ah, Nathan, you finally decided to join the party," Pierre said. "Where is Amy?"

"She is talking to a new friend about *Three Men in a Boat*," said Nathan.

Eve led Nathan through the noisy crowds towards the tail end of the deck. "So, do you believe me now?" asked Eve.

"It seems that way, but are you telling me that there is nothing going on here?" said Nathan.

"Well, Nathan, these are all adults, and they decide what they want to do; of course there is plenty going on here, you just can't see it."

"Really? But where?"

"Nathan, this is a digital world. Let me show you the secret." Eve took him to another flight of stairs and went down to the lower deck.

The scene took Nathan by surprise; a hundred men and women were crowded in the large hall, talking, hugging and kissing; some were one-on-one, but many were involved in a multiparty embrace. Frequently, these entangled bodies would bump the panel door opening and disappear inside. So here was the comrade love-sharing party.

"Sorry, Eve, it's too crowded for me here and I need some fresh air…" Nathan was cut short by Eve's lips. She held his neck tightly and sealed his mouth with a true French-style kiss.

"Oh…please stop…" Nathan tried to get free from Eve's embrace, but her grip was quite strong, and then she pushed forward, sending both of them crashing through a door on the panelled wall.

Inside the door, there was a room like a hotel suite. Nathan hadn't had time to survey the surroundings because Eve was still holding him tightly and kissing him passionately. Their bodies crashed forward, bumping into the wall; the wall opened up another panel door. Before they fell inside, to his surprise, the corner of his eye caught two other people in the room. They were tangled together, kissing each other the same way he and Eve were doing, but that wasn't the surprising part. The surprising part was that these two looked exactly like Eve and him, a copy of each of them.

Nathan didn't have time to think. Their bodies landed on a double bed in another hotel suite-like room. As soon as they were settled on the surface of the bed, Eve pushed Nathan down and straddled him. She put her hand to her face and pulled her facemask off. Nathan couldn't believe his eyes: in front of him, the blonde Eve had suddenly changed into the red-haired girl in his dream. She was Mary O'Brian.

Mary didn't give Nathan much time to think. "Take your mask off," she commended with a throaty voice.

Nathan did as he was told, showing no resistance at all; this even surprised himself. Before he managed to take a deep breath, Mary sealed her lips over his. Staring at her blue eyes just an inch above him, Nathan felt heatwaves starting to boil up inside him; he held her cheeks with both hands and kissed her back with equal force, and soon they had both sunk into their own world.

Nathan lay on the bed, still in a state of shock; he couldn't believe what had just happened. The girl he had dreamed about since he had seen her in the bar in Amsterdam was actually right in front of him, in the process of putting her clothes back on her naked body. She was the most beautiful girl he had ever met in his life, with an almost Barbie-like body, full breasts, thin waist, long legs, but not her face. The piercing blue eyes under the red hair emitted toughness and determination, absolutely nothing like a doll.

"Hi, Mary." Nathan felt a bit awkward speaking her name for the first time. "That was a wonderful experience, the best in my life."

"Me too; I also enjoyed it very much."

"You know what? It's also my first sexual experience in the last fifteen years." Nathan knew it wasn't completely true, because from his personal viewpoint, it'd only be a couple of weeks, despite the fact fifteen years had passed for the rest of the world. He said it to impress her.

"Really? How?" Mary just put her jeans back on.

"Well." Nathan thought for a moment. Although desperately wanting to impress her more, in the end he decided not to tell her about Master Wuwei; he told her the same story as he had told everyone else.

"Oh, that's why you are an OBU virgin," Mary said thoughtfully while putting her last piece of clothing on.

Despite the fact that they had just made love, the atmosphere had changed, not like the romantic aftermath Nathan had imagined. Looking at Mary, who was now fully dressed, Nathan rolled off the bed, and put his own clothes back on as fast as he could manage.

"Sorry, Nathan, for being so abrupt," said Mary. "What just happened was not part of my mission; I just couldn't restrain myself. I hope you don't mind."

"Of course not. As I just said, it's the best thing that has happened to me in my whole life."

"All right, Nathan, I assume you know something about who I am and what we are doing."

"Yes, I have done some Internet research, so I have some rough ideas."

"Yeah, right, trust your little Internet research to tell you the truth," Mary said.

"Well, of course I don't completely believe what I found but it's a starting point."

"Nathan, do you want to know the truth?"

He didn't say anything, simply nodded.


"Nathan, tell me what you have found out about me."

The question made him feel a bit awkward. "I searched and they all said you are…"

"A terrorist, right? Please don't feel awkward about it; I am used to people calling me that."

"All right." He felt the words flowing more easily. "You belong to an organization called Salvation of Humanity, or SOH, that claims OBU will eventually destroy humanity, so the only way to save the human race is to totally destroy OBU."

"Go on," said Mary.

"SOH has carried out terrorist activities around the globe to sabotage OBU utilities and has caused innocent casualties along the way."

"What about me?" Mary gazed at Nathan.

"Well, it seems that your group's methods are quite different from the old bombing and shooting tactics. Instead, you employ high-tech attack strategies, such as releasing computer viruses into OBU, and those have appeared to be relatively successful."

"Anything else?" Mary stood up, pacing a bit in the confined space.

"Well, I found thousands of threats, but those are the main points."

"Okay, what's your view on me?" Mary stopped pacing, coming to a stop standing right in front of Nathan.

"Well, it's rather difficult and awkward to say."

"All right, this may make it easier for you: tell me your opinion about OBU. Do you think it's good or evil?"

"As I mentioned, I have only really known about OBU for the last couple of weeks, so my experience is very limited. However, from what I have seen, heard and experienced, although OBU is not a perfect world, it has solved the biggest threats to modern society, such as global warming and other environmental disasters."

"That's totally understandable, particularly from your background. So, you think it's wrong for us to try to destroy OBU?"

"Well, from an environmental and especially pollution-focused point of view, I think OBU has done a marvellous job." Nathan avoided answering her question directly.

"All right, let's discuss that more later. Nathan, do you think that people now have more freedom than before?"

"It seems that people are free to go anywhere and do anything as long as they are within the boundaries of the law." Nathan didn't look Mary in her eyes while speaking these words.

'Illusions. What you perceive is what they want you to perceive; none of that is the truth but distorted and censored information."

"Please explain."

"On the surface, OBU is a paradise that gives people ultimate freedom to say and do anything they like; whilst most people are using OBU to realize their sexual fantasies, and I have to agree it's the biggest sexual revolution in human history, fewer and fewer people know or care about what is going on behind the scenes."

"Behind the scenes?" asked Nathan.

"Yes, everyone is being closely watched and monitored. OBU is like Big Brother, it's the perfect world to get everyone in check."

Nathan thought about it for a moment. "I suppose that it'd be necessary to monitor unlawful activities." He looked away from her.

"But it'd be a different story if they were using OBU to censor different opinions and crush freedom of speech."

"I haven't heard about that."

"No, you wouldn't have, and that is exactly the point," said Mary.

Mary sat down next to Nathan, so close that he could smell her body fragrance. Nathan was embarrassed to sense the reaction from his body, so he adjusted his position to hide his awkwardness.

"It's true that people are free to say whatever they like anywhere in OBU without bearing any consequence for two reasons: one is that freedom of speech guarantees people this right; the second and the real reason is that it is impossible to monitor everyone's activities and every word they speak—the amount of data required would make that task unattainable. As a result, OBU would only be able to check on some limited targets, not the general population."

"So, we do have freedom in OBU after all," said Nathan in relief.

"Don't be so fast to draw your conclusions," Mary said. "When you talk in a bar, at a party or in a gathering, you are only able to speak to a limited audience, but when you put your opinions or ideas on the Internet, news sites, blogs, or any of these mass message sites, Big Brother can flex its powerful muscles. They can filter and censor every single thread, news article and conversation on these sites. Which is relatively easier compared to people's personal interaction data in OBU."

"Are you telling me that people can say whatever they like in OBU to other people but are unable to spread their messages to a large-scale audience?"

"Yes, that's exactly what has happened in the OBU age."

"What would happen if someone tried it?"

"Depending on the seriousness of the message, the message would be eliminated immediately, and the person would be interrogated, imprisoned or even assassinated if required."

"Assassinated? Are you telling me the government would assassinate their own citizens?"

"Who would know the truth? Every day there are thousands of people who die of drug overdoses or in various other accidents, so it's not so difficult for the secret police to kill a few dissidents and hide the deaths among those incidents."

"Do you have any evidence to support your claims?"

"It's difficult to collect evidence from others, but we do have firsthand data related to our organization. I know you would say it's a different story because SOH is a terrorist organization, but doesn't every citizen have the basic human right of a fair trial and presumption of innocence? I can tell you countless cases where the secret police killed first and asked questions afterwards."

"Were the people attacking you in the bar the secret police?" asked Nathan.

"Yes, they were OBU field agents, elite assassins who are equipped with the latest deadly weapons and technology in OBU." Mary paused; Nathan didn't ask any questions, so she continued. "That's why you haven't been able to see or hear anything from SOH, the reason why we are trying to destroy OBU. Anyway, the lack of freedom of speech and the censorship are not our main reasons to launch this war against OBU."

"What's the reason then?"

"Nathan, OBU is slowly destroying humanity; if nobody does anything to stop it, in a few decades, the human race will be wiped from the surface of the earth."

## Chapter 19

"What do you mean by that exactly?" Nathan asked.

Mary locked her gaze on Nathan, speaking slowly. "The birth rate around the globe has been declining continuously since OBU started fifteen years ago, at an alarmingly high rate. We hacked into the government's and other world organizations' databases, obtaining data to support our initial suspicions."

"Are you telling me that OBU is affecting human fertility?"

"Yes. Our experts' estimate is that, if the trend keeps going, in twenty years' time, the decline in the rate of birth around the world will reach a point of no return. It'd basically mark the end of humanity." Mary sounded really gloomy.

"But how could OBU affect human fertility?"

"We're not quite sure exactly but our experts suspect that long-term exposure to OBU damages the quality of the sperm," said Mary.

"You keep saying 'our experts'; who are they?"

"They are experts in human fertility research fields and the reason I refer them as 'our experts' is because they share our concerns and agree with our actions."

"But how could the government not act on those facts?"

"Well, the politicians are very short-sighted, only interested in their next vote, so no one is interested in looking further than that. Besides, OBU Corporation, as the largest and most powerful organization in human history, influences the opinions and outcomes of that research and controls the policies behind making it global knowledge."

Nathan thought about it. "If what you've said is true, surely OBU Corporation would be worried about it too, because there wouldn't be an OBU if no humans existed on Earth."

"Sadly, it's the reality, or OBU's version of reality, like a person knowing that drugs, smoking and alcohol will kill them but they're just unable to get rid of the bad habits. Besides, OBU Corporation believes that they will be able to find a cure to remedy the fertility problem soon."

"I have worked in Africa for a couple of weeks now; not very long but I know a bit about what is happening over there. Based on my observations, the OBU participation rate is pretty low there, so the fertility problem is not prevalent around the globe."

Mary stood up, pacing around the room again. She stopped. "They will soon be sucked into OBU just as everywhere else has been. Nathan, the birth rate has been declining alarmingly; although it may not seem like a big issue today, it will accelerate very rapidly if given another fifteen years. By then two or three generations will be fully affected by OBU, and then there will be no hope to reverse the trend."

Nathan contemplated what he had just heard. "That's just great," he said gloomily. "We, as a race, have very little hope of survival. Without OBU, we could die out through global warming, but with OBU, we could be wiped out by fertility problems."

Mary sat beside Nathan again. She wrapped her arm around Nathan's neck, her face only inches away from his. "That's the problem with our society; when technology creates one problem, we try to use new technology to solve it but as a result, more often we just create an even bigger problem than the previous one."

"What should we do then? I am not sure destroying OBU would solve all the problems. For instance, how do you deal with the global warming problem?"

Mary's eyes became brighter. She moved away from Nathan.

"I have to agree that OBU did help solve some of the environmental problems, and also helped with the invention of many environmentally friendly technologies, but most important of all, OBU has changed people's perceptions about their way of living, such as eating slow, local, organic food and OBU traveling. Therefore, if OBU were gone tomorrow, it wouldn't bring global warming back straight away so we have time to continue employing environmentally friendly technologies and practices. Nathan, if we don't get rid of OBU soon, there won't be any humans left in this world, so what's the point of having a clean environment if there is nobody here to enjoy it?"

"Well, I can see your argument, but I still need time to think things through," Nathan said slowly. "But why are you getting me involved?"

"Nathan, there is a prophecy that says only an OBU virgin can help us bring OBU down. Since you are the only OBU virgin we know, that's why we are having this conversation today."

"Prophecy? Don't tell me you believe that superstitious stuff."

"Well, it depends. When I first met you, I could tell from your expression that you had seen my real face, even though I was wearing the most updated mask then."

"Yes, it's true. But I haven't managed to replicate the moment ever since. Mary, was that the reason you were at the bar in the first place, to see me?"

"It was," Mary said simply.

"But you risked your life by doing that; in fact, the field agents almost got all of you killed."

"Thanks to your bravery and outstanding fighting skills, I survived. Rescued by you, my knight on a white horse." Mary's eyes were shining.

"That's all right," Nathan mumbled. He felt a bit embarrassed, as he was not used to this kind of compliment, particularly from his dream girl. He calmed down a bit and then said, "But how would I be able to help you to bring OBU down?"

Mary pulled her long red hair away from her face. "We know from our experiences that it's ineffective to use conventional methods such as bombing to sabotage OBU utilities, and that's why my group has been trying to introduce computer viruses in the last few years. Although we have managed to cause a few regional breakdowns, it's nowhere near enough to destroy the whole OBU globally."

Nathan didn't say anything, so Mary continued.

"Our computer experts have concluded that the only way to do it is to introduce the virus right into the OBU HQ, as it has direct links to all regional OBU networks around the world, but the problem is nobody is able to identify where the OBU HQ is, let alone infiltrate it."

"And I would be able to identity the HQ somehow?"

"From the instance when you were able to see through my mask, considering even OBU's field agents were unable to, we believe you possess the ability to somehow interpret OBU's codes into visual images in your mind; therefore, you might potentially be able to find where the HQ is."

"But I haven't been able to replicate that ability since then."

"Nathan, just be patient; the ability is still in your head and it will come back one day."

"Mary, can I ask you a question?"

"Yes, of course, please do."

"Mary…" Nathan tried to think how to word it but decided to just say it. "Is what happened, I mean, before our conversation, part of your strategy to recruit me into SOH?"

Mary blushed.

"No, I did it only based on my own decision; in fact, although I informed my organization about you, no one in SOH believes my theory. What happened was just because I like you and want to thank you for saving my life. Of course, if you decide to join SOH, I would like to get to know you better and who knows what could happen between us." Her blue eyes gazed at Nathan for a very long time.

"I'll need time to think about it," said Nathan. "Is Amy also a member of SOH?"

"Yes, but she didn't know you were going to meet me today. Nathan, regardless of whether you decide to join SOH or not, could you please keep our meeting a secret; please don't mention it to anybody, including Amy."

"Okay, I will. But how do I contact you if I do decide to go along with you?"

"I'll contact you soon." Mary glanced at her watch. "Nathan, we had better get moving."


"Gary, how do guns and bombs work in OBU?" Nathan asked. The Thames river cruise had finished but he didn't go straight to sleep, instead he went straight to his jumper, talking to Gary.

"Well, everything in OBU is to do with our brains; similar to hypnosis, when one believes he has been shot

131

and is going to die, his brain just shuts down his body and dies," said Gary.

"If that's the case, then you wouldn't die if someone shot you in your back, because you're not aware the bullet's coming," said Nathan.

"It doesn't work that way; even if you're not aware of the bullet, your brain still receives that bullet's signals, so you would still be dead," said Gary.

"The Dutch police told me it's the violent signals that cause brain damage and therefore death," said Nathan.

"That's a common misunderstanding about OBU. The helmet, the gateway to OBU, has a built-in safety to protect the users; even if those safety measures fail, the signals being received from OBU are so weak that it's impossible to cause someone's instant death," said Gary.

Nathan thought about that concept for a moment. "I suppose if all of these situations are based on our brains interpreting the signals, if someone somehow convinces his brain not to believe the signals, he wouldn't be hurt by the guns, right?"

Gary paused for a few seconds, thinking quite hard about Nathan's question. "I think you have made quite a good point; in theory, it's possible, but no one could train his mind to go beyond the norm. It'd need a giant leap of faith, and I very much doubt anyone would be able to do that."

"I suppose you are right, but why do people invent guns and bombs in OBU? I just don't understand," said Nathan.

"They are mainly for military training purposes, but, well…killing is human nature, isn't it?" said Gary.

Nathan didn't respond; he had fallen into deep thought. He soon signed off and turned in for the night.

Nathan said good morning to Amy, and then sat at the table to have breakfast. He felt a bit awkward after his meeting with Mary. Of course, he didn't tell Amy about it and she wouldn't know anything but he still felt funny in front of Amy.

"Eve seems like a lovely girl. Did you have a good time during the cruise?" asked Amy.

"She is okay." Nathan didn't look at Amy, busily eating his cereal.

"I would say she is much more than okay." Amy studied his face. "You look really happy; you haven't stopped smiling all morning."

"Really? I hadn't noticed it myself." Nathan smiled.

"You guys spent the whole cruise on the lower deck; was it a good party down there?" Amy asked casually, though there was a hint of something else under her breezy tone.

"Oh, nothing special or unusual was happening on the lower deck; people were drinking, chatting and socializing with each other, not much different from the upper viewing deck really." Nathan told himself that he had mostly told the truth, because that was what had happened on the bottom deck, if one didn't bump into the panelled doors in the wall; therefore, he felt quite comfortable keeping a straight face as he was not lying.

"Quite different from my imagination then; maybe I should venture to the lower deck as well."

"You should; by the way, how did you get on with Peter? He seemed like quite a nice guy."

Amy poured herself a cup of tea. "Peter is a very nice guy; handsome, intelligent, knowledgeable and with a sense of humour. Yes, we had a good time. He told me lots of history about the buildings along the Thames."

"It sounds really good; are you going to meet again?" asked Nathan.

"I don't think so; it was one of those one-off moments. Anyway, what about you and Eve?"

"Well, I suppose that we are in the same boat on that front: also a one-off event." Nathan felt a bit guilty lying about it. He knew clearly that Mary would contact him again, probably soon.

"I am done." Amy stood up. "Let me know when you are ready to go." She went to her bedroom.

Nathan felt that there was jealousy in Amy's tone, but maybe he was just being paranoid.

The day passed uneventfully; however, Pierre was sick, so he didn't turn up to school. At the end of the day after all the students had left, Lucie stayed a bit longer; it was unusual for her because she was always the first to leave, dashing to her parties.

"Can I have a word with you please, Amy," said Lucie.

They were in Nathan's classroom; it was quite spacious. Nathan was busily tiding up his desk, putting the papers, books and other teaching aids away. Even though Lucie and Amy were at the other end of the room, quite a distance away, he could still hear their conversation clearly. Nathan felt quite awkward overhearing other people's private conversations, so he tried to get what he was doing done as quickly as he could, and then left the room.

"Amy, I don't know if I should say this to you, but because Pierre isn't here today, I might as well use the opportunity to tell you," Lucie said.

"Tell me what?" asked Amy.

"I think that Pierre is in love with you," said Lucie.

"No way, he just wants me to attend your 'all for one and one for all' French-style love parties," said Amy.

"Well, that's his way of showing you his love," said Lucie.

"If that's the case, it's definitely the weirdest way to show your love. I thought you French guys were good at romantic stuff; wouldn't he be able to think up some more imaginative and creative ways?" said Amy.

"Well…" Lucie seemed a bit awkward. "I suppose that it's Pierre's individual way of doing things. Anyway, despite it being weird or awkward, it's true that he has fallen in love with you. I want you to know that telling you this is my own decision, and he has nothing to do with it," said Lucie.

Amy thought for a moment. "It could be a guy thing. Maybe it's because I keep declining his invitations; therefore, he's become obsessed with the idea."

"I don't know, Amy; I have to go." Lucie turned to Nathan, raising her voice. "Nathan, I believe that you met quite a few new friends during the cruise yesterday, and they are having another gathering tonight; some of them asked me to invite you."

Amy picked up her bag. "I'll see you tomorrow then, Nathan. Have a good time at the party."

"Amy, why don't you come with us? Peter could be there as well," said Nathan.

Amy laughed drily. "I have heard enough about *Three Men in a Boat*. Goodnight." She walked out of the door.

**Chapter 20**

The party was in a mansion in Paris. Nathan wasn't sure if this was a real mansion or just a digital creation. Anyway, it was spectacularly fitted with crystal chandeliers, Persian rugs, ancient furniture, and famous oil paintings. Nathan nodded to the butler, who greeted them inside the large, heavy double front doors.

People were in groups, drinking and chatting in the large hall; nearby, on the wide marble stairs, on chairs in the corners, and inside the hallways leading to different rooms, Nathan could see people kissing and carrying out all kinds of intimate activities, so it was clearly one of the comrade love-sharing parties Lucie and Pierre had mentioned after all.

Lucie said goodbye to Nathan and then joined a group in the corner. Nathan didn't know why he was there; anyway, he kept walking upstairs. The corridor on the second floor was more crowded than the hall on the ground level. He felt a person tugging on his elbow; turning around, he saw Eve was smiling at him.

Before he could say anything, Eve put her arms around his neck, sealed his lips with hers, and gave him a full French kiss. Their bodies bumped into the wall. To Nathan's surprise, the wall opened up into a hidden door, and suddenly they were in another room.

As soon as they were inside the room, the wardrobe door opened, and a guy walked out. He looked like a copy of Nathan. Without a word, Eve pushed Nathan into the wardrobe; whilst still embracing and kissing the new 'Nathan', Eve closed the wardrobe door with her back.

There was a brief darkness and then brightness again. Nathan found he was in the middle of a large warehouse; large containers packed in rows formed wide corridors. Mary stood right in front of him.

"Welcome to our training facility, Nathan." Mary hugged Nathan, then kissed him on his cheeks, but no more French kisses.

"I thought you were disguising yourself as Eve when you kissed me then."

"No, she is one of my comrades. Sorry for not warning you beforehand. We have to use a decoy to act as you at the party, in case the OBU field agents are watching you."

"The field agents are watching me? Why?"

"We are not sure they are, but it's always better to be cautious," Mary said. "Nathan, are you in or out?"

Nathan thought for a second, and then nodded.

"Okay, that's great, so we are formally comrades now." Mary shook his hand, but that made Nathan feel a bit weird. "However, this is only my personal initiative, and we are still waiting for formal approval from the SOH commanders."

"What is this place and what are we doing here?" asked Nathan.

"We have quite a few top computer experts who are more than capable of creating the digital gateway for us. This is a training facility where you can learn how to use all kinds of military weapons, bombs and drive various vehicles, etc."

"Why do I need this military training?"

"Nathan, I know you are very good at hand-to-hand combat, but you can't fight the agents' guns with your bare hands. Have you used guns before?"

"No. I don't like guns. Their sole purpose is to kill."

"Nathan, I agree with you, but if we want to save lives, unfortunately we have to kill in order to achieve it." Mary led Nathan to a table at the end of the corridor; on the table, different kinds of guns were displayed.

Mary picked up a handgun. "In OBU there are replicas of almost every type of gun in the real world."

"I can't believe it and I can't understand why anyone would want to bring guns to OBU," said Nathan.

"Well, destruction is human nature, I suppose. The main reason is for training purposes; soldiers can be trained in OBU much more cheaply than in the real world." Mary put the handgun down and picked up an automatic assault rifle.

"It's actually quite a lot of work to create software that can shoot bullets. Although I am no software engineer or programmer, my understanding is that the software for guns has to produce a fast interface with other datasets, so the reaction between guns and human brains would be fast, like bullets; this also applies to other materials in OBU, so bullets and bombs can damage buildings and objects as they would in the real world."

"So bullets and bombs are just pieces of software, and they create a fast interface with other datasets and software to cause damage," mumbled Nathan.

"Yes, that's right," Mary said. "Pick up a gun, and let's get the ball rolling."

Nathan said goodbye to his students and went back with Amy to their apartment. In the evening, they went down to the basement gym as usual. Today Nathan and Amy chose to climb up the Swiss Alps as they hadn't done it for a while.

They made their way inside the cabin to get changed. Nathan went inside a cubicle. After double-checking and making sure it was the correct locker, he opened the door and walked into it. It would have been strange if anyone had been looking, but almost immediately after Nathan disappeared inside the locker, he walked out again. The locker was extremely large, more like a walk-in wardrobe, and thanks to the digital advantage of OBU, it meant they were easy to use, so users did walk in and out of the lockers quite often, so maybe it wasn't that odd after all.

However, the truth was that Nathan didn't walk out at all; instead he pushed the back of the locker open, like another gateway, and walked into the digital warehouse where he had started his first military training with Mary yesterday. The person who looked identical to Nathan and had in fact walked out of the locker was Peter, wearing a mask of Nathan's face underneath another set of masks that matched what Nathan was wearing at the moment; therefore, when the agents saw through Peter's outer mask, they would see it was Nathan's real face underneath. The tricky part was to make sure that the agents were unable to see through the mask of Nathan's real face. Mary had ensured Nathan that SOH had quite a few top computer programmers and the masks they produced were equipped with the latest anti-seeker software, and were changed daily, so there was little chance the agents would be able to catch them.

Nathan was quite happy with the choice of his decoy; it seemed that Amy and Peter got on quite well together, based on the Thames cruise. Somehow it made him feel less guilty about lying to Amy. Nathan didn't really know why he felt guilty towards Amy, he just did.

Walking in the large space under the warehouse's high ceiling, Nathan knew it was a digital space well hidden in OBU and covered with layer upon layer of security.

Rows and rows of huge containers divided the huge warehouse into long corridors. At the other end of the corridor, Mary smiled at him.

As soon as Nathan was close to her, Mary put her arms around him, giving him a deep French kiss. The passionate union lasted for a very long time, but just as Nathan felt himself losing control, Mary suddenly pulled away from him as abruptly as she had started the session.

"That will be all for today, so let's start our real training."

Nathan nodded, trying to get himself to calm down.

Mary laughed while watching Nathan. "Sorry for that; maybe I shouldn't greet you in that way next time."

"Oh, no; it's a very nice welcome and I love it," said Nathan.

Mary picked up a handgun from the table. "The reason that I asked you to go to the gym first is to synchronize your muscles with your mind; otherwise, your eyes would be able to move much faster than your body could act."

"I thought our muscles wouldn't matter in OBU as everything is to do with our mind here."

"Yes and no; it's true that you can move faster in OBU than in the real world due to your thoughts being much faster than your muscles' movements. But you are still bound by your own physical ability; basically, someone who has fast reaction times in the real world would do better in OBU as well," Mary said.

Nathan thought for a moment. "Are you telling me how fast we move in OBU is proportional to our ability in the real world?"

"Yes, this is done by way of the computer-human interface programming, so to present the real world to

OBU users in the real sense; basically, people have more or less the same speed and strength here as they possess in the real world." Mary signalled Nathan to also pick up a handgun from the table. "Nathan, we started your introductory lesson last time, so you know the basics about guns."

Nathan picked up a handgun from the table.

"Don't forget to put a magazine in," said Mary.

Nathan felt a bit embarrassed for forgetting such a basic thing and just holding an empty gun. While pushing the magazine into the handgun, he asked, "I don't understand why we still need magazines in OBU. I would imagine that a digital gun could shoot forever and have unlimited bullets inside; they are only a piece of software after all."

Mary shook the gun in her hand. "Everything in OBU is represented as visual images for the users and they are designed for military training for the real world. Besides, the bullets are specially interfaced between software, so they do take space to store them; as a result, we still need magazines and bullets for guns in OBU, identical to in the real world. Any more questions before we start?"

Nathan shook his head.

"Look at the glass bottle on top of the container on your left; now try shooting it."

Nathan aimed and pulled the trigger. He missed.

"Try to squeeze the trigger and control your breath," said Mary.

Nathan tried again and missed again. He finally hit the target on his fifth try.

"Nathan, like any other skill, it takes lots of practice to become a sharpshooter. Have you heard about the ten thousand hours rule?"

"I've heard about it," Nathan said thoughtfully.

"You are very good at hand-to-hand combat; how long did you train to be able to fight like that?"

It was actually overnight, but Nathan didn't tell anyone about that, because nobody, including himself, would ever believe it. Now, thinking back, maybe he did have fifteen years of training under Master Wuwei's magic.

"As I said before, I don't remember what happened to me, but I assume that I must have done years of training to gain those fighting skills. Have you done your ten thousand hours?"

Mary shook her head.

"No, I haven't. Even if you did finish the ten thousand hours, not everyone could become a sharpshooter, it really depends on one's understanding of the gun. It has to become a part of your body; when you can control it the same way as you control your limbs, as easily and naturally as you breathe, then you have mastered the art of shooting."

"Come on, Mary; show me how good you are. From the way you're talking, you must be quite good at it."

Mary smiled. "I am not that great; but okay, please load the disc thrower."

## Chapter 21

Nathan spotted a machine sitting beside the table. He picked up a clay disc and loaded it into the thrower's tray.

"Ready to shoot," said Mary.

Nathan hit the trigger to release the clay disc. Mary casually swung her gun up, shooting the disc into a puff of pink smoke.

"Quite impressive," said Nathan.

A proud smile appeared on Mary's face. "Nathan, load three discs into the tray."

"Really?" Nathan did as requested. His jaw dropped as three different colours of smoke burst in mid-air. "Wow, you are good, shooting three discs at once."

"It's not much use shooting whilst standing still, as in the battlefield, you will most likely be in motion." Mary walked to the next row of containers; Nathan followed. She stopped at a forklift. After climbing into the driver's seat, Mary said, "Nathan, stand beside the table there; now put one bottle on your left, one on your right, and hold one on your hand. Right, just like that."

"Are you going to shoot the bottles?" Nathan said uncertainly.

Mary laughed. "Trust me, Nathan. This is a simulated hostage situation. I have complete confidence I won't hurt you, please trust me."

Nathan nodded but was still quite nervous inside.

Mary drove the forklift backwards. It moved quite fast, almost like a racing car, so it was obviously a modified forklift. Mary then raced towards Nathan at full speed; still thirty feet away, she raised her gun with one hand, but kept her other hand on the steering wheel, and fired three shots.

Nathan felt the bottles beside him and in his hand explode simultaneously and then he felt pain on his arm. Looking down, he saw the shattered glass fragments cutting through his forearm, drawing blood.

Mary stopped the forklift beside Nathan. After seeing the blood on his arm, she jumped from the driver's seat. "Oh shit, did I shoot you?"

"No, you didn't shoot me; just a piece of broken glass."

"Let me have a look at it." Mary pulled his sleeve up; it was a long, bloody gash along Nathan's forearm. "I need to get a first aid kit and wrap you up."

"It's really not a big deal." Nathan suddenly thought about something. This was not real, just a signal from a piece of software that represented a piece of flying broken glass which told his brain that it cut through his skin and drew blood. What happened if he chose not to believe it? It was only an illusion after all. Nathan concentrated and breathed deeply, trying to relax his mind.

Meanwhile, Mary was hurrying back with a first aid kit. "What happened to the wound?" Mary looked at his arm, puzzled. Nathan's forearm was as good as new; there was no sign of any wound or blood.

Nathan smiled and told her what he had just done.

"Nathan, I knew you were special."

"It's not that special; quite basic, actually. I mean, to not believe the wound is real."

"Nathan." Mary's eyes were shiny. "It is basic and anyone could say it but you are the only one I know who could actually make the wound go away." She thought

144

for a second or two. "In that case, we may be able to speed up your training."

"How?"

Mary sat down on a chair nearby.

"Time in OBU is generally the same as in the real world. If you spend two hours here, when you go back to the real world, you'll also have lost two hours there, but with some digital alteration, we could expand time within OBU."

"Expand time?" A thought burst into Nathan's head, but he didn't say anything.

"Yes, we could expand time; you could spend two hours here but only miss one hour in the real world."

So, if one could expand time in OBU, why wouldn't Master Wuwei be able to expand time in the real world? Maybe it'd be more accurate to say that Master Wuwei had contracted time within his hut, so for Nathan it was only overnight but for the rest of the world, fifteen years had passed. However, Nathan didn't speak it out loud; instead, he said, "I assume that you could expand it much more, say expanding one hour in the real world to a day, a week, a year in OBU."

Mary stared at Nathan, not saying anything for a long time. Finally, she said, "In theory, it'd be possible, but in practice, an ordinary person would only be able to withstand a two-to-one ratio."

"What would happen to the person if you were to do more than a two-to-one ratio?"

"Well, the person could lose his memory, or suffer from brain damage in a worst-case scenario. There were a few cases like that when the time-expanding software was created initially, but now it's banned." Mary gazed at Nathan. "Because you just demonstrated your ability to control your own mind, you may be able to utilize the function to speed up your training."

Nathan got really excited about the prospect. "I would definitely like to give it a go," he said.

Mary pulled out a piece of printed paper from her pocket.

"Here is the menu on how to expand time; see the control panel on that container? I won't be able to be here to train with you, but we do have a few training programs you can use to help you; they would appear as people that you can talk to and interact with. Here is the contents of your training."

Mary hugged Nathan, kissing him on his cheeks.

"Good luck with it. I would suggest you take it easy and start slowly. I will meet you at your school tomorrow after all the students have gone home." She left.

Nathan walked to the control panel.

"How long should I expand the time here?" he asked himself. If he had been able to spend about eight hours in Master Wuwei's hut which had been the equivalent of fifteen years in the real world, he should be able to do the same here, he decided. He estimated that if he spent five years in OBU, it would only be around three hours in the real world. Five years full-time would be well over ten thousand hours; as a result, when he came out the other end, he would be a pro in military training. Smiling to himself, Nathan pushed a few buttons on the control panel.

## Chapter 22

After choosing his time expansion option, Nathan opened the training file Mary had left for him on the table, picking up the first page on top of the pile of papers. The title showed a sharpshooter training menu. The next page on the pile was the menu for land driving, including all kinds of cars, tanks and other military vehicles: sailing boats, including river cruises, speed boats and even miniature submarines; flying machines including helicopters, fighters, and also different types of private jets. Interesting, thought Nathan to himself.

The next page was on spying techniques, including computer hacking, assassination techniques, tracking, interrogation techniques, lie detecting by observing people's behaviour, world and regional politics, etc. Nathan didn't know how many subjects and areas he could cover during the five-year period but decided to start it in the same order as the menu pile; it seemed logical to get the basic training first.

There were passwords in the menu page to activate the training program. Nathan felt amused by the bizarre concept. Because everything was panning out as visual images, it would be almost like a magic spell.

Sure enough, after he said the password, the piece of paper flew out of his hand. It floated upwards towards the high ceiling, and then, with a loud *bang*, exploded like a firework. The menu page broke into thousands of pieces in mid-air and showered down over the containers in the large warehouse. Nathan watched with a grin. It was like in the PowerPoint presentations he used to do, an introductory special effect, but in a much more spectacular fashion. Then everything around him suddenly changed; he was no longer in a huge warehouse full of large containers, but in a Wild West mining town in the gold rush age in the USA. The programmers had an unusual sense of humour, thought Nathan to himself.

A sheriff walked out from the door of the wooden police house. "What's your name, son?" He spoke in a thick American midwestern accent.

"Nathan." Nathan knew the sheriff was merely a piece of software here to train him, but he couldn't help but admire how real he looked.

"Right, Nathan; you want to become a sharpshooter, right?"

"That's the aim." Nathan felt a bit nervous even though he knew it was ridiculous to feel nervous in front of a piece of software.

"Put your gun belt on and show me how good you are." The sheriff threw a gun belt towards him and it landed in front of Nathan's feet. He waited for Nathan to get ready; when the gun was in Nathan's hand and in firing position, the sheriff took his hat off, throwing it in mid-air.

Nathan emptied the whole clip of bullets into the sky, hoping one of them might hit the target. The hope disappeared immediately after he picked up the sheriff's hat from the dusty ground; there was not a single hole in it.

"Nathan, we have a lot of work to do." The sheriff put the hat back on his head again.

The training was fun and stimulating. Nathan had started three types of training simultaneously, not only saving time, but also allowing him more variety and more fun. By alternating his activities between sharp shooting, driving and spying courses, he could also find new thrills before getting bored with the repetitive exercises.

When he wanted to end the activity, Nathan would speak the password, and the surroundings of that training environment would disappear back to the warehouse setting so he could activate the next program.

Nathan couldn't help but admire how much the digital technology could do in creating the realistic training settings. The same digital space of the warehouse had been transformed into the Pacific Ocean for his boating; central London for his spying; New York's Long Island for his car chasing and gun shooting; the Sahara Desert and the Arctic Circle for his endurance tests.

The most fun part of spy training was meeting the attractive girls in bars, parties and luxury hotels, a pure 007- and Cold War-style fantasy. Nathan even suspected that these girls might actually be human because he had quite in-depth conversations with them as part of his lie detecting and interrogation technique training. These girls, or the programs, were either so sophisticated that they were almost human, or they really were human. Anyway, he loved the high-flying, fantastic luxury spy lifestyle. He loved the private jet, luxury suites in the casino complex, super expensive sports cars with the most stunning girls, and the power he held to save the world from evil forces.

Time passed quickly; Nathan lived as if he was in real life. He went to sleep, got up and had a shower; dressed to start a new day engaging in different activities; he dined and travelled; however, in the back of his mind, he knew all of these things were illusions of the computer program, and even the time was not real. Nathan did a quick calculation: by expanding three hours of time in the real world to five years in OBU, he was stretching every minute of his life into ten days in OBU; not a bad deal.

Time passed quickly when one was having fun, and finally his five years of training finished. When the last training setting disappeared into thin air, Nathan stared at the gloomy, bleak warehouse full of containers again. He sighed; the fun was over, and it was time to face reality again, but it wasn't all depressing; Nathan was very much looking forward to meeting Mary again. Although he had only parted from her three hours ago, he did have five years of memories in between.

The next morning Nathan and Amy sat down to have breakfast.

"How did the training go last night?" asked Amy.

Nathan wasn't sure if he should share everything with her, so he kept it general. "It was fantastic. I loved them all. Have you done it yourself?"

Amy laughed. "Yeah, I did; like rides in Disneyland."

"Right, exactly. Did you enjoy your conversation with Peter?"

"Well, Peter is very knowledgeable and fun to have a conversation with…" Amy let the sentence drop away. "Anyway, are you going to do the training again tonight?"

"I think so; I just couldn't get enough of it."

"A boy's fantasy, eh?" Amy smiled. "Well, enjoy it while it lasts. See you tomorrow morning then."

Nathan met Mary at the warehouse again. Amy, together with Peter, who was disguised as Nathan's decoy again, went to visit Paris. They might attend a love party. Amy needed to be cheered up; she was a bit too uptight, thought Nathan.

"So, did you enjoy your training last night?" said Mary.

"Very much," said Nathan.

"Oh, I can see how much you enjoyed yourself." Mary was reading a pile of papers, presumably the reports of Nathan's training results. She gasped. "Holy shit, Nathan; you did five years in three hours."

Nathan nodded, smiling but saying nothing.

Mary walked around him, watching him with great curiosity. "You look pretty normal, but it would not be a surprise to find out your brain is cooked."

Nathan patted his own head. "It's as good as new; a bit warm but far from cooked."

"I can't believe it; no one could have done that. I mean I have never heard of anyone achieving it. Just simply impossible; no human brain could withstand the stress," Mary said.

"Well, I don't know how but it seems I have managed it." Of course, Nathan didn't want to reveal his encounter with Master Wuwei.

"Let's have a look at what you have achieved in your five-year full-immersion intensive training program." Mary flipped a few pages. "Sharp shooting, driving, and spying. Oh, I see, it seems you quite enjoyed yourself with those female spies in casinos, hotels, parties and clubs; so no wonder you loved the training so much."

Nathan felt his face getting hotter. "It's all part of the training." He laughed drily but felt slightly embarrassed.

"Yes, of course it was." Mary put the pile of paper down on the table. "Okay, Nathan. Let's see what you have achieved." She pointed at the clay disc thrower. "Shall we start with this?"

"No problem." Nathan picked up a handgun and a magazine from the table. Without looking, he slid the magazine into the gun in one sleek move, as if he had been doing it his whole life.

"Very impressive," Mary commented. As she was about to push the trigger to release the clay disc, Nathan stopped her. "Why don't you pile more discs into the tray?"

"Of course." Mary loaded two extra discs into the thrower.

"More," said Nathan.

"Typical boy mentality, always wanting to win. Okay, I would like to see you beat my record." Mary loaded one more disc.

"More," grinned Nathan.

"Are you kidding me?" Mary turned to Nathan. "No one without an accelerator has managed to shoot more than four discs."

"Accelerator? What's that?"

"Let's get this done first, and then I'll explain it to you." She was about to hit the thrower's trigger when he stopped her again.

"Hang on," Nathan said. "To save time, please load ten discs so we can get this done with."

Mary's jaw dropped to the ground. "Nathan, don't bullshit me. There is no way you could do that."

"Let's find out, shall we?" Nathan stood there, like a cowboy in the Wild West.

Mary put extra discs into the throwers' tray until they totalled ten altogether. "Fire!" She pushed the trigger mechanism.

Nathan's movements were casual, calm, smooth, slick and silent; as if with just a single glance, he had memorized all the discs' positions, their movement velocities and flying directions, the wind speed and other environmental factors; as if he didn't shoot with his eyes

152

and hand, but with his mind. The gun in his hand became part of his being, an extension of his limb.

Ten puffs of colourful smoke popped up under the warehouse's high ceiling like fireworks.

"It's impossible," mumbled Mary.

"Mary, tell me about this accelerator."

Mary sat on the table. "Due to our brain's ability to cope with signals from OBU, people generally perform the same in OBU as they would in the real world. I mean their hand-eye coordination, like target shooting and hand-to-hand combat ability. To date, the best record for clay shooting was four, so my record of three discs is not too bad after all." Mary laughed.

Nathan smiled, but didn't say anything.

"Then they invented this accelerator; it's basically able to speed up the interface between human brains and OBU; the filed data has shown that it can almost double the user's speed."

"Have the field agents been equipped with the accelerators?" asked Nathan thoughtfully.

"Yes, they have."

"Could anyone else have them as well?"

"No," said Mary. "This is because the accelerators are hardware that has to be surgically implanted into the user's head; in addition to that, not everyone is able to handle it."

"So the field agents selected are particularly gifted ones."

"You can say that again. They are a small group of elite agents who can appear and disappear in any place in OBU instantly because they have ultimate access to all the databases in OBU. They are fast, deadly and invincible. An ordinary human, regardless of how good you are, would have no chance of fighting them, so it was amazing that you beat them in the bar to save me."

"So you think that the field agents let me go intentionally, and they have been keeping a close eye on what I have been doing since?" said Nathan.

"Yes, and that's why we are so cautious each time we meet up."

"What do they want to find out from me?"

"Well, we guess that they want to find out who you really are, and what your connection with us is; ultimately to use you to get to us."

Nathan thought about it for a while and then said, "How good are these agents? I mean how many discs could they manage to shoot down at once?"

"Not completely sure about their best record, but based on our source, they could easily shoot down eight discs," said Mary. "There are three super agents we know of; one is called 'Gunslinger', and the other 'Cowboy' and they are both extremely good with their guns. We have heard that their best record could be twelve discs." Mary wrapped her arms around Nathan's neck. "Today you almost beat their records by shooting down ten discs. I love you." She gave him a very long and very wet French kiss.

"But I am still slower than the Gunslinger and the Cowboy," Nathan asked after his mouth was free. "What about the third super agent?"

Mary shook her head. "We don't know anything about him; in fact, we don't even know if it's a him or a her. It is very mysterious even to our double agent inside the organization."

"Do you have a vague idea how good he is?"

"No. Let's assume he is better than the other agents, but you are a very close match for him." Mary kissed Nathan again.

"Why is he so mysterious that even your mole inside the organization doesn't know about him?"

"Because nobody has ever seen him without a mask."

"So how do we know if he even exists? He could be anyone," asked Nathan.

"Yes, he could but one thing is that no mask could disguise one's ability. This super-agent has been involved in a few operations against us; we have never seen someone so fast and deadly with his hands and gun."

"So based on my test results, I'm unlikely to be able to beat any one of those three super agents, let alone help you to bring OBU down."

Mary thought for a moment and then said slowly, "There are two factors that prevent us from destroying OBU: one is that we actually don't know where its HQ is, and that's why your ability to see through OBU code would be extremely useful…"

"But I haven't been able to regain that ability ever since the first time," interrupted Nathan.

"You may be able to one day, hopefully. The second factor is that, even if we manage to somehow identify and break into OBU HQ, the super agents would be there to guard the site, but none of us has any chance of fighting against them."

"Including me…" mumbled Nathan.

"Nathan, you have a far better chance than any of my people ever would; trust me, your ability will continue to improve, and I have full confidence in you." Mary fingered the pile of papers on the table, finding the page she wanted. "I want to test your lie detecting abilities."

With a snap of her fingers, they both stood inside a luxury suite overlooking a spectacular view of the ocean. Nathan recognized it as the casino complex that had been used to film one of the 007 films.

Mary stared into Nathan's eyes, only an inch away; he could feel her breath.

"Nathan, I love you. Tell me if I am lying or telling the truth."

Nathan gazed at her blue eyes. "You like me, quite a lot I dare say, but it's not love, yet, so you are lying. I suppose that you are trying to use your affection to lure me to fight for you. Am I right?"

Mary blinked her eyes.

"Nathan, I do like you, a lot. I don't know if it's love or not, but I think about you all the time. Now tell me if that is also a lie?" She sealed his lips with a deep kiss.

"It's not a lie." Nathan just managed to catch his breath before Mary threw him to the bed.

## Chapter 23

"I am quite happy with your assessment," grinned Mary.

Although they had gone back to the warehouse again, Nathan could still feel Mary's flesh against his skin. This was fantastic; he wished they could have these kinds of assessments more often.

"I'll report the results of your assessments back to SOH, and hopefully they will formally approve you and you can join us soon," said Mary.

"Join SOH? I haven't made up my mind yet." Nathan wasn't joking; his voice was quite serious.

"Come on, Nathan; join SOH for me, for our love." Mary hung on his neck; her lips were almost touching his, but not quite.

"I don't know. It's a hard decision. So far, I can see the arguments for both sides, but I'm not quite sure which is worse, global warming or the decreasing birth rate. Let's face it, OBU has solved so many of the world's biggest problems already…"

Mary pushed her lips onto his, cutting his words off in the middle of his sentence.

"Trust me, if by getting rid of humanity you could solve the world's problems, I would prefer to live and deal with the problems left. What's the point in having a clean environment if no humans are left on this planet to enjoy it?"

Nathan knew it was hard to argue with Mary, and he still didn't know which way he should go, so he decided to change the subject. "Since I have passed the assessment, well, I assume I did, will I get a gun in OBU as well?"

157

"No, you won't." Mary was still hanging on his neck. "This is because the field agents can detect guns easily."

"Do you mean that they use software to search all the databases and uncover people's masks? It'd be impossible to do so, considering the billions of people in OBU," said Nathan.

"Well, I wouldn't be that confident." Mary let him go. She sat on the table, full of guns and piles of papers. "Firstly, the agents don't check everyone, but target a few suspects, so they could manage it easily. Secondly, bullets, similar to explosives in the real world, have quite unique fingerprints, so it's relatively easy to detect them. Guns are banned in OBU around the world, including in the USA; therefore, if you were caught carrying a gun in OBU, you would be put in jail for a very long time, so now you understand why you can't have a gun."

"All right, but don't tell me no one carries guns in OBU apart from the police and agents; surely the organized criminal organizations and SOH have ways to avoid being detected."

"SOH is not an organized criminal organization; we are the good guys, okay," said Mary seriously.

"Okay, I am sorry to put it that way, I didn't mean it like that."

"You have to understand that we are trying to save humanity," Mary continued after seeing Nathan nod firmly. "To answer your question, it's possible to hide guns under masks but with certain risks. Although the advanced digital masks could prevent the detection of guns in most cases, the agents could always have even more advanced detecting software, the seekers; therefore, if not absolutely necessary, we avoid carrying guns."

"What about other types of weapons, such as knives, swords, bows and arrows? Could these weapons be hidden more easily?"

"Yes, they could be more easily hidden than guns but are still banned in OBU; most of the time we don't carry any weapons. We fight with software and computer viruses, not with guns and swords," said Mary.

"I don't know about that; if that's the case, why did I have to do all of that military training?"

"There are always exceptions. That'll be all for today. Nathan, I will meet you at your school tomorrow evening and hopefully I'll have good news for you." She kissed him one last time. "I am really happy, and I like you very much; thanks for everything, Nathan."

"Me, too."


Mary, still in Eve's mask, walked in after all the students had left. Peter followed her in. Soon Pierre, Lucie and Amy also walked in.

"Wow, Nathan, is this your new girlfriend?" Lucie winked at Nathan.

Nathan smiled. "Let me introduce everyone. Eve, Peter, this is Lucie and Pierre."

"Peter." Lucie shook Peter's hand. "Amy has told me quite a lot about you; maybe we should get together sometime."

"When the opportunity arrives, it'd be my great pleasure," said Peter.

"What do you do for a living, Eve?" Pierre shook Mary's hand.

"Peter and I also work for OBUarity; we are working on the logistics of technical aids for developing countries," said Mary.

"Oh, I see. So what's next? Are we all going to the party together?" Pierre looked at Amy while speaking.

"I…" Just as Mary started the sentence, a group of people burst in through the door.

Each of the intruders held a handgun, aimed at Nathan and his friends. The guy in front of the group shouted, "Police! Don't move; put your hands behind your heads. Do it now!"

Nathan did as requested. He scanned the newcomers calmly; there were six of them, all dressed in military combat uniforms. His first thought was that someone had tipped them off and they were here to arrest Mary. What should he do? Beat up the police and save Mary? Nathan wasn't sure about that, because unlike last time, the police had guns; if he decided to fight, it'd definitely get someone killed. He'd never killed anyone in his life and didn't want that to change tonight.

"Cuff them all," commanded the leader to the rest of the police. "Get into the van, quickly," he ordered again after everyone's hands were cuffed behind their backs.

Nathan, followed by his friends, climbed into the police van parked outside of the classroom. After everyone had been pushed into the back of the van, the back doors were shut with a thump. It became quite dark.

"What's happening? Does anyone know why we are getting arrested?" Lucie said in a terrified voice.

Nathan didn't say anything and then he heard Pierre's voice. "It must be some kind of mistake; we should be okay when they find out they got the wrong people."

Then everyone fell silent; nobody said anything until the van stopped.

The back doors of the van opened.

"Get out! All of you," the leader shouted.

It was a warehouse, similar to the one Nathan used for his training, full of rows and rows of large containers. The van was parked in the empty area, presumably the loading space, just inside the sliding gates of the warehouse. The police forced Nathan and his friends to line up against the row of containers, and the police officers stood in a line opposite them; their guns were still held in their hands.

"I am afraid you have made a mistake," said Pierre. "We work for OBUarity, you can check with OBU to verify our identities."

"Shut up," said the leader. He then walked to Nathan.

"We know you beat up police agents in Little Amsterdam, and therefore saved the most wanted terrorist, Mary O'Brian. Based on our latest information, you met her again recently, so tell us where she is now."

It was a big shock to Nathan. His brain was working at high speed to assess the situation. What should he do? He didn't dare look at any of his friends, afraid of giving the police any ideas. "I don't know what you are talking about."

"Are you denying you are Nathan, and that you saved Mary O'Brian in Little Amsterdam?" shouted the leader.

"I am Nathan, but I discussed that incident with the Dutch police already. How do I know if you are really police? If you are, why aren't we in a police station?" said Nathan.

"Yes, why weren't we taken to a police station?" demanded Pierre.

The leader walked a bit closer to Pierre. "Because we are dealing with the most wanted and most dangerous terrorist in the world. The reason we are here is that we can interrogate you without having to follow protocols."

"We have our rights. You can't treat us like this," shouted Pierre.

"No, you don't have any rights in this interrogation centre. If you don't shut up now, I will have to use this to shut you up permanently." He shook his gun in Pierre's face. The leader then turned to Nathan. "Listen to me, Nathan, just tell us where Mary O'Brian is."

"I have never met her before and have no idea where she is," said Nathan.

"Okay, you want to play this the hard way." The leader walked up to Amy, putting the gun to her temple. "I will count to three; if you don't tell me by then, I'll put a bullet in her head. One…"

Oh shit; how could this be happening? Nathan's mind was on fire. What should he do?

"Two…" The leader was interrupted by Pierre.

"You can't do that; I will sue you…"

A loud bang, and the gun in the leader's hand exploded. Nathan saw a bloody hole appear on Pierre's forehead. The leader spat on the ground. "Damn French; I hate them."

Nathan couldn't believe his eyes; Pierre was dead, right in front of him. This guy, whoever he was, must have lost his mind. He had just killed an innocent person in order to force him to tell them where Mary was. It was beyond ridiculous; it was mad. It had to be stopped; Nathan made up his mind. He concentrated his mind, focusing on the handcuffs behind his back, telling himself there were no handcuffs there, it was just a signal trigger to his mind so he couldn't move his hands freely, because his mind believed it was real. He kept concentrating to free his mind; there were no handcuffs at all.

It may have felt like a long time but in fact it was only a short moment. Nathan felt his hands come free, but he kept his hands where they were, not wanting to alarm the kidnappers yet. He estimated the distance between him and the leader, and all the other kidnappers' positions; he wasn't sure if he could take them out before they pulled their triggers. Most of the guns in the kidnappers' hands hung by their sides and pointed at the floor, so it would give him the short time he required; they would hesitate initially, and then raise their guns. His advantage was the element of surprise and his speed.

The leader gripped Amy and put his gun against her head again. "Let's start the game again. I hope that there are no interruptions this time. Okay, one…two…"

"Stop it," Nathan shouted out. "I'll talk. I'll tell you everything you want, but please let her go, please. No more killing," Nathan begged; his voice sounded like he was weeping.

The leader lowered his gun and walked towards Nathan. His expression showed some disgust and disappointment. He stopped in front of Nathan, only a foot away. "Well, I am…"

Nathan didn't give him time to finish his sentence; he moved like lightning. He flashed his hand out, gripping the leader's gun with his right hand, and chopped the leader's neck with the edge of his left hand. The leader immediately fell limply to the floor.

As soon as he got hold of the leader's gun, which was in his hand only a split second after his attack, Nathan swung it and fired at the rest of the kidnappers in rapid succession, in fact, more like a continuous burst of bullets. Five bloody holes appeared on the rest of the five kidnappers' foreheads. Nathan was confident that they were all dead before their bodies had hit the ground; this was much easier than shooting ten clay discs.

When his eyes landed on Mary's face, he was surprised by her expression: shocked and disbelieving. What was going on here? Just as Nathan was wondering this but hadn't had time to open his mouth to ask, a huge explosion blasted the warehouse's gate away.

Without thinking, Nathan automatically threw himself onto the ground; out of the corner of his eye, he saw Mary and Amy were doing exactly the same, but Lucie and Peter were frozen to the spot. "Get down to the ground," shouted Nathan, but it was too late. A moment later a rain of bullets showered in and cut them both down to the ground.

Nathan rolled quickly; he noticed that Mary and Amy had also got themselves a gun each. Nathan turned his head towards the gate, seeing a group of people moving in. Their guns were aimed in all directions, ready to fire, but their vision was temporarily blocked by the smoke created by the explosion.

Nathan didn't give them time to adjust.

His gun fired continuously, while his body rolled on the ground, fast. Nathan had seen eight attackers moving in, and they all seemed very good; his first round of assaults only managed to hit four targets, and the rest quickly disappeared behind the large containers.

Nathan felt like his right arm had been hit by a fast train, and the gun fell from his hand down to the ground. Glancing down, he saw his right arm and right leg had been shot and the pain was incredible. He turned, seeing both Mary and Amy lying in their own bloody pools, but they were both alive, so he breathed out in relief; being shot was actually making Mary and Amy safer, because the attackers wouldn't bother to kill them now.

Nathan knew how good Mary was. Despite knowing nothing about Amy's ability, he remembered her telling him she had also been trained; from Amy's fast reaction to the explosion, Nathan would say Amy was not far behind Mary in terms of combat and shooting skills and experience, therefore, whoever had managed to shoot three of them almost at the same time was extremely good indeed.

He noticed that Mary was trying to tell him something, but due to the distance, he was unable to hear her words; after she had repeated the words a few times, Nathan figured them out from her lips' movements.

Mary was repeating the word 'Cowboy'.

So Mary must have seen the super-agent and it had to be the Cowboy who had shot at Mary, Amy and Nathan. The only reason Mary was able to recognize the super-agent was because the Cowboy never wore any masks: he had complete confidence that he didn't need one.

The situation was very dangerous indeed. Nathan was up against four agents and one of them was the Cowboy, one of the three best super agents in the world.

## Chapter 24

Nathan did a quick assessment on the situation: Mary, Amy and he were all wounded but were all still alive; obviously the Cowboy had spared them intentionally because the bullets could easily have been embedded in their heads and hearts. He also knew his own scores: he had killed four intruders by punching holes in their foreheads, but his opponent was much better, hitting his targets six times, two bullets for each of their right arms and right legs. He turned, shouting at Mary and Amy, "Are you all right?"

"Still breathing if that's what you want to know," shouted Mary while pressing her left hand over her right arm and putting her uninjured leg over the wounded one to stop the bleeding. Amy was doing the same; she didn't say anything, just nodded.

Nathan then looked at the pool of his own blood around his body. His brain was operating faster; he knew they would all be dead if he couldn't come up with a solution soon, and it needed to be very soon. He felt dizzy from loss of blood, and excruciating pain was shooting from the bullet wounds. First thing's first, he needed to fix up his wounds if he had any chance of fighting back.

Nathan closed his eyes, concentrating his mind on his injured knee. The wound was not real, just an illusion created by the software and an interface called bullets; he didn't need to accept it and he could reject it... Nathan remembered he had done this in training with the glass bottle that had cut his forearm, but this was much worse; nevertheless, the principle was the same, and if he had done it once, he should be able to do it again.

When it was anything to do with one's mind, the last thing you wanted to do was have to rush and hurry; Nathan knew the key point was to relax and take things slowly. He kept his eyes closed, relaxing his muscles from his head down to his toes, like you would do during a meditation class, but his opponents didn't give him the luxury of time to sit there and meditate for as long as required.

"Really impressive! You knocked down four of my mates."

Nathan opened his eyes; the four remaining intruders stood just ten feet away from him, standing in a half circle. The voice was from the guy in the centre of the half circle. Based on the way he carried himself and the way that Mary was staring at him, Nathan could be reasonably sure that he was one of the three best shooters among the field agents, the Cowboy.

The Cowboy never wore a mask because he had no need to hide his face as all of his opponents were long dead. He had a long face and sharp eyes, just as one would imagine a sharpshooter to possess; he dressed like, well, a cowboy, with a gun belt and holster. He obviously had outstanding skills and an equally enormous ego; Nathan told himself. There was no way he could outshoot the Cowboy, so he had to outsmart him.

"You must be the famous Cowboy; I heard a lot about how good you were but never imagined you were actually this good." Nathan gestured towards himself and then his two comrades.

"What's your name?" asked the Cowboy.

"Nathan; thanks for not killing us."

"Nathan," said the Cowboy thoughtfully. "How come I haven't ever heard about you before?" He stared at Nathan for a few long seconds. "I have to give you credit for being such a faster shooter yourself. You know what, Nathan? While I admire your ability, it's a pity that I have to kill you now to remove the threat, because since our team was established, no triple zero agent has being killed in the battlefield, but you managed to shoot four."

While engaged in conversation, Nathan was meditating on the inside, and his situation had improved quite significantly. Mind over matter, and it was never so true as it was in his situation now; he had successfully used his meditation to not only stop the bleeding but also fully restore the functionality of his injured arm and leg. In other words, he was as good as new but to avoid alerting his enemy, Nathan didn't remove his hand from his injured arm; he kept the same posture.

"So you are the elite field agents, the triple zero agents, like 007," said Nathan.

"I am triple-0 3," said the Cowboy.

"So you are only the third best agent; I assume that 0001 and 0002 are better than you," said Nathan.

"That's up to the individual's opinion," snorted the Cowboy.

Nathan looked down, seeing his gun lying in a pool of his own blood next to his leg; he smiled and then looked up. "Since you are going to kill me soon, why don't we play a game?"

"A game?" The Cowboy's eyes also landed on the gun covered in Nathan's blood.

Nathan sat up a bit straighter, appearing to be struggling, but in fact he did it quite easily; the pained moaning was acting for the benefit of the agents. He used the opportunity to check if his body had recovered, and he was happy with the result.

"Yes, a game. I want to bet with you; regardless of whether I win or lose, you have to promise not to kill my friends." Nathan turned, seeing Mary's astonished expression. *She must think I'm completely mad,* thought Nathan. Amy, on the other hand, seemed quite calm.

"Don't worry about that, because I won't kill them. I'll take them back and torture them to get information about the whole of SOH," laughed the Cowboy. "I'll look after your friends very well." The rest of the agents joined in with the laughter.

"Good." Nathan adjusted his sitting position again, accompanied by more pained moaning. "I have said you are very good, and it seems your track record has proved the point; you have never been beaten before."

"I am all ears. So?" mocked the Cowboy and the rest of the agents laughed loudly again.

Nathan lifted his chin up to point at the agents on both sides of the Cowboy. "I will bet that, if you let me pick up my gun, I can shoot and kill all of your three agents and yourself." Nathan panted; his head rested on his right shoulder for dramatic effect.

Loud laughter burst out inside the warehouse. The Cowboy laughed so much that he bent down on his knees; finally he stopped laughing. "Nathan, you have chosen the wrong occupation; you are much better at telling jokes than shooting." The laughter was getting louder and louder.

Nathan turned to see sadness on Mary's face, but Amy's expression remained blank. He waited until all the laughter had stopped. "What do you say about my bet? Cowboy, you have nothing to lose; four guns against my one."

The Cowboy walked a few steps closer to Nathan; he gazed into Nathan's eyes for a long time. "Nathan, I

169

admire your courage as a soldier, but please don't insult my intelligence. I shot you and your two friends when you were uninjured and now you are telling me you can manage to kill all of us with your wounded arm?"

"Yes, that's exactly what I mean, but with my left hand. Come on, Cowboy, you are going to kill me anyway, so why don't we all have some fun meanwhile?" said Nathan.

The Cowboy stepped back in line with the other agents. "Nathan, I respect you as a worthy opponent, a real warrior and soldier, so I will let you die with dignity." He turned to the other agents. "Holster your guns, all of you."

The three agents holstered their guns with slick, fast movements.

The Cowboy also holstered his own gun. He hung both of his arms by his sides, his right hand next to his gun holster, cowboy-style, before a shootout in the Wild West. "Nathan, pick up your gun, slowly."

Nathan removed his left hand from his bloody right arm and picked up his gun from the pool of his blood. He wiped the gun on his trousers a few times. "Cowboy, thanks for this opportunity; regardless of the outcome, I will always respect you as a true opponent. One more tip, Cowboy, don't miss my head."

"Are you going to shoot in that sitting position?" asked the Cowboy.

"No, I will stand up and die with dignity." Nathan struggled to get to his feet, with much more grinding of his teeth and theatrical moaning. Inside he let out a breath of relief; he had just confirmed that his self-healing had worked. He put weight on his left leg, the uninjured leg.

Nathan slowly put the gun into his belt, eyeing the agents in a half circle around him. He knew clearly that he was not faster than the Cowboy, and the other three agents were not much slower than him; even if he managed to kill the Cowboy, he wouldn't be able to survive the bullets from the other three agents. It was tough but he had no choice; this was his only chance and he had to play his bet.

His eyes locked with the Cowboy's; the air suddenly became solid in the warehouse.

## Chapter 25

Mary dragged her wounded leg behind her and approached Nathan. Amy had already crawled to his side. Nathan lifted his eyes, glancing at the half circle of agents' bodies, and smiled; he had outsmarted and beaten his enemy, and saved the two women he cared for the most in his life. A sharp pain shot through his body, reminding him about the bullet holes in his chest; blood was oozing out.

"Are you going to die?" Amy said while using her jacket to stop Nathan's bleeding.

"I hope not." Nathan managed to smile. "It seems that my heart is still pumping."

Mary put her hand on Nathan's neck, checking his pulse, and said, "I don't understand how the Cowboy could miss your heart." She stared at his blood-covered chest for a few seconds. "I am sure the bullets should have hit your heart based on where the entry wounds are; tell me what happened."

Nathan closed his eyes while trying to use meditation to heal the new wounds on his chest, also recalling what had happened in his mind.

Nathan knew that he wouldn't be able to shoot faster than the Cowboy even if he was completely unwounded, and had absolutely no chance of surviving the gun battle with the other three agents fighting alongside the Cowboy, so he had to think outside of the box. He then thought about Tao; the opposite was true: if he couldn't beat his enemy by being a faster shooter, could he win with slower shooting? Of course, it was unthinkable for an ordinary person under ordinary circumstances, but he was not an ordinary person under ordinary circumstances.

As soon as the concept burst into his mind, Nathan immediately, almost by instinct, knew what he would have to do next; he had to play with the Cowboy's ego: he had never been beaten in his entire life.

Nathan offered to fight all of them at once and it was no surprise that the Cowboy ordered the rest of the agents to holster their guns. That had put Nathan one step closer to survival but still nowhere near close enough to defeat the Cowboy.

Nathan knew clearly that the bullets from the Cowboy's gun would hit his body first. What he relied on was his mind power. Even though he had confirmed his self-healing ability by meditation, he also knew it was not good enough to deal with a fatal hit to his heart or head. His mind was simply unable to heal him fast enough to prevent his body from shutting down; he would be dead before he could do any meditation.

Therefore, the only option left was to meditate beforehand. He didn't know how the idea came to his mind, but it did: if he could self-heal by believing the wounds weren't real, why shouldn't he be able to believe his heart was not where it was; in other words, he should be able to shift his heart to another part of his body, maybe far enough to the side to avoid the bullets. All of these happenings in OBU were just a matter of mind games anyway.

Even if it was possible to shift his heart away, he couldn't guarantee the bullets wouldn't hit his head, and there was no way he could move his brain outside of his head, so he told the Cowboy to shoot at his head; he bet his life, together with two of his friends' lives, that the Cowboy wouldn't shoot at his head and his heart-shifting method would work. It was a farfetched bet but he had no other option.

The Cowboy was fast, indeed; his bullets hit Nathan's chest twice before Nathan punched a bloody hole in the Cowboy's forehead; Nathan didn't want to take a chance by aiming at the Cowboy's heart because the Cowboy could have been wearing some kind of bulletproof vest, so he went for the unprotected skull.

The Cowboy's expression was beyond surprise; he couldn't believe what had happened. Nathan's left arm flashed out as fast as lightning, and he must have seen the bullet shoot out of the gun's barrel to bring an end to his existence.

It was a relatively easy task to finish off the rest of the three agents; Nathan was quite confident that he could beat three of them in a standoff. At the moment, his gun was in firing position while the agents were still in the process of drawing theirs. To prove the point, Nathan punched a bullet hole in each of their foreheads in the first round, and then another in their chests in the following round, well before their guns were up.

Nathan felt his meditation had worked; the pain of his chest wounds had gone, so he opened his eyes and smiled.

"I guess that I was just lucky; maybe because of the shooting angle, the Cowboy's bullets missed my heart." He decided not to explain all the details to them yet, as he had other much more important matters to deal with.

Nathan took Amy's blood-soaked jacket off his chest. "I am okay now."

Amy's eyes opened wide. "How?"

"Nathan has a very powerful mind-control ability that enables him to heal his wounds and injuries in OBU," said Mary.

"Let me see if I am also able to help you girls." Nathan held Amy's hand, letting his mind travel to Amy's body through his hand to hers, his mind's eye focused on her wounds. After the first few rounds of self-healing, he had become quite efficient in this new mind-mending technique; a few minutes later, he opened his eyes. "Amy, stand up."

"I can't," said Amy.

"Yes, you can. I have just healed your wounds. Trust me. Now stand up as you would normally do," Nathan ordered.

Amy pushed herself up. "My God, I can't believe it." She kicked her leg and waved her arm madly.

"Shall we do something about you now?" Nathan held Mary's hand.

"Mary, do you know what's going on here?" Nathan asked after Mary had recovered from her gunshot wounds.

"Just wait a minute." Mary stood up, walking to the control panel mounted on the side of a large container. She pushed a few buttons; soon the warehouse gate reappeared and sealed them in from outside. When all was done, she came back to Nathan and Amy.

"What a bloody mess this is!" Mary put her fingers through her hair, speaking in a low groan.

"Mary, calm down. Please tell us what is going on." Nathan put his hand on Mary's shoulder and spoke softly.

Amy had remained silent since recovering from her wounds; she was just staring at Mary and Nathan.

175

Mary lifted her head.

"All right, I will explain but it will have to be brief as we don't have too much time. I have set up the double-time expansion function so that should give us a little more time."

Nathan didn't say anything, just nodded.

Mary took a deep breath. "After I reported your assessment results back to SOH, HQ was very impressed, so they wanted to do a final test on you to check if you were an undercover agent."

"What? So the kidnapping was a test conducted by SOH?" asked Nathan.

"Yes, it was, because you seemed just too good to be real; many believe no one could have achieved those results unless he was an agent in disguise," said Mary.

"I can't believe it," mumbled Amy quietly.

"So your people were willing to kill Pierre to test whether I was an agent or not?"

"Is it true, they really did kill Pierre?" Tears filled Amy's eyes.

"Of course it is untrue; it was an act, a software trick to make it look real, otherwise you wouldn't have believed it." Mary laughed drily.

Nathan doubted it was a software trick because he saw Pierre die with his own eyes, and the death was very real to him; but he decided to give her the benefit of the doubt and believe it for the time being. "What happened with the agents? Please don't tell me they were not real agents, also part of the test."

"Oh no, they were the real agents," said Mary.

Amy's sobbing was getting louder. "Poor Pierre, he was trying to approach me so hard...for so long...I should have..."

Mary looked at Amy. "I am so sorry about Pierre." She then stared into Nathan's eyes. "Nathan, we are not out of trouble yet; in fact, we are now in an even more dangerous situation."

"What are you talking about?" Nathan turned to Mary.

"Thanks to your fast shooting skills, now SOH believes that you are a real agent and that I have also turned against them," said Mary.

"Be reasonable, Mary. Even if I hadn't killed the kidnappers, whom I know now were guys from SOH, the agents would have killed them anyway, so what's the difference? Besides, I truly believed that they had killed Pierre and were going to kill Amy."

Mary sighed. "I know that, but SOH don't and won't believe it. Therefore, we are now on SOH's hit list; they hate traitors more than their enemies."

"That's just great," said Nathan.

Amy had stopped crying and was listening to this new revelation intensely.

"That's not all. Nathan, you have just wiped out an entire elite unit of field agents single handed; it's never happened in OBU history, so now they know how dangerous you are. As a result, they will hunt you down at all costs."

"Why would they be so serious about me? Revenge?"

"Oh no, not revenge. If you can kill one of their best units, you could possibly gain forced entry to OBU's HQ and few could stop you; it's about the survival of OBU, so they won't stop until you are dead." Mary paused, and when neither Nathan nor Amy said anything, she continued.

"Not to mention we heard the words from the Cowboy himself, he was just 0003; that means there are two more agents that are better than him, so your future battles will be much more difficult, if you are able to survive at all."

"It does sound dangerous; what should we do now?" asked Nathan.

Mary thought for a long time and said hesitantly, "I would suggest that you and Amy try to run and hide for as long as you can; meanwhile, I will try to explain and persuade SOH to believe the truth of what just happened."

"Where could we hide, Nathan?" asked Amy. Her worry was so obvious it even showed on her face.

Nathan's brain was operating at high speed. He knew Mary was right and they were indeed in a more dangerous situation. After more careful thought, he said,

"Mary, I appreciate your offer to talk to SOH but I won't let you do it for my sake. You could get yourself killed or become their hostage to use against me; besides, even if SOH believes you, I still have even more powerful and deadly forces to fight against."

"So what do you suggest then?" asked Mary.

"I am not going to hide or run; instead, I am going to London. I believe both HQs of SOH and OBU are in London, right?" said Nathan.

"London? That's suicidal," said Mary.

"Yes, Mary's right; it's too dangerous to go to London now. It'd be better to hide somewhere here in Australia; maybe some remote area that has no OBU or Internet connections," said Amy hopefully.

"Amy, even if we are able to hide for a while, they will find us eventually; rather than waiting for them to find us, why not get to them first? Attacking is the best defence strategy. London is the last place they would expect us to be, so it would be safe for the time being until we can work out ways to push forward."

Mary thought for a moment.

"Nathan, I think you are right. We would have to fight against OBU alone, and also avoid SOH as well. Okay, I will also go underground in London. I will meet you at London Heathrow Airport."

## Chapter 26

This was Nathan's very first-time visiting Heathrow, the busiest passenger airport in the United Kingdom in its heyday, but what was in front of his eyes now couldn't be further from his imagination. The surroundings where the tiny crowds waited to go through the immigration customs looked worn and dirty, desperately in need of some repairs and upgrades. However, this was not a total surprise to Nathan based on his flying experience starting from Sydney.

Due to OBU's monopoly on leisure, business and adventure travelling, most passenger airlines around the world had gone bankrupt, and the few still flying were subsidized heavily by their own governments. Nathan and Amy flew with Australia's national carrier, Qantas, but one couldn't really call it a passenger plane. Most of the planes still in service had been re-fitted as freight carriers, and a small number of them kept a few seats in the front rows of the cabin, once first-class seats, for the occasional travellers. So in that sense, Nathan was actually lucky enough to be flying first class on his first trip to Europe.

Nathan turned to Amy, who gave him a tired and nervous smile. He sighed but at the same time breathed out in relief; they had at least managed to escape from Sydney before the agency discovered the disappearance of the Cowboy and his elite unit.

Mary obviously had quite substantial knowledge about the agency and how they were operating; she told Nathan that the Cowboy had lots of freedom, basically operating outside of any laws. Members of SOH had reported on numerous occasions that the agency's elite units had

180

killed innocent people either by mistake or as collateral damage but of course they were unable to tell the world the truth, because whenever they tried to put it on the Internet or OBU, their words would be deleted automatically by the monitoring software. As for the deaths of the innocent people, their families and relatives would be told that they died for some kind of health-related reason or unavoidable natural accidents; there wouldn't be any investigations by any police detectives or law-enforcement agents. However, the freedom the elite unit enjoyed was also their downfall, because nobody would know where they were until much too late, so Mary was quite confident that Nathan and Amy would have time to make their escape.

After logging out of OBU, Nathan and Amy didn't pack anything extra except a small backpack each. They withdrew money from an ATM, maxing out their daily limit, as from then on they would have to use cash to avoid being traced.

Since there were so few travellers, the security and ticketing in Sydney International Airport was negligible; they just bought the tickets and got on board the next plane heading to London. He doubted if the customs officer had bothered to enter their names and destination into the database.

Amy shivered and Nathan felt cold too. It was pretty chilly even inside the airport building. They had both put on all the warm clothes they had brought with them, but it was still not enough; Nathan and Amy had a hard time adjusting themselves from the summer weather in Sydney to the stone-cold chill of London's winter.

There was a short queue in front of Nathan and Amy of people who had come to London from the collection of several planes that had recently landed. Fortunately, they moved forward rapidly and soon they were in front of the immigration desk; he and Amy pushed their passports into the small gap under the glass screen, where a stern-faced guy sat.

"Is this the first time you've visited the UK?" asked the customs officer in a bored voice.

'Yes, it is." Nathan tried to sound as calm as possible.

The officer turned the pages of Nathan's passport and then Amy's for a while, and then stood up. "Mr. Nathan Jenkins and Ms. Amy Kelly, I am afraid that you both have to come with me to answer a few immigration questions."

Nathan exchanged a look with Amy, who shook her head slightly. "Is there anything wrong with our passports, sir?" asked Nathan in a concerned voice.

The officer nodded. "Nothing serious, but I do have a couple of questions; it's just a formality and shouldn't take too much time. This way, please."

Nathan turned around and glanced back; they were the last passengers, and all the other immigration booths were empty. He noticed the worried expression on Amy's face, and he couldn't blame her for that because he was worried himself.

Nathan and Amy followed the officer, walking through a door and along a long corridor, and then through another couple of doors into yet another corridor. The corridors were long and seemed endless; after many turns and more doors, Nathan couldn't help but ask, "How much further do we have to go, sir?"

"Not far at all; here we go, that door is my office."

It was not really an office, but a storage space, quite spacious in the centre, with many cabinets standing along the walls. There were no desks or chairs, and a group of guys who looked like luggage handlers were gathered in the middle of the space.

The officer quickly walked to the group. "Nathan Jenkins and Amy Kelly." He spoke loudly.

Nathan turned, just in time to see two large guys, also dressed like luggage handlers, walk in from outside and close the door behind them. This didn't look good; Nathan did a quick assessment of the situation. There were six in front of them, and two behind; they were all large, muscular guys, like rugby players, and he was unsure if they were armed or not. Although he had beaten a group of agents with his bare hands in OBU once, Nathan had no confidence that he could reproduce the same result here because this was not OBU, and he had never actually fought body-to-body with anyone in his whole life; there was always a first time for everything, he told himself.

Nathan glanced at Amy and he noticed that her body was tensed. It was a good sign; she at least would be able to defend herself for a while, but she wouldn't last long against these large guys. Nathan was six feet tall and athletic, but all of these guys were not only a few inches taller but also much thicker than him. He nodded, while using meditation to move his Chi (inner energy) around his body to get himself ready for the coming confrontation, and said, "What's this about, gents?"

"Well, Nathan, we want to invite you to visit our HQ. In case you haven't worked out who we are, we are SOH." One of the guys spoke; he seemed to be the leader of the group.

SOH, not the agents, wanted revenge. Nathan knew there wouldn't be an easy way out today and there was no point arguing his case with these guys at all. "All right; it's between you and me, so let the lady out of here."

"I am afraid I can't do that. Nathan, we heard you are very good at fighting, at least in OBU, but I strongly suggest you make this easy and come with us voluntarily. We don't want to make a mess here," said the leader.

Nathan scanned the group of SOH members with cool eyes; they looked tough, and tattoos and scars covered their faces and thick arms. "All right, let the lady watch from the side, and I'll play with you." He pushed Amy sideways so that she was standing against a cabinet and he threw his backpack on the floor beside her feet, then he turned his body slightly so he could see the two guys behind him as well.

"Nathan, I hope your fighting skills are as good as your reputation suggests. You two check him out." The leader waved his arm and two guys stepped towards Nathan.

Nathan knew that, even if he could beat these two, the rest of them wouldn't let him and Amy out. Besides, they were very likely armed, with knives or even guns hidden underneath their jackets, so he had to be smart and get out of this confined space as soon as possible. Before engaging with the oncoming attackers, he quickly glanced at Amy, tipping his chin slightly towards the door; he was satisfied when she nodded back slightly. After that, the first guy's fist almost hit his face.

Nathan backed up a step, using his palm to block the next punch from the second guy. These two were actually quite good at hand-to-hand combat; they must have had lots of training. They could have been ex-soldiers from special military forces. Nathan didn't fight back, instead he only ducked, backed up, and blocked the constant rain

184

of blows and kicks; without looking back, Nathan knew that his body was zigzagging across the room and was fast approaching the two big guys who guarded the door.

Everyone in the room shouted excitedly. They shouted for the guys to kick Nathan's ass, break his nose, crush his arms and legs and every part of his body. The fighting looked almost like stunts on a movie set; despite the two ex-soldiers' fierce attacks, none of their power blows actually landed on Nathan's body. Nathan seemed always to be just able to twist his body and avoid being hit at the last possible moment. Nathan never formed fists during the whole fight but used his palms to deflect the blows.

Nathan didn't know how he knew all of these movements, or how he saw or sensed the attack speed and angle; his body and limbs reacted automatically, without even thinking, by pure instinct. Nathan could see exactly which blow would land where and when. Still not glancing back, Nathan knew that he was only a couple of feet away from the two guys standing in front of the door. He also knew one of them was going to headlock him from behind to let the others beat the shit out of him. Nathan didn't need to look; he could sense it.

Nathan saw the guy's arms closing in on him on his way to headlock him from behind; he pretended not to know, still moving backward to avoid the blows coming from in front of him. Just before the arms closed on his neck, Nathan acted: he dropped suddenly, missing the arm narrowly. Nathan turned his body slightly and his shoulder bumped right into the guy's chest behind him, sending his body flying back, hitting the side wall, and collapsing on the floor.

By using the force from bumping the guy away, Nathan leaned forward; his left hand flashed out and his fingers spread out: the eagle claw! Nathan didn't have

185

any memory of learning the Kung Fu term but the concept jumped into his mind as his body acted it out. His fingers, like eagle claws, gripped the attacker's wrist with lightning speed; with a jerk and a tug, the sound of bones popping told Nathan that his shoulder, elbow and wrist joints were all dislocated.

Nathan let him go as he hollered and clutched at his arm. Lifting his leg, he kicked at the second attacker in quick succession. Nathan's first kick landed on his kneecap, the second in his stomach, sending him back-flipping through the air. Nathan found it hard to believe that it was possible to kick such a large guy into a back flip, but he had seen it with his own eyes.

Even before the back-flipping guy had landed on the floor, Nathan twisted his body again. The edge of his right hand, the 'palm blade' in Kung Fu terms, chopped at the neck of the last guy standing in front of the door; the force of the chop caused him to fall away from the door silently.

Before Nathan could say anything, Amy leaped to his side; she opened the door and dashed out. Nathan followed closely and closed the door behind him.

They ran along the corridor, not quite sure which direction to go in but just running, bumping doors open and turning corners. Nathan slowed down when the sounds of people chasing faded away.

He looked back; once they were sure there was no one behind them, he stopped. Amy also stopped, panting heavily beside him. Nathan took a few deep breaths. "What the hell was all of that about?"

"Don't know how SOH knew we were on that flight so quickly," said Amy, still breathless.

Nathan thought for a moment. "Let's get out of here first and worry about that later."

Just as they turned the next corner, two guys appeared in front of them, both dressed in the uniform of luggage handlers.

Nathan was going to launch his assault but stopped after hearing the words coming out of the first guy's mouth.

"Have you booked a river cruise for today?"

It was the first sentence of Nathan and Mary's contact code. Nathan turned at Amy, and then said, "Yes, I have, but it's for tomorrow."

The guy smiled. "No worries; tomorrow is also fine."

All the words matched. "Are you friends of Mary's?" asked Nathan.

"Please follow me; this way." The two of them turned and led the way; Nathan and Amy followed.

After a few turns, they went into a room. Nathan had no idea that there were so many corridors and rooms in the complex; it was like a maze. Once they were all in the room, the second guy closed the door behind them. It was a changing room with a row of lockers. Nathan was about to ask but the first guy signalled him to wait. He opened a locker and took out a bag.

Nathan watched him curiously as he took out a pile of clothes, seemingly luggage handlers' overalls, the same as they both wore, and finally two sets of square plastic boxes the size of a novel.

"Put the overalls on, both of you, quickly," urged the first guy.

Without a word, Nathan and Amy put the working clothes over their own clothes; the overalls fit both of them perfectly. The first guy walked around them a few times. "Not bad; what do you think, Steve?"

The second guy, Steve, nodded.

"Okay, we need to hurry. Steve, you help Nathan with his mask, and I'll do Amy's," ordered the first guy.

Steve asked Nathan to stand in front of a mirror that was mounted on the wall, and then opened one of the plastic boxes; inside was what looked like a makeup kit. He picked up a thin layer of skin-coloured plastic; Nathan didn't realize what it was until Steve lifted it up to his face. It was a facemask, customized to fit Nathan's face. It seemed that Steve had done this many times before. He knew exactly what to do, adjusting and gluing the thin layer onto Nathan's face, applying some colour by using a brush on the edges where the mask merged into his skin. The whole process only took a few minutes.

Nathan was amazed by how effective a facemask and some makeup could be; he was staring at a complete stranger in the mirror. He turned his neck to see himself from different angles; the mask matched his own skin colour perfectly. Lastly, Steve pulled out a hat from the bag and put it on Nathan's head. The hat covered the mask's edges where they merged into his hairline.

"A new handsome look, eh?" asked Steve, who stood back, studying his work.

"Good job, Steve," said the first guy.

Nathan turned. Seeing Amy was a big surprise; Amy was no longer herself. In fact, she didn't look like a girl at all. Nathan was staring at a strange young male, a guy he had never seen before.

"Okay, Nathan, your name is Mark; and Amy, yours is John. Mark and John are the owners of the faces you two are wearing now, so if by chance anyone asks you questions, try to speak as little as possible. Particularly

188

you, Amy, keep your voice as low as possible," said the first guy.

"Wouldn't people find our voices and accents wrong for Mark and John?" asked Amy in as low a voice as she could, like she was told to.

"Not bad with your voice, Amy. Mark and John are relatively new here so not many people know them. Your main concern is to fool the OBU cameras," said Steve.

"I see," said Nathan thoughtfully. "What happens if the cameras measure our skulls? You know, it's hard to fake bone structures."

"Well, I doubt the cameras will measure everyone's skulls. Nothing is absolute, let's just go and hope for the best." The first guy walked out and signalled for Nathan and Amy to follow him. "Since very few passengers travel nowadays, the whole airport has become a freight hub which requires lots of luggage handlers," said the first guy as they walked along the maze-like corridors. Finally, they reached the open air; in front of them, buses were parked along the roadsides, and long queues of luggage handlers snaked slowly onto the buses.

"Right, we came out at the right moment," said the first guy as they joined the queue.

**Chapter 27**

Nathan hadn't been to London before. He had seen the city in pictures, movies, and had recently visited it in OBU, but looking out of the bus window, he had to say what he saw was quite different from his memory from his OBU visit. Unlike the pretty, modern city landscape in OBU, many of the buildings were badly worn and desperately required an overhaul, so what he had seen in OBU must have been the enhanced digital version of the city, thought Nathan.

They got off the bus near an aboveground train station; Nathan and Amy then followed the first guy as he jumped onto a train. However, Steve didn't come with them, but stayed on the bus instead. There were not many passengers on the train and the few there didn't speak a word. The train travelled into the underground zone; they were now in the centre of London. Nathan and Amy silently followed the first guy as he got off the train, walked to a different platform and then got on to another train. Finally, they walked up the stairs, which were really just escalators that had stopped working; it was a long way up.

The ground floor was inside a large complex; judging from what was left in the construction site, Nathan guessed this place could have been a luxury shopping mall in its heyday, but now all the walls were stripped to bare concrete. The first guy looked at Nathan's confused expression and smiled.

"This was a department store before OBU and has been in disuse for more than a decade; some company tried to convert it to an apartment building but either ran out of money or went bankrupt, so this half-stripped building has been emptied for years." He waved his arm around. "There are many empty, half demolished and abandoned buildings in London's centre. If you walk outside along the streets, the only things moving are the OBU cameras mounted on buildings or flying above the streets, and there may be a few wild dogs and feral cats."

Nathan shook his head but made no comments. Amy had kept quiet the whole time.

They walked around inside the building for a while, into the part that hadn't been stripped; they climbed up the stairs that were covered with worn and dirty carpets, and finally stopped in front of a few rooms. Nathan guessed they could be offices inside the department store.

"There are no OBU cameras mounted inside the building, so we can do whatever we want here, but we are not alone; I would say almost all the empty buildings are occupied by different groups of gangs and this is, of course, my territory." The first guy pointed to their left. "The toilet and shower are that way and still working." He then pushed a door open. "Amy, here is your room. You can take your mask off if you want; freshen up and make yourself comfortable. I'm going to have some private words with Nathan."

Amy nodded as she walked into the room, closing the door behind her.

"Nathan, this way." The first guy gripped Nathan's hand, dragging him towards the door at the other end of the corridor.

Nathan felt quite awkward having his hand held by another guy. "Hey, mate, you don't need to drag me…"

"Shut up; just come with me." The guy's voice suddenly changed; it sounded really familiar, but Nathan couldn't put his finger on it. He knew he had heard that

191

voice somewhere. Nathan was still feeling awkward as they stumbled into a room together. The guy aimed a kick backwards to close the door, and then looped his arms around Nathan's neck; his face was approaching Nathan's.

"Hang on, mate, that's going a bit too far." Nathan pushed the guy to arm's length. "Mate, I appreciate your help, but I am not into…"

"You are such an idiot; look at my face." The guy used his hands to grip the skin underneath his chin, and he pulled a layer of skin away, off his face. Nathan couldn't help but gasp: underneath the mask, Mary was smiling at him, like a flower blossoming in a spring breeze.

"You are right, I am such an idiot; I should have guessed it was you in the first place." Nathan felt badly embarrassed.

"Tear your mask off," ordered Mary in a husky voice while her hands were busily unbuttoning Nathan's belt.

They both breathed heavily and tried to tear each other's clothes off as fast as possible; soon they jumped under the covers in the big bed in the middle of the room. Nathan stared at Mary's blue eyes only a few inches away underneath him, and then kissed her deeply. He could feel her bare breasts again his chest, and her flat stomach and smooth thighs. It was such a long time since he'd touched a girl's flesh; the excitement made Nathan's head feel light, and his blood was boiling.

"I love you so much," Nathan said in between kissing Mary while his hands were busily exploring her body.

"Wait a moment." Mary held his hand, stopping his movements.

"What's the matter?" Nathan was puzzled.

A shy smile appeared at the corner of Mary's mouth. "Nathan, please be gentle…I am still a virgin…"

Nathan stopped, staring at Mary in disbelief. "Are you kidding?"

"No, it's for real." Mary pulled his head down and kissed his mouth gently. "Nathan, have you been with a virgin before?"

Nathan shook his head; no, he hadn't. The couple of girls he had met before Cathy weren't virgins, and neither was Cathy herself, and that was all his experience with girls.

"Do you think you are able to handle me?" Mary kissed him again.

Nathan thought for a moment. "I think I will manage." He held Mary, kissing her delicious mouth for a very long time until they had both run out of breath; then they both sank deep into another world.


The lovemaking was passionate even going towards the violent side; sweat poured off their bodies. Afterwards, Nathan lay beside Mary, panting heavily. Mary lay on her back, both hands on her tummy, stroking herself gently.

"Nathan, I hope I can get pregnant after this."

"Oh shit, I complete forget about using a condom. Pregnant? Are you serious?"

"Yes, I am deadly serious." Mary climbed on top of Nathan. "Nathan, you were an OBU virgin a few weeks ago, so you are still healthy in your reproductive capability department, probably the best man any girl could hope for to father a baby."

"Mary, are you sure you want to have a baby with me? I mean, we only met such a short time ago."

"Nathan, do you love me or not?"

"Yes, I do love you."

"So what's the problem then?" Mary held Nathan's hand, putting it on her tummy. "We may need to work harder to make sure it happens."

"I    can't    wait."    Nathan    kissed    her    again.

## Chapter 28

"I have to go now," Mary said after she had put her clothes back on. "There are two sets of helmets in that cupboard for you and Amy. Please log in to OBU and meet me at the river cruise boat I told you about before. I will introduce you two to my comrades and then we can discuss what to do next." She walked towards the door but stopped. "Nathan, please make sure you stay in this room and Amy stays in her room."

Nathan laughed. "Amy and I have been sharing a flat for weeks; what's this? Jealousy?"

Mary shook her head. "Jealous I may be, but it's for safety and practicality mostly. Anyway, please pass the helmet to Amy and I'll see you both in OBU soon." She then disappeared out of the door.

Nathan sat there, still remembering their steamy lovemaking; he could still smell Mary's body fragrance in the air. He was unable to get the smile off of his face even when he knocked on Amy's door.

"Come in," answered Amy.

Nathan walked in and saw Amy sitting on her bed; she had removed her mask. "So how is the virgin Mary?"

Nathan's jaw dropped. "How did you know?"

Amy smiled bitterly. "Nathan, I knew it was Mary when we first met her in the airport. A woman's instinct, you might say; I guessed it from the way she looked at you and the way she was speaking even though she tried to speak in a low voice. I confirmed my suspicions when she helped me to put my mask on, because there is no way a guy could do things like that."

Looking at Amy's bitter smile, Nathan sighed inside; he had known Amy had a crush on him a long time ago, and it seemed that it hadn't gone away. He wished that he could give her a chance and love her in return, but he just couldn't.

"Of course, you girls are much better observers than us guys. I only found out much later," he said, embarrassed, particularly as he was remembering what had happened on his bed just then. "Here is a helmet for you. Mary asked us to meet her on the river cruise boat soon." He passed it to her.

"Thanks. Nathan, I am glad that we still share a flat, except the distance between our bedrooms doors is much greater now," said Amy.

Nathan didn't know what to say; he nodded in silence and then said, "All right, I'll see you soon in OBU then." He walked out of Amy's room feeling awkward, very awkward indeed.

It was a big contrast between the ghost town of real London and the booming tourist city in OBU. Nathan and Amy walked along the Thames among thousands of tourists from all over the world; they wanted to see and experience the famous city that was at the centre of European civilization.

Nathan and Amy each wore a digital mask; he knew that Mary would know what they looked like because she had provided the masks for them. Even though he had been in OBU and had been wearing masks for a while now, Nathan was still not used to it; he felt like he was living in a masked party all the time.

The river cruise was a booming business; there were so many cruising boats up and down the Thames all the time, it was no surprise that Mary liked to use a boat for their secret meetings. Nathan and Amy walked on board like all the other visitors; he had no idea where to find

Mary because she could be anyone in the crowd around him.

The digital version of the cruise boat could contain many more people than in the real world; thousands of people could all fit onto the different level decks without feeling crowded. Nathan and Amy walked towards the bottom deck; people were talking noisily in all kinds of languages, like a giant party. Nathan had been here before, but at the moment, he had no idea where to look or go.

A waitress holding a plate full of drinks passed them. "Would you like a drink, ma'am and sir?" she asked.

Nathan wanted to say no but he caught the waitress's eyes and saw a glimmer of a smile in them; they had to belong to the only female he knew so well at the moment, Mary. He smiled. "No thanks. Could you please tell me where the bathroom is?"

"Of course; walk along the corridor to the end and the door is on your left. Beware as the door blends into the panels so you may have to push a few panels to find it." The waitress walked off to serve others.

Nathan and Amy found the bathroom. He locked the door of his cubicle. Soon the side panel of the cubicle opened like a door and he stepped through it. Rather than walking into the next toilet cubicle as common sense would suggest, Nathan stepped into a large hall. Next to him, Amy also emerged; this was a digital dimension Mary had created under the cover of the cruise boat.

The hall looked luxurious, almost like a sixteenth-century French palace Nathan had once visited in OBU, but at the moment, he had neither the time nor the interest to pay attention to the surroundings. Sitting on the spacious couches under the large window that looked out at the landscaped garden and water fountains, a group of people stared at him and Amy; Mary was standing behind the crowd, still in her waitress outfit and mask.

"Hi, you guys made it," Mary said brightly. "Everyone, let me introduce you to each other. This is Nathan and Amy, and I am sure you guys have heard about them quite a lot by now." The group laughed and greeted him and Amy.

"Nathan and Amy, please take off your masks." After the request was fulfilled, Mary continued. "So I would like everyone to remove their masks so we can know each other better. I believe this could be the very first time some of you have actually seen each other's real faces. Let's start with me first."

Mary pulled her mask off. "I am sure you all know my face, as it's on all websites and every public gathering location in OBU."

The group laughed.

Mary then introduced the guys next to her who pulled their masks off in turn. "Steve, James, John, Mark, Victor and David…"

So Mark and John were real people who were the owners of the masks he and Amy wore in the airport, and they did look exactly the same as the masks; these guys, six of them, all looked like they were from a worker's union: tough, bulky and strong; and they all had Irish accents, so they were clearly from Mary's neighbourhood. However, Nathan didn't ask any questions, just smiled and said hello to everyone.

Mary turned to Nathan. "I have tried but failed to convince SOH that it was a misunderstanding and an accident what happened in the warehouse when the pretend kidnappers were killed, so we are still fugitives hiding from SOH's revenge hunts. These are my loyal comrades and I trust all of them with my life."

Nathan nodded but still didn't say anything.

Mary stopped and then spoke with an air of mystery. "And last but not least, please meet our computer guru." She waved her arm at the back of the crowd.

Until then Nathan realized that Mary hadn't introduced the last person in the room; this guy was dressed and looked much the same as her Irish mob, which could be the reason why he hadn't paid much attention to him. When this guru stood up and greeted him, Nathan couldn't believe his eyes; this could not be true. He glanced at Amy, who was equally surprised to hear that voice.

Sure enough, after the guru removed his mask, underneath the face that appeared belonged to a person Nathan knew very well, Gary West, his high school mate and uni buddy.

"Holy shit! Gary. I can't believe this; you are a member of SOH," shouted Nathan.

"Hi, Gary," said Amy.

"Well, Nathan and Amy, sorry for not being able to tell you earlier; I had to follow Mary's orders," said Gary.

"Wait a moment," Nathan said. "Gary, tell me that meeting Mary during my first visit to the bar in Little Amsterdam did not just happen, but you organized the whole thing."

Gary glanced at Mary once; she nodded so he said, "When you said you were an OBU virgin, I informed Mary and she wanted to meet you in person immediately."

"That explains quite a lot," Nathan said thoughtfully. He then suddenly thought about something else. "Gary, did you also kill the two lawyers in Little Amsterdam?"

Gary opened his arms and shrugged. "Well, it was necessary, because if the police heard what had happened to them, the agents would know how special you were, and you would have been arrested immediately. But surely you don't feel any sympathy towards those two thugs."

"No, I don't, but they didn't deserve to die, or at least it should have been left to a jury to make the judgment," said Nathan.

"We don't have the luxury to do that," Mary said. She walked to the front of the crowd. "Welcome the Aussie gang to London." Her expression then became serious. "Our situation does not look very good. The agents are hunting us as they always were, and now SOH are on our tails as well; they all want us dead. I was panicking, but Nathan persuaded me, and I agree with him, that our best strategy is to push forward. Running is not an option, because either the agents or SOH members would find us sooner or later, and we would also soon run out of places to hide."

Mary scanned everyone's faces, satisfied with what she saw and then continued. "My dear friends and comrades, we have no way out so our only hope is to find the headquarters of OBU and destroy it. That's our only way to survive."

She looked into each set of eyes, and said slowly, "If you want out, please say so and I won't force you to stay but you have to promise to keep our secrets; and also best of luck to you in escaping from the agents and SOH. Does anyone want out?"

Mary waited but no one replied so she spoke again. "Gary, I'll let you explain our overall plan and the next move."

Gary glanced at Nathan before speaking. "As we all know very well, the only way to destroy OBU is to introduce a virus into its headquarters because the virus would spread out through the entire OBU system instantly; unfortunately, it's been impossible to do so until now." He looked at everyone, and then continued.

"There are three elements that make the task impossible. One, we don't know where the headquarters is; we know it must be here in London somewhere. We believe that the HQ is a digital hub in OBU; therefore, it doesn't exist in the physical world, at least not all in a building somewhere in the city. It could well be spread around the world, so we have to locate it in OBU."

Gary checked his audience to see if they had followed him and then continued.

"The second task is to break into the HQ. We have limited manpower and resources in OBU, so it would have to be a secret break-in, and it'd be tough, considering how much security would be in the HQ."

"What's the last element then?" asked David impatiently in a thick Irish accent.

Gary put his hand up. "I am just getting to it. Assuming we somehow find where the HQ is and also manage to break into it, the last line of defence is the elite agents. You are all familiar with the agents and know well how many SOH members they have killed. Basically no one can survive facing them. Because of the implanted accelerators in their brains, they are much faster and stronger than any of us."

Mark looked at Nathan with suspicion. "So you are telling us this guy, Nathan, could beat the elite agents?"

Mary stepped forward.

"I haven't told anyone about this yet, and I am sure the agency wouldn't be very keen to broadcast it either: singlehandedly, Nathan not only killed the kidnappers from SOH, but also wiped out the whole elite unit led by the Cowboy."

"The Cowboy? *The* Cowboy?" Gary shouted at Mary.

From the gasps around the room, Nathan assumed they were all quite impressed by what he had done.

Mary nodded. "Yes, the Cowboy and his entire elite unit; Nathan shot them all dead. I had never seen someone who is actually faster than the Cowboy."

No, I was not faster than the Cowboy, Nathan said internally. However, he understood why Mary lied about it; she wanted to boost her troop's confidence. Nathan just smiled and didn't offer to say anything.

The expressions on the Irish mob's faces changed from suspicious to surprise, and finally pure admiration. They swamped forward, hugging and patting Nathan on the back.

"Mate, thank you so much; the Cowboy killed my brother," said John.

"I thank you on behalf of my cousin; he was also killed by the Cowboy," said Mark.

It seemed that they all had someone they were related to who was killed by the Cowboy and the elite unit. They cried, cheered and lifted Nathan up into the air. Soon the meeting turned into a celebration. Mary opened a few bottles of Champion and lots of Guinness, and everyone really enjoyed themselves.

## Chapter 29

This was one of the very rare occasions in Nathan's life when he got drunk, but he didn't care; these Irish men's passions moved him so much. Amy also completely let herself go; her normal self-control was gone and she took part in the wild Irish dances until she collapsed onto the floor. Mary was the wildest party animal Nathan had ever seen in his whole life, although admittedly he hadn't been to many wild parties either.

Mary hugged and kissed almost every male in the room, making Nathan feel a bit jealous but he didn't show it due to the spirit of the celebration. However, Gary, on the other hand, kept to the sidelines; he just sat there, drinking and smoking. Nathan knew Gary wasn't into the dancing and hugging business. Finally, things calmed down. By then, everyone was so drunk they were unable to stand up, so they all lay on either the couch or the floor.

"Gary, could you please tell Nathan your brilliant idea to extract information from OBU staff." Mary laid her head on Nathan's chest; they were both lying on the floor.

"Well." Gary blew out a big cloud of blue smoke. "Since Nathan showed his ability to record and pass emotions and feelings through jumpers to others, I have this idea to use it on one of the OBU staff."

"I don't follow." Nathan's spinning head didn't help him to digest Gary's idea at all.

"Gary, you need to explain why we need to do it that way." Mary turned, kissing Nathan gently.

Nathan could feel jealousy from the whole room, including Amy and Gary.

"All right," said Gary. "We can't use either force or drugs to extract information from OBU's staff, because the software would be detected and then they would change the location of the HQ. Yes, moving the entire building to a new location can be done easily in OBU; therefore, the information we got would be useless."

"How could my jumper help?" Nathan said. Mary was playing with his hair.

Gary laid his head on the couch's back, staring at the ceiling. "If we somehow put a jumper on a member of staff and let you connect to him via your jumper, then we could extract information without leaving any trace; he wouldn't remember a thing afterwards."

"But I have no idea how to do that," said Nathan. Mary was stroking his face.

"Well, you actually don't need to do anything." Gary put the rolled-up dope away and drank a large mouthful of gold liquid. "I will give you a drug that makes you feel relaxed and in the mood to want to show off and tell people about your own secrets, so when you connect your jumper to the OBU staff member's, he will be affected by your mood, and do the same."

"You must be joking; I don't want to tell anyone about my secrets." Nathan frowned.

"Nathan, I only said you would be in the mood to want to tell people about your secrets, but you would not do it if you didn't want to; the drug will only help you relax but by no means can it force people to make confessions. Otherwise, nobody would need torture techniques anymore," said Gary.

"That's a big relief," mumbled Nathan. "So how would you get him to tell us about his secrets then?"

"If he is with a beautiful and seductive girl who is doing a lap dance for him, he would tell her anything she asked," said Gary.

"Where can we find this seductive lap dancer?" asked Nathan.

"She is not far from your nose," said Mary while kissing Nathan again.

"What? You can't be serious." Nathan pushed Mary away a bit, staring at her eyes.

"Why not? Don't you think I am attractive enough?" asked Mary with a grin.

"I mean it'd be very dangerous; too much of a risk for you." Nathan struggled to work out his arguments.

"If we don't crack OBU, we could all be dead soon, so whatever the risk it's worth taking." Mary sat up. "If nobody has any objections or comments, we will carry out the plan tomorrow evening. Now let's discuss the details."

The building Nathan and Amy were staying in was by no means luxury accommodation; although it looked like an abandoned construction site, they did have basic facilities within the premises. It was remarkable that there was still a gas supply, so someone was able to fix the original hot water system on their floor. A basic kitchen with a gas cooktop and stove was more than enough to cook their daily meals. For fugitives, Nathan and Amy couldn't complain too much. Mary had stored plenty of food in the fridge for them, and also promised that more would be delivered later.

It was dinnertime the next day, and both Nathan and Amy sat down to have their evening meal. It was a pre-made pizza, a put-in-the-oven-type ready meal.

"Nathan, I know that you are madly in love with Mary so I'm unsure if I should say this," Amy said.

"So it's something to do with Mary then?"

"Yes, it is."

"Well, go ahead."

"How do I put this?" Amy hesitated but decided to proceed. "You still remember that the SOH kidnappers killed Pierre. Mary said it was a staged show to test if you were an undercover agent."

"Of course, I remember it. What about it?"

"The more I think about it, the less convinced I am…"

"Are you telling me it was an intentional act? To actually kill Pierre?" Nathan interrupted.

"Initially I only had doubts but now I am convinced it was; they wanted you to completely believe it was for real."

Nathan thought about it for a moment; he had to admit that there was some truth in Amy's words as the killing did look extremely real, but it was not that hard to fake anything in the digital world of OBU. "Let's assume it was for real, what's your point?"

Amy sipped some of her tea, and then said, "My point is that SOH killed an innocent person just to test your loyalty."

"We are still unsure about that and you have no proof at all, suspicions at the most."

"Of course, I don't have any proof," Amy said slowly. "Here are more speculations: I strongly suspect that it could be Mary who tipped off the Cowboy."

"That's absurd. Why would anyone in their right mind do that? Remember we could have all been killed, including Mary herself; surely Mary didn't want to organize her own death. How do you explain that?"

"Although I didn't know Mary very well in person, I had heard a lot about her; she is ambitious and passionate about destroying OBU. Obsessive, I would say. After so many years of struggling, she hadn't seen any lights at the end of the tunnel, and then you came, and began changing everything." Amy paused. "She discovered your extraordinary abilities, but she still needed to know if you were able to stand against the elite unit."

"What would happen if I couldn't? Wouldn't she have ended her last hope by sending me to my death?"

"And her own death as well; Nathan, I believe that she would rather die than not be able to destroy OBU. Yes, I believe she gambled that you would be able to kill the Cowboy; if you failed, she was prepared to die with you, so really, she wasn't that bad towards you after all." Amy laughed drily.

Nathan shook his head; he didn't believe a word Amy had said but at the same time, he couldn't stop wondering if it was true. "Why are you telling me this? What do you want to achieve by telling me this?"

"I thought you might be interested to know; obviously not, so I apologize for having said it."

Nathan gazed into Amy's eyes for a few seconds. "Amy, we are all in very dangerous situations, and it's crucial we stick together. Please don't say this to anyone else."

"I won't."

"Okay, let's get ourselves ready for the nightclub."


Nathan sipped his soda water; Amy and Gary sat beside him. They were inside a noisy and crowded nightclub; flashing lights and blaring music filled the air around him. Nathan had his earphones in, bobbing his head as if listening to and enjoying his own music, but in fact, the earphones were his jumper, which was connected to Mary's.

Nathan had asked Gary how they knew their target was an employee working in OBU's headquarters. Gary said that they had observed these guys for a long time and the target selected tonight was no coincidence. Nathan turned off the visual signals on his jumper because he couldn't make himself watch Mary acting like a lap dancer, wriggling over the guy's lap. He closed his eyes, trying to push the image out of his mind: the guy's greedy eyes so closely ogling every inch of Mary's body.

Glancing around casually, Nathan could see the Irish mob scattered around the nightclub: Steve and James were near the entrance; John and Mark were at the two exits; Victor and David were at another table on the other side of the private booth where Mary was performing for the OBU guy.

Gary as usual was smoking, also with an earbud in so as to control the staging of the operation. Nathan heard Mary's voice. "Darling, are you enjoying my show?"

"Very much. What's this?"

"My favourite music; you'll enjoy it and have a good time."

Nathan then heard the soft music from his jumper; he knew that Mary had put her jumper on the guy's head.

Gary opened his eyes. "Nathan, drink it now."

Nathan picked up a small glass that Gary had prepared for him; it contained the drug making one want to speak out about his secrets. Not sure how it worked, Nathan just played along. He gulped the sweet liquid and soon felt a warm wave washing up his body, right to his head, and he felt happy, very happy. The images of Mary's delicious body appeared in his mind, and Nathan wanted to tell her how much he loved her; he wanted to use all the vocabulary he knew and all the vocabulary that ever existed to tell Mary about his love towards her; he wanted to die for her. Then he heard a male voice.

"I love you so much; you are so lovely."

"Really?"

"Oh yes. I will do anything for you."

"All the guys say that to me, but none have ever done anything for me," said Mary.

"I am different; you know I work in OBU's headquarters, but I shouldn't tell anybody about this."

"Then you shouldn't tell me; I don't want you getting into trouble, just for me."

"Yes, I want to tell you to prove I love you; I don't care if it brings trouble to me or not…"

Nathan couldn't stand it any longer; he turned off the sound. It was okay because Gary was listening to it and also the conversation was being recorded.

"Are you all right?" Amy asked in a concerned voice.

"Not feeling too good; might be the effect of the drug." Nathan wasn't completely lying; apart from the jealousy he felt knowing that his beloved girl was performing an intimate act for another guy, the drug did make him feel uneasy. His limbs felt weak; he felt drowsy, like he was getting completely drunk. He put his hand into his pocket, feeling the gun there. Normally they wouldn't risk bringing guns with them into OBU, but this was different. Before they came today, Gary had given each of them a gun; he told them that he had wrapped the guns with special anti-seeker software so hopefully no alarm would be triggered. Sure enough, their guns hadn't been detected by the nightclub's weapon detectors when they entered the premises.

Time passed so slowly that Nathan kept checking his watch. Finally, Gary looked up at him and nodded.

Nathan breathed out a big sigh of relief. It was over. Turning around, he saw Mary walking out from the private show booth.

Time to go.

As he stood up, a wave of nausea overwhelmed Nathan. He used his hand to cover his mouth and ran for the bathroom. He spent the next few minutes vomiting violently into the toilet; maybe the effect of the drug, he thought while bending over the toilet. Gradually he calmed down a bit and felt able to think more clearly; the vomiting seemed to help get rid of some of the drug, but he still felt quite drowsy and had no strength in his limbs.

Nathan walked out of the bathroom that was located near the entrance and saw Mary and the rest of the group standing near one of the two exits. He tapped his jumper and said, "I am coming…" but was interrupted by a sudden burst of shouting and screaming from the entrance. He turned around, seeing a large group of police arrive; among them, there were a few plain-clothes guys.

## Chapter 30

Nathan heard Mary's gasp in his earphone. "The Gunslinger!"

Nathan immediately knew what she was talking about. "Which one, Mary?" he asked urgently.

"The one walking in the middle, in sunglasses and a black leather jacket. Nathan, get over here quickly. We have to run," said Mary.

Nathan quickly assessed the situation. "Mary, it's too late for me to get out now. There must be police outside the exits as well, so you had better use a different escape route. I will make a distraction."

"Oh no, Nathan, I can't leave you here. The Gunslinger will kill you," said Mary.

"Mary, listen to me carefully; you can't help me here, and I promise that I won't die here. Just go after I get their attention."

"Nathan, I'll be back to rescue you. I promise," said Mary.

Nathan nodded. By then, the police, the Gunslinger and his elite unit had turned the music off, ordering all of the people in the room to stand along the wall for ID checks. Nathan walked forward, pushing through the crowd. As he got closer to the agents, Nathan stepped onto a chair, and then stood on the table next to it. He raised both his hands high in the air and shouted,

"Ladies and gentlemen, please calm down; these police officers and plain-clothes agents are here to find me." He acted as if he was drunk. In fact, it was not that far from the truth; he still felt drowsy and weak in his limbs. After getting everyone's attention, he continued. "Hey, you, the guy with sunglasses and a black jacket, are you the

211

famous Gunslinger? I know you never wear a mask, so it must be you."

Gasps rose from the crowds; it seemed many knew about one of the fastest gun-drawing agents. At the same time, guns were aimed at Nathan, and the agents shouted, ordering him to get to the floor.

"My hands are in the air and I only want to have a few words with the Gunslinger," Nathan shouted.

The Gunslinger put his arms up to signal the police and agents to lower their guns. The crowd between Nathan and the agents had already moved towards the walls so now Nathan faced the Gunslinger, less than ten feet away. Out of the corner of his eyes, Nathan saw Mary and her comrades using the opportunity of being pushing towards the wall to sneak into one of the private booths; Gary must have set up a secret escape exit inside the booth. After that, he felt much better; at least Mary and the rest had escaped.

Nathan knew that he would need to give Amy as much time as possible, because when the agents arrested him, they would trace him and find his hiding place in the real world.

"Who are you? What do you want to say to me?" the Gunslinger said calmly.

Nathan studied him carefully; the Gunslinger was quite tall and slim. Nathan could see his gun holster inside his leather jacket. His face was peaceful and relaxed, perfectly self-controlled. Nathan knew well that even if he were at his best, he would not be able to beat the Gunslinger. Nathan put his hand up to his face and pulled his mask off.

"I am Nathan Jenkins and I'm pretty sure I am now on your most wanted list, right?"

More noises rose from the crowd and people tried to move as far as possible away from Nathan.

"Nathan Jenkins; yes, I would like to have a few words with you." The Gunslinger walked forward a couple of paces.

Nathan jumped off the desk but fell onto the floor. The agents around the Gunslinger laughed loudly, but not the Gunslinger himself; his cold eyes were gazing at Nathan.

He was only half pretending when he fell to the ground; Nathan wanted his enemy to believe he was completely drunk. Hopefully it'd give him some kind of advantage, even if he was unsure what that could be at the moment. However, he did feel heavy-limbed and lightheaded, so it was also half real. Nathan sighed inside: based on his previous experience with the Cowboy and his elite unit, the Gunslinger didn't need to draw his gun to shoot Nathan tonight, because any of the agents from his elite unit would be able to put a bullet into Nathan's body before Nathan could get his gun out of his pocket, but they didn't know that. Nathan had to play with their suspicions and give Amy as much time as possible to escape, away from the half-built department store.

"Why do you want to talk to me?" Nathan climbed up, trying to stand there steadily.

The Gunslinger stared at Nathan's eyes for a few seconds, and then spoke slowly and calmly. "I was told that it was you who had shot the Cowboy and his entire unit dead singlehanded: how?"

Nathan wobbled a bit, staggering a step backwards, but managed to stand still again. "We had a standoff, and I was faster than the Cowboy. You know the result;

obviously I was in a better state then." Nathan tried to speak as clearly as he could, unsuccessfully.

"Hard to believe you would be faster than the Cowboy," the Gunslinger said. "Well, I suppose that there is only one way to find out." He pulled his black leather jacket open, showing the gun holster on his belt. "I assume that you carry a gun with you. Please feel free to fire whenever you are ready."

The crowds behind Nathan and the Gunslinger, including the police officers and the agents, quickly moved away as far as possible; no one wanted to be in the firing line.

Nathan couldn't believe he had ended up like this; to be honest, Nathan knew he wouldn't have a chance even if he hadn't taken the drug earlier. Due to his mind training with Master Wuwei, Nathan was much faster than normal people, including most agents, but not the Cowboy and the Gunslinger; these two guys were undoubtedly faster than Nathan with their implanted accelerators. The brain-cyber interfaces would enable them to have extremely short reaction times. Nathan had tricked the Cowboy, but his luck wouldn't last tonight; the Gunslinger would figure out how the Cowboy was killed and would definitely shoot at Nathan's head.

Nathan thought for a moment and decided he couldn't die yet; he needed to give Amy more time to escape. What could he say to delay the Gunslinger's bullets? Nathan had to say something intriguing to the Gunslinger, so he wouldn't want to kill Nathan right here.

"I know it seems I am the last one likely to be able to kill the Cowboy, one of the fastest agents in OBU, but unfortunately it is a fact: he died, and I lived." Nathan paused, as if trying to remember what to say next. "I am not going to draw my gun tonight because I have drunk too much, so if you want to find out how fast I am, you can wait until tomorrow after I get over the hangover. What do you say?"

The Gunslinger didn't change his posture one bit; his eyes locked on Nathan's. "Nathan, was this how you killed the Cowboy, by playing such a trick on him?"

"I wasn't drunk then, if that's what you mean," said Nathan.

"Nathan, I know you are pretending to be drunk. You're waiting for your chance; but here it is, your last chance. I'll shoot you regardless of whether you draw your gun or not," said the Gunslinger.

Nathan decided that he had less chance to get killed if he didn't have a gun in his hand; surely the Gunslinger wanted to find out how he had killed the Cowboy. "What are you talking about? Where is my gun?" Nathan shook his head, and both his hands.

"You asked for this," said the Gunslinger.

Not many people were even sure if the Gunslinger had drawn his gun at all because they only saw a blur of movement in his right hand, and then two gunshots burst in the air. They turned their gazes to Nathan; both of his wrists were bleeding badly.

The Gunslinger looked disappointed. He turned to his agents. "Take him away."

**Chapter 31**

Nathan was tied up on a chair in an interrogation room. Since he hadn't seen Amy being brought in, Nathan assumed that she had escaped, so he exhaled a deep breath in relief. The blood on his wrists had dried. Nathan knew the bullets hadn't gone through his wrist bones, in fact they had just scratched his skin, so it may have looked a bit of a mess, but they were only superficial wounds. It seemed that the Gunslinger had just wanted to demonstrate his shooting ability.

Nathan didn't use his mind control to self-heal the wounds, because he didn't want the agents to know about his secret yet. Although the wounds were still there, he did manage to use his mind to stop the pain, so his wrists didn't hurt him as badly as they appeared to; the agents had intentionally made the handcuffs rub the wounds whilst dragging Nathan into the room. Nathan pretended to wince but kept a cold smile on his face.

Nathan didn't worry about the gun in his pocket. Gary told him that he was the only one who could use the gun. If someone else touched it, it would just appear as a piece of dirty tissue; in other words, the gun software would self-destruct as it turned itself into a piece of tissue.

Then everyone left the room until only the Gunslinger remained. He towered over Nathan.


"Okay, Nathan, here there are only two of us, so tell me how you managed to kill the Cowboy. I don't believe you are faster than him for a second; it's complete bullshit. You must have played a dirty trick on him."

"There is nothing to talk about. As I said before, if you really want to find out what happened to the Cowboy, you need to see it yourself. Wait until my wrists are healed, and I feel better, give me a gun and I'll show you how the Cowboy was killed; hopefully you'll have the guts to see it," said Nathan.

"Tough guy," said the Gunslinger.

He was not sure how, but Nathan knew the punch was coming; there were just some extremely subtle changes of expressions or slight shifts of body weight, but Nathan was able to see them instantly and that's how he could move first and defeat his opponents. However, he could neither move to avoid, nor use his mind power to deflect the hit. The blow almost broke his jawbone, possible breaking a couple of his teeth. Nathan tasted salty blood in his mouth. It was painful, so Nathan used his mind to reduce the pain level a bit to make it bearable.

"What's that for?" Nathan spat out a mouthful of blood.

"Keep talking; otherwise, more pain is on the way." The Gunslinger rubbed his own fist. He had obviously hurt himself a bit with the punch.

"Nothing to talk about; I was just faster than the Cowboy," said Nathan.

"All right, let's see if you are as tough as you think you are." The Gunslinger brought a leather bag from the corner of the room and put it on top of the table beside Nathan. After taking the contents out and spreading them over the tabletop, he said, "These are the introduction, the basic torture tools. I will use these special knives to cut different parts of your body to see how long you can last before you tell me everything."

Staring at all of the different types of surgical-looking instruments, Nathan felt sick to his stomach. He agreed that they would not only inflict lots of pain, but also create a big mess on him; his body would be hacked into

217

a blood-covered mess. Nathan sighed inside; it seemed that he had to use his mind-control self-healing to deal with the oncoming torture. He closed his eyes for a moment and then opened them again as the wounds on both his wrists healed.

"You are wasting your time. Have a look at my wrists," said Nathan.

"You are a freak! How did you do that?" shouted the Gunslinger. He stared at Nathan's wrists in disbelief.

"Mind games, isn't it?" Nathan said. "Everything in OBU is a mind game; if you believe it, you get hurt, but if you don't, there is no physical harm done."

The Gunslinger thought about it. "I agree with you in theory, but nobody has been able to deny the signals from OBU, until now." He paused and then said, "Was this how you tricked the Cowboy?"

"No," said Nathan.

The Gunslinger walked back a few steps, drawing his gun. "If I put a bullet in your head, are you still able to self-heal?"

"You shouldn't do that unless you want to kill me; it's true that I am able to self-heal, but I am only able to heal myself afterwards, not fast enough to prevent the damage done to me," said Nathan.

"Well, I suppose there is not much point in using these knives then." The Gunslinger packed the torture knives away and took something else out of the bag; a helmet similar to the one used to log in to OBU.

"What is it?" asked Nathan nervously.

"Don't be alarmed." The Gunslinger put the helmet on Nathan's head, and then stepped back. He picked up a remote control-like object from the tabletop. "Before we start, you may want to know the helmet on your head is nothing more than a torture instrument, the ultimate pain producer because it inflicts pain right into your brain. Well, enjoy it." He pushed the button.

The pain was initially like a dentist drilling directly into Nathan's teeth and hitting the nerves, and then the intensity increased dramatically. Nathan felt like his body was being torn in half. Within seconds, Nathan felt darkness cover his eyes. When Nathan opened his eyes again, he saw the Gunslinger's evil grin; what an evil beast he was! He enjoyed others' pain.

"I trust that you enjoyed the treatment." The Gunslinger grinned.

Nathan took a deep breath. "You know what? Although you torture me like this, I won't do the same to you when you are in my hands. I will simply put a bullet in your evil brain and shut you off for good. Remember, this is a promise."

"Thanks a lot; I am so thrilled and can't wait for that day, but for now, you have to enjoy my hospitality. Nathan, tell me where Mary O'Brian is before I push the button again."

"I am sure by now you have located my body, so you know where she is as well as I do."

"Oh yes, we found your body," the Gunslinger said. "Now tell me where Mary O'Brian is."

"Untie me, and I'll show you where she is," laughed Nathan.

"Yeah right, nice try. Here is the second round of pain." The Gunslinger pushed the button again.

The pain hit Nathan like a giant blow, so hard and fast it threw him completely. It was so strange that when one was beyond the pain threshold, one could not feel the pain at all; that's what happened to Nathan. Nathan found himself floating in the corner of the room, watching his own body tied up on the chair as the Gunslinger watched him with a satisfied smile. It was like an out of body experience in OBU, a double out of body experience.

Nathan turned around and surprisingly found that he could actually see through the wall; he could see the digital outlines of the building. Nathan pushed the wall behind him. Like the weightless floating he had seen on the space station on TV, his body floated forward like a balloon; this was fun. Then Nathan heard his body from where it was tied up on the chair; he was moaning. In no time, he found he was inside his own body again.

"Are you enjoying the ride?" the Gunslinger asked.

"Very much," Nathan laughed. At that exact moment, he figured out what had happened to him; somehow, the torture helmet had introduced such a high level of pain to Nathan's brain that not only did it switch his pain sensors off, but it also enabled him to access the ability he only experienced once, when he met Mary for the first time in the bar. The new discovery filled Nathan's mind with joy; he laughed loudly.

"Oh shit, I must have overdone the bloody cage," the Gunslinger said.

"What happened, boss?" Two agents opened the door and ran into the room.

"Nothing to worry about; I am enjoying the ride," laughed Nathan like a drunk man.

The two agents looked back at the Gunslinger, who said, "This guy is a freak; it seems the cage didn't work on him." He paused and then waved his hand. "Take him away and log him off OBU. I am going to use a real knife to cut his skin in the real world." He then turned to Nathan. "I hope you will still be laughing then."

The two agents unlocked Nathan from the chair and were dragging him away when a commanding voice floated into the room.

"Leave him in the room."

Nathan felt the voice was familiar but at that exact moment, he couldn't put his finger on it. Then a person walked in. Staring at the newcomer, Nathan's jaw dropped.

It was Cathy, Nathan's ex-girlfriend.

"What are you doing here, Cathy?" Nathan asked.

Cathy didn't answer his question; in fact, she didn't even look at him. She waved her arm at the Gunslinger and the other two agents. "Please leave us alone, gentlemen."

With only the two of them in the room, Cathy pulled a chair from the table and sat in front of Nathan. "Nathan, how could you get yourself caught up with Mary O'Brian and her terrorist organization?"

Nathan was still puzzled. "Hang on, Cathy, what are you doing here?" From the way Cathy talked to the Gunslinger and the other agents, Nathan had guessed her role, but he still wanted to hear it from her own lips.

Cathy moved a strand of her hair behind her ear. "Well, I told you that I worked for an environmental protection agency last time."

"But I wouldn't imagine an environmental agent has anything to do with these thugs and assassins." Nathan pointed his finger at the door.

"Please calm down, Nathan." Cathy patted Nathan's arm. "They are not thugs or assassins; they are agents of the special anti-terrorist force."

Nathan moved his body away from Cathy. "Yeah, right, anti-terrorist agents; so you are an anti-terrorist agent as well then?"

"Yes, I am also part of the agency, except I very rarely get involved with field work."

"Do you mean the killing, torturing and kidnapping?"

Cathy shook her head slowly and then spoke patiently. "Nathan, sometimes it's necessary to use extreme measures to deal with extreme circumstances…"

"Like torturing me to death, for example," Nathan interrupted.

"I am sorry for what happened to you, Nathan. If I had known earlier, I would have been here long before the ordeal. Anyway, tell me how you got yourself entangled with Mary O'Brian, the most wanted terrorist in the world."

Nathan studied Cathy for a moment, trying to ascertain whether she was telling the truth. "There is not much to tell; I agree with what Mary and her people are doing so I joined them in the fight against OBU."

Cathy's face looked saddened. "I can't believe these words are actually coming out of your mouth. Nathan, remember how hard we fought against the greedy corporations to protect the environment? Remember when I showed you the benefits OBU brings to this world? Look at my eyes; do you truly want to bring global warming, pollution, and environmental disasters back?"

Nathan gazed at Cathy's eyes, and could see that she truly believed what she said. Sighing, Nathan reached out, patting her arm. "Cathy, I haven't forgotten that and I don't want to bring the environment disasters back, but OBU is not the solution; using OBU to solve the environmental problems is like drinking poison to satisfy your thirst…"

"What are you talking about?" Cathy interrupted Nathan.

"Cathy, don't pretend you don't know the truth: human fertility has been steadily decreasing since OBU was introduced. If the trend continues, when it reaches the critical point, humanity could be wiped from the surface of the earth."

"That's just Mary O'Brian's bullshit; there are some reports talking about fertility problems, but they existed long before OBU age, and that's why we have IVF technology."

"I don't think any IVF would be able to save the human race if there are no sources of quality sperm left."

Cathy hesitated and then said, "Look, Nathan, I read some of the reports along the lines you are talking about. I have to admit that there may be some potential issues like that in the long term, but they are nowhere near as serious as Mary O'Brian wants you to think. Besides, there are lots of efforts being invested into solving the problems; believe me, it's in everyone's interests to rectify it."

"I also understand that the sperm quality and quantity decrease is directly related to the nature of OBU; it's the hours men spend in OBU that causes the problem, so I don't see any solution except getting rid of OBU altogether," said Nathan.

"The scientists are working on the solution and they will find one sooner or later; besides, without OBU, we wouldn't be able to survive under the mounting environmental disasters anyway," said Cathy.

"Cathy, we have already had a few clean energy breakthroughs, so we are in a much better position to deal with global warming compared to a decade ago, but the rate at which fertility is decreasing is so urgent that we can't afford to wait another decade."

Cathy's expression became rigid. "Not everyone is in OBU all the time; it may be true for those who are in OBU all the time, but the majority of the population in other parts of the world are still living a normal life in the real world, so it's ridiculous to state that humanity faces the danger of being wiped out."

"Cathy, please don't fool yourself. We know most of the world's population has embraced OBU, and only a small proportion of people in remote and poor areas have limited access to OBU. But these groups are declining very rapidly as the OBU Corporation is working hard to ensure they can join the digital paradise."

Frustration appeared on Cathy's face, quite obviously now. "Nathan, you have been brainwashed by Mary O'Brian, so it's hard to persuade you to think rationally. She would certainly use her body to get you under her control; believe me, you are neither the first nor the last man she has captured with her body…"

"That's ridiculous to insult her like that; I am doing this not because I have slept with her, but because I believe the truth…"

"The truth? Nathan, I can show you the evidence that Mary O'Brian has slept with every single man in her unit. In fact that's how she recruits her members; sadly you are only one of her many male lovers."

"Really? In case you want to know, I made love with Mary in the real world here in London, just yesterday, and she was still a virgin then," said Nathan.

Cathy laughed uncontrollably. "Virgin? Nathan, where have you been during the last fifteen years? Almost all girls growing up in the OBU age are virgins, but it has nothing to do with the facts both boys and girls have been sleeping with hundreds of others, so your virgin Mary has had as many lovers as any other girl in the OBU age. Wake up, Nathan, Mary O'Brian is just using you for her own purpose."

Nathan thought about it, and had to admit that there were some truths to Cathy's words. From the way the Irish mob interacted with Mary, it was possible that Mary had experienced affairs with her comrades along the way, before he had appeared in her life. It made Nathan feel jealous towards all those unknown lovers before him. Somehow, his mind went back to Amy; Amy wasn't like that, sleeping around with everyone. But the problem was he didn't love Amy; Nathan was quite sure that Amy had an eye on him. Why was fate so unfair to everyone? Nathan sighed.

"Cathy, what you said may be true, but I believe it's the right thing to do to get rid of OBU in order to save humanity, and it has nothing to do with the affair between Mary and me."

Cathy thought for a long time before finally standing up. "Nathan, it seems that you have made up your mind, and I do hope you know what you are doing. Anyway, I have asked them to give you tonight to think things through, but it'll be out of my hands by tomorrow morning." She turned and walked out of the room.

## Chapter 32

Nathan curled up on the bed under the thin blanket. He was locked in a small room with no windows. Looking around the limited space, he wasn't sure if it was a jail cell, but it definitely served the purpose of containing him. During his torture sessions, they had moved his body here so when he logged out of OBU, he found himself in this room alone. Nathan really hoped Amy had safely escaped.

During the last few hours, Nathan couldn't help but think about Cathy's words over and over again. Was it true that Mary had used her body to recruit all the men in her organization? Nathan tried to put it into perspective; it would be understandable if it worked for Mary, and it had nothing to do with him because she hadn't known him then, but it still hurt him, a lot. Nathan tried to get the images of hundreds of men making love with Mary out of his mind without much luck. He stood up and began pacing around the room, cursing himself for not being able to think rationally.

After a couple of hours of internal struggle, Nathan gradually calmed down a bit and started thinking about what would happen to him when the sun rose the next morning. Based on his estimate, it should be around three or four in the morning, so in another few hours, he would have to face the Gunslinger's torture again, but in the real world where his mind control would count for nothing. The thought of those knives cutting through his skin sent a spasm of terror along his spine. What should he do? Of course he wouldn't want to betray Mary, but Nathan was really doubtful about how long he would last in the face of the torture. The worst part was, even if he decided to

226

betray Mary, Nathan had no idea where Mary and her men were, so he wouldn't be able to provide any useful information at all; therefore, the only fate for him was the oncoming torture. Nathan closed his eyes and wished this was all just a bad dream; when he opened his eyes, he would find himself waking up in his bed and everything would be perfectly okay. He would laugh at his own dreams and tell his friends about it. Unfortunately, when his eyes opened, Nathan found he was still inside the cold room.

He had to get out of here; although Nathan knew it would be impossible, he still examined the walls and door inch by inch, hoping to find any defect that he could explore further. Then he heard some noises, quite different noises from the sort you would expect in the early hours of the morning, so he put his ear on the door. A few thuds possibly indicated bodies dropping to the ground. Then someone was knocking on the door.

"Nathan, are you in there?" It was Mary's voice.

"Yes, I am right here," answered Nathan.

"Thank God. Nathan, stay away from the door, get back as far as possible; we are going to blow it up. Tell me when you are ready."

Nathan moved to the corner of the wall and squatted down with his knees to his chest and both hands on his ears. "I am ready," he shouted.

There was an explosion, and the door was blasted open. Among the smoke and dust a figure rushed in. "Nathan? Are you here?" It was Mary's voice. Outside, the sound of gun-fire intensified.

Nathan stood up. "I am here."

"Oh, Nathan, I got you. Mary embraced him tightly. "Let's get out of here." She dragged him out of the door.

227

Outside in the corridor, Amy and the Irish mob were shooting towards the other side of the building. "Let's get out of here," Mary shouted.

"Mary, give me a gun," said Nathan. "I will cover for you guys to get out."

"Don't be ridiculous," shouted Mary. "We are here to rescue you."

"Don't forget I am a sharpshooter; I want to kill the bastards who tortured me and also killed many other souls. Mary, stay with me, let the others out first," Nathan shouted back.

Mary hesitated for a second before drawing a handgun from her belt and passing it to Nathan; she shouted at the others, "You all go; Nathan and I will cover you!"

Nathan weighed the gun in his hand; he had handled guns for years in OBU, but this was the first time he had actually held a gun physically. He clicked off the safety and tried to relax his muscles. His eyes were focused on the other end of the long corridor as he and Mary moved back along the wall towards the door. Their movements were quiet yet rapid. Nathan's eyes never left the smoke and dust under the pale lights along the bullet-riddled corridor.

They were both at the gateway when Nathan spotted movement; without thinking, he lifted his gun and fired three shots in quick succession. In that split second, Nathan was confident that he had punched three holes in the three foreheads at the other end of the long corridor. Then he heard gunshots behind him.

He quickly spun around and could just see Amy levelling her gun towards their left; following Amy's line of vision, Nathan saw three bodies drop at the next corner of the street. He didn't expect Amy to be here as well.

"Get into the car, quick!" shouted Mary.

Three cars were parked in front of the building. Nathan and Mary jumped into the nearest car and it shot forward even before the door was closed. Nathan was impressed by how organized and efficient Mary's rescue operation was: it would be less than a minute from the time the door was blasted to their getaway.

After a few turns, they drove at normal speed. Nathan still hadn't heard police sirens, so he let out a long breath in relief.

After a few more turns along some back alleys, their car drove into a car park under a large building; he hadn't seen any other cars and assumed they had split up to avoid being followed.

"This way," Mary urged Nathan and Steve as they followed her through the door into the building.

Nathan followed Mary going down into a basement again, but Steve didn't come with them. They walked through a few more doors, and Nathan found they had emerged into the London underground railway system, the Tube. Mary and her men must have made these into their secret passageways, thought Nathan as they hurried along the train tracks. A couple of hundred meters later, they entered a door on the wall of the Tube tunnel.

It was amazing to go through these underground mazes; at the same time, Nathan understood the necessity of avoiding being detected by the police and the agents. After a few more turns, and climbing up and down some stairs, they arrived in another basement, and he knew that they had reached their destination. He saw not only living facilities but also Amy and the Irish mob; they must have entered the place via a different entrance. Thinking about it, Nathan suspected the path Mary took him through

229

could only belong to herself. Ultimate secrecy even unknown to her comrades, but she shared it with him, showing her total trust in him. It made Nathan feel warm in his heart.

"Nathan, welcome to our underground resistance centre." Mary waved her arms around. "We have all the essential living facilities we need, electricity, water, food and bathrooms." She then turned to the others. "Well done, guys; it was a completely successful operation! Now you can relax a bit; freshen up and we will have a meeting to work out our next move."

Mary looped her arm around Nathan's elbow, dragging him towards a room at the far side of the compound; he presumed it would be her bedroom. Nathan could sense the Irish mob's jealous stares on his back, and he felt really good about it. They may have shared a few intimate moments with Mary in the past, but he would be the first man to share her bedroom and the reason he was so sure about it was because Mary was still a virgin until she had made love with him recently. However, the delightful thought was soon dampened after Nathan glanced at Amy's sad expression. Amy quickly turned and walked into her bedroom.

Mary's bedroom was very basic: a double bed, a small desk and a chair beside it. This didn't surprise Nathan as in OBU age people lived on nothing more than the most basic needs, because their luxury indulgence would be satisfied in the digital world.

"Sorry, it's quite messy here." Mary put a few items away. "You are the first person to ever visit my bedroom."

Nathan stood there, feeling a bit awkward. "No problem; it's totally fine…" he mumbled.

Mary closed the door and launched herself on Nathan. "I was so worried I was going to lose you, Nathan; thank God we got you out." Her lips sealed his before Nathan could manage a response.

The kiss soon heated both of them up to boiling point; they tore off each other's clothes and fell onto the bed. The near-death experience made them appreciate the value of life more and intensified their joy of being in love; it was the most intense and most exciting lovemaking Nathan had ever felt in his life.

When the passionate storm was over, while Nathan lay on his back, naked and panting heavily, Mary clung onto him and whispered into his ear, "I love you so much…"

"I love you, too…" Nathan thought about something. "How did you manage to find where I was being kept?"

Mary smiled. "I put a tracking device inside your shoe; those agents were so arrogant as to think we were all desperately running for our lives. The last thing they thought we would contemplate was a rescue operation."

"I am impressed," Nathan said and really meant it.

Mary stroked Nathan's chest. "Did they torture you last night?" she asked gently.

"Yes, they did a bit in OBU." Nathan told Mary what happened.

'Those bastards. I am so sorry for your suffering…" Mary kissed Nathan's neck gently.

"I am all right, and thanks for getting me out just in time; they were going to torture me in the real world."

Mary didn't say anything but embraced him tighter.

Nathan thought about asking Mary if she had recruited all her team by sleeping with them but decided against it; Cathy could have told him a lie. Even if it was the truth, it had happened long before Mary met him, so it had nothing to do with their relationship. Nathan closed his eyes, enjoying the delicious moment with his dream girl.

## Chapter 33

"Nathan, can I have a word with you please," said Amy. They'd just had their dinner. Mary and her Irish mob were discussing something at the other end of the compound.

"Sure," said Nathan.

"Could we talk in my room please," Amy said while glancing in Mary's direction.

A question mark popped into Nathan's mind; he hesitated for a second. "Okay."

"Amy, what would you like to talk about?" Nathan asked after they had entered Amy's room.

Amy stood there, gazing into Nathan's eyes for a long time.

"Amy?" Nathan said.

Amy's face reddened. She quickly moved her gaze away, a bit embarrassed. After a few more seconds of silence, she finally said, "Nathan, you know I love you…"

Nathan sighed loudly inside. "Amy, I am sorry…"

Amy interrupted. "Please let me finish first. I fell in love with you when I first met you at the bakery. Initially I thought I only had a teenage crush on you, and it would be over soon. Every day I was so excited and so looked forward to seeing you at the bakery. I was so happy to just see you and stand beside you; I didn't have many thoughts beyond that. I clearly remember the day you came to work so depressed and devastated after Cathy dumped you. At the time, I felt so sorry for you, but at the same time, although embarrassed to admit it, I felt hope for the first time; I could have a chance to get closer to you." Amy sighed deeply.

"Then you just simply disappeared; everyone thought you had died. I felt like my whole world had collapsed, and I felt like I was dead in my heart. Although I tried to forge some relationships through the years, none of them worked, because in my heart, you were my first and only true love…" Tears filled her eyes.

Nathan didn't know what to say but managed to mumble a 'sorry'.

"No need to feel sorry." Amy wiped her tears away with the back of her hand. "It's not your fault, purely my own matter. The moment I heard you had come back alive I truly believed it was God's will to give you back to me. My frozen heart after fifteen long years finally thawed out." Amy turned her gaze back to Nathan again.

"Nathan, I know you don't love me but I still want to tell you that I have had such a lovely time working with you all these days; they were the happiest time ever in my whole life. Thank you so much."

"Amy, I am sorry, but you know I love Mary…"

Amy patted Nathan's arm gently. "I know that. Nathan, this is very difficult for me to say but I have to say it. You may have fallen madly in love with Mary, but I am not convinced she feels the same way towards you."

The expression on Nathan's face said it all.

Amy smiled drily. "I know you may think I am saying this because I am jealous, and I am, but I also want to tell you the truth. Mary is using you to realize her goal of destroying OBU."

"No, she is not using me; I too believe that OBU should be stopped."

"Nathan, you are not the only one she has used. I've had quite a few conversations with the Irish mob. They could see that I love you so they told me about what happened between Mary and them. Mary has slept with all of them; they all fell hopelessly in love with her, most still are, but now Mary has started with you all over again in front of their eyes."

Nathan thought carefully. "Amy, I appreciate that you care for me, but I love Mary, and I don't care if she had any relationships with others before my time. I am sorry for sounding rude, but please don't mention this to me again."

As Nathan turned around, already walking out of the room, Amy said, "The main purpose of this conversation is not your relationship with Mary."

"I am listening." Nathan turned, looking at Amy.

"Nathan, Mary can't win against OBU; she will be killed or captured sooner or later. Why don't we get out of here before it's too late; you were almost killed last night."

Nathan said in a serious tone, "Amy, I understand if you want to get out now, but I will stay and help Mary against OBU. If there is nothing else to talk about, I would like to go back to Mary." He nodded to Amy, and then walked out in silence.

Nathan was aware of Amy following a few paces behind him, but he kept walking. Mary stopped talking to her Irish comrades, lifted her gaze to Nathan and then to Amy with a question mark on her face, but before anyone could open their mouths, an alarm went off loudly.

Mary and all the Irish men's faces changed.

"Oh shit, the agents have found our nest," Mary cursed. She quickly looked around. "Okay, everyone, spread out, and we'll meet in OBU as usual. Mark, you take Amy with you, and Nathan, you come with me. Go."

"Nobody move! Put your hands in the air or I'll put a bullet in her brain."

To everyone's astonishment, Amy pointed her gun at Mary. Before Nathan could say anything, Amy spoke again. "Nathan, don't even think about it; I know you have shot down ten discs, but I did manage to get four, and since my gun is ready to fire, you can be sure that I will be able to kill her before you even draw your gun." Amy spoke slowly and clearly; her hands were steady.

While raising both his hands in the air, Nathan's brain was thinking at a crazy speed. What the hell was going on here? "Amy, I promise that I will solve whatever problems you have with me, but for now, we need to get out of here before the agents arrive," Nathan said in a calm, even tone.

"You, James, raise both hands up, now! Otherwise, I'll shoot Mary and you together."

James slowly raised both his hands.

"Please, Amy, at least tell me what this is about; if it's to do with me…" But Mary interrupted him.

"Amy, don't tell me you are an undercover agent from OBU?" Mary asked in disbelief.

Amy's hands were steady, and her voice was very calm. "Mary, I have to admit you are quick; yes, I am working for OBU." She then turned her gaze to Nathan. "Nathan, I am doing this for you; please wake up. Mary and her men will be killed sooner or later and now is the time to get out safely."

Nathan could hear noises coming from behind Amy and assumed the agents would be pouring in soon. He believed Amy had told the truth and that she was fully capable of killing Mary well before he could draw his gun. He had to play this right; otherwise, everyone would be killed.

"Amy, I love Mary and will help her to destroy OBU even if I lose my life; I appreciate your kind offer to save my life, but I have made up my mind. If you still love me like you told me a few minutes ago, please let us leave; otherwise, please kill me first." Nathan watched Amy's eyes carefully. He calculated his chances of drawing his gun, but it was too late. Suddenly two dozen agents and police officers poured out from one of the bedrooms that must have doubled as a secret exit.

"Don't move!"

"Lie on your stomach on the ground!" a policeman shouted.

"Shut up!" Amy shouted loudly. Everyone stared at her, momentarily quiet. "Lower your guns, I have everything under control here." She then turned to Nathan. "Nathan, you will always be my true love; I am so sorry about this, but I have to do it." Amy swung her gun towards Nathan.

"Ma'am, please don't shoot; we want to take them alive…" an agent, who appeared to be the team leader, shouted but never got a chance to finish his sentence.

Amy's gun swung past Nathan; her body twisted in high speed and her gun fired in rapid succession. The leader and three other agents were shot in their foreheads instantly.

The moment Amy has spoken, from her eyes, Nathan could tell what she was going to do next. He desperately wanted to stop her, but it was far too late for him to do anything, except to draw his gun as fast as he could manage.

Nathan acted even before Amy's gun went off. While Amy was still in motion he leaped up, withdrawing his gun in mid-air. He let loose a whole clip of bullets before his body bumped into Mary and knocked her to the ground. Nathan's bullets had hit the agents almost at the same time as Amy's; Nathan was aiming mainly at the agents and was quite confident that he got eight of them.

Nathan felt a pain in his right arm as if it had been hit by a train, and his gun was flung out of his hand; he was quite impressed by how quickly the agents had reacted. Underneath him, Mary's gun fired rapidly. Without looking, Nathan heard the Irishmen and the rest of the agents and police exchanging fire in the cramped space. He hit the floor; the pain from the impact on his wounded arm almost knocked him out, and then his eyes caught the gun nearby on the ground beside Mark, who had three bullet holes in his chest, dead.

Nathan picked up the gun with his left hand, still in a rolling motion, and spread another clip of bullets upwards into the foreheads of another bunch of agents and police. No need to count, his instinct told him that he scored six in his second round.

The furious gun battle finished as abruptly as it had started; the last policeman fell to his knees. Nathan did a quick assessment; all agents and police were down, and so were the six Irishmen. Mary seemed unhurt, and on her way to standing up. Amy's hands covered the gun wound on her stomach as blood poured out.

A groan issued from Steve and Mary went to him. Nathan got up, walking to Amy. "Amy, are you okay?"

Amy spoke in a voice so weak that Nathan had to put his ear close to her mouth to hear. "…help Mary…destroy OBU…so she…loves you…for real…I want you…happy…"

"Amy, I won't let you die." Nathan desperately tried to help but knew it was clearly too late for her.

"Nathan…please…kiss me…"

Nathan's tears dropped on Amy's face while he kissed her on her lips.

"It's so…lovely…I finally get to…kiss you…Nathan…I love you." Amy's head dropped but the happy smile still lingered at the corner of her mouth.

A gunshot made Nathan lift up his eyes; Mary lowered her gun, but she was still holding Steve. Steve's body was covered with bullet holes; Mary had ended his suffering.

Mary stood up, walked to Nathan and quickly checked his arm. "It seems that the bullet went through but missed your bone." She tore off a piece of her shirt and bandaged his bleeding arm.

"Nathan, we need to get out of here now."

Nathan nodded. He stood up, feeling a sudden black cloud over his eyes, and almost collapsed. Mary held him, dragging him into the secret passage they had used on the way in.

They walked through the Tube tunnels and underground drain and sewage systems for a very long time until they finally arrived in another basement under another building. Nathan had no idea where he was. It was Mary's second secret hideout that she had only visited a couple of times, just to make sure everything was in order. It had the basic living facilities and medical supplies.

Nathan re-examined his arm and confirmed the bullet had gone through his forearm and had indeed fortunately missed his bones. When everything was done, Mary collapsed onto the ground with both hands holding her face as she sobbed uncontrollably.

"How could this have happened?" She repeated these words over and over.

Nathan made a cup of tea for each of them. After sipping some hot tea, Mary gradually calmed down.

"Nathan, do you think that the reason Amy betrayed us was because of jealousy?"

"I don't know and may never know." Nathan told Mary the last words from Amy. "Mary, I will help you to destroy OBU, for Amy and all the friends we have lost."

Mary held Nathan tightly, gazing into his eyes. "Nathan, you know I love you, don't you?"

"I do," Nathan said, but Amy's words still echoed in his head. Why did Amy believe that Mary was just using him? Nathan had to admit he couldn't really understand how women's minds worked.

Mary's expression changed; she looked more depressed than ever. "What can we do now, after losing every man we had?"

Nathan suddenly remembered something very important. He went on to tell Mary how he was tortured to unconsciousness by the Gunslinger in OBU, and how he discovered he could see through people and even the building's digital masks. "It may be the intense torture signals that somehow triggered this special ability in me that I only had once when I met you for the first time; I did see through your mask then."

"I remember your expression when our eyes met for the first time." Mary looked into Nathan's eyes, speaking in a soft voice. "It's our fate to be together." She kissed him softly.

"We need to discuss this with Gary. I am quite confident we will be able to break into OBU's HQ," said Nathan.

"Are you sure you will be okay with your arm?" Mary looked down at the bandage.

"Not a big deal, only a scratch." Nathan stood up. "Let's go."

## Chapter 34

Gary met them at a crowded café in SOHO, downtown London. It was such an amazing contrast between the ghost town of real London and this thriving digital version of the same city in OBU. They sat in the corner to avoid any unwanted attention. Overseas tourists were chatting in all different languages around them. Like all facilities in OBU, the digital café had almost infinite capacity: no matter how many customers walked through its doors, no one would feel crowded at all and they could all have window seats with a view of the crowded street outside.

"I am so sorry for what happened," said Gary.

"How did you find out about it so quickly?" asked Nathan.

"I have my own sources." Gary didn't offer more details. "What's next?"

Nathan told Gary quietly about what happened to him after the torture session and his newly gained ability to see through masks in OBU.

"Really? That's fascinating." Gary drank some of his coffee and then continued, "Based on the information Mary extracted from the lap dancing session, I have cracked the security codes. Now with Nathan's new ability, we should be able to locate where the HQ is, so we are on course to get the job done."

"No, we are not," said Mary slowly.

"Do you mean the Gunslinger?" said Nathan.

"Yes. We will still be unable to pass him even if we manage to pass through all other obstacles," Mary said gloomily.

"The break-in was never meant to lead to an open battle; hopefully we won't see anybody at all. Otherwise, the Gunslinger will be the last one we'll have to worry about," said Gary.

"But still, what if he is there?" asked Mary.

Nathan thought for a moment. "Leave him to me, I will take care of him."

"I am sorry to say this, but you are no match for him," Mary said. "Mark stayed behind to see how you dealt with the Gunslinger; he saw exactly what happened to you."

"That's not a fair assessment." Nathan turned to Gary. "Thanks to your brilliant idea of letting me drink that drug, I could hardly stand up steadily then. Believe me, I can deal with him, and this is the only way to move forward."

Gary thought about it and then said, "I suppose it is our only option." He then looked at Mary. "I will need time to work out the details of the break-in; meanwhile, you guys can have a good rest, pull yourselves together."

Gary left.

During the next couple of weeks, Mary and Nathan lived an almost normal life. Apart from occasionally wandering into OBU, they spent much of their time in the basement. Despite the limited space and minimal living standards, they were happy and enjoyed every minute of it.

Each time after their exhausting lovemaking, Mary would pat her naked tummy and tell Nathan that she could feel a new life hatching inside. This gave a completely new meaning to their intimate actions, not merely taking pleasure in the act, but also fulfilling their mission to create a new life.

243

In between the passionate lovemaking, they cooked, washed dishes and sneaked outside of the building to enjoy what nature could offer: rain, moon, wind, clouds and sunshine. They discussed and wondered why people needed all the extras that were now regarded as modern-day essentials and why everyone couldn't just live a simpler life and still have just as much fun.

The wound on Nathan's arm was healing but it would need many months to fully recover and function at full capacity. Fortunately, during his military training in the time-expanded warehouse, he had trained himself to use his left hand as well. At the time, he had only switched which hand he trained with to break the repetitive single hand shooting which became boring after a while. He had also hoped that one day it'd be useful. In the end, after the five years of intensive training, Nathan was almost able to use his left hand as easily as his right. The efforts had clearly paid off in the shootout; his left hand had enabled him to shoot down the Cowboy and the last six agents in the last battle.

Their time together in the basement was like a holiday and like all the most enjoyable holidays, it ended too soon. As Nathan finished cooking their dinner that night, Mary told him that Gary had just left a message and wanted to meet up with them.

Nathan and Mary met Gary in a Starbucks cafe on Oxford Street, the busiest part of Central London. Like other digital versions of cafes in OBU, this international chain was huge and packed with people. As soon as he spotted them walking into the café, Gary stood up and signalled them to follow him out.

Walking along Oxford Street among thousands of overseas tourists and locals, Gary said to Nathan, "Based on your observations, I have mapped out the locations the HQ has appeared in during the last two weeks. Although it changes its location daily, a certain pattern has emerged. Maybe because there has not been anyone capable of cracking its digital camouflage, apart from Nathan of course, the pattern so far has been easily predictable. To prove my point, let's have a wild goose chase along London's streets today."

"What are you talking about?" Mary asked. "What are we chasing?"

"The HQ, naturally." Gary pointed to the subway ahead. "We take the Tube and resurface at Westminster station opposite the London Eye."

"Are you predicting the HQ will be at the London Eye today?" asked Nathan.

"Oh, no, not at the London Eye," Gary said as they got onto the train. "If my prediction is correct, it should be at Westminster Abbey."

"Well, there is only one way to find out," said Mary.

It was quite an interesting phenomenon, that although there were so many fantastic features created by the digital revolutions in OBU—basically people could do anything they liked, such as flying in mid-air, diving deep into oceans and thousands of other adventurous fantasy rides—the basic pre-OBU attractions such as the London Eye were still a must-see for many overseas tourists.

Today was no exception.

They rubbed shoulders with the everlasting crowds who were crossing the Westminster Bridge over the Thames to visit the London Eye, and arrived at Westminster Abbey not far from the Tube station with the same name.

"It doesn't look like anything close to a HQ to me." Mary studied the great church carefully.

On the other hand, Nathan had seen what he was looking for. To ordinary eyes, it was simply Westminster Abbey and if one walked in the door, he would find himself in the church that everyone had seen so many times on TV, but what Nathan had seen was the real digital version under the camouflage of the church mask: the OBU headquarters. The extravagantly decorated building demonstrated the power and wealth of OBU, the globe-dominating corporation. The logo of OBU was seemingly made from thousands of diamonds. The irony was that the digital diamonds were not worth more than plastic ones, maybe a few different lines of coded program. Besides, the only people who could see them were all OBU employees.

Since he hadn't seen anybody go in or out of the building, Nathan suspected that there were secret entrances elsewhere in and out of the HQ. "Gary, your prediction is correct; I can see the building, exactly the same as I have seen it during the last two weeks."

Gary smiled in satisfaction. "To be on the safe side, we should come back a few more times to confirm that my next few predictions for the next few days are also correct."

"What's the location for tomorrow then?" asked Mary.

"Buckingham Palace," said Gary.

"It seems OBU love the old tradition then; the newest and the oldest go together nicely," laughed Nathan.

"I am impressed, Gary; good work." Mary patted Gary's back fondly. "I know you have explained this to me before, but I still don't get it: why would they need to set their HQ somewhere in OBU?"

"Well, The HQ is just a huge database, or the centre of all databases in OBU. In order for the employees and other databases to access it, the HQ has to give out its access address or AD as the term is used in OBU. Because everything in OBU is represented as visual images, it is much easier to camouflage it on top of an easily recognized building or landmark," Gary said. "In fact, it has nothing to do with the building it sits on at the moment; if you walked into Westminster Abbey now, you would still not see more than the church itself. To get into the HQ, one has to have the right access privilege."

"Well, it's still as clear as muddy water to me but never mind," Mary said.

"So, if we had the correct security codes and entered it, we would see the HQ itself, rather than the church; similar to the concept of different dimensions, am I right?" said Nathan.

"Bingo," said Gary.

"Do you mean that normal people could still enter the Abbey while the HQ staff are doing their business on top of these visitors?" asked Mary.

"They share the same digital space but in different dimensions, so they wouldn't be on top of each other," explained Gary.

Mary thought about it and decided not to ask any more questions.

"Gary, what does the virus look like?" asked Nathan.

"We are not talking about it here." Gary turned and walked away. Mary and Nathan followed.

In a large meeting room in an unknown location, a group of people sat around a large oval-shaped table. The person at the head of the table was seated in front of a large OBU symbol, with a 'chairman' sign perched on the table in front of him. He cleared his throat a couple of times before speaking. "Can anyone tell me what happened?"

The person in a black suit behind a 'chief security officer' sign (CSO) said, "We lost a whole unit of field agents in London in the operation to arrest Mary O'Brian."

"How could the operation have gone so badly?" asked the chairman.

"I am afraid it's beyond my department." The CSO turned. "Cathy, would you please explain the details of the operation."

Cathy, Nathan's ex-girlfriend, with a 'special services' sign in front of her on the table, said, "Our undercover agent, Amy Kelly, had been with SOH for over a decade and has reported to Mary O'Brian directly for the last five years. She was also our deepest undercover agent inside SOH. Two weeks ago, she reported back the exact location of Mary O'Brian's hideout, so we launched the operation to arrest Mary O'Brian."

"So?" asked the chairman.

"Due to the location being so deep underground, we were unable to receive the agents' signals so didn't know exactly what was happening." Cathy took a deep breath and then continued. "When the backup unit arrived, all of our agents, together with six SOH members, and Amy Kelly, were all shot dead."

"Was Mary O'Brian also dead?" asked the chairman.

"No, it appears that Mary O'Brian escaped," Cathy said.

"But how?" said the CSO. "We sent in two dozen of our best field agents."

"Our best guess is that Nathan Jenkins killed most of the agents, and Mary O'Brian's men killed the rest," Cathy said without any emotion.

"Who is this Nathan Jenkins?" asked the chairman.

Cathy glanced at the CSO, and then spoke slowly. "Nathan Jenkins is my ex-boyfriend. He disappeared fifteen years ago, and everyone assumed he was dead but he reappeared a few weeks ago. According to his own words, he woke up one day and found that he was fifteen years in the future. Based on his ignorance about OBU, it's reasonable to believe that he was absent from society during the last fifteen years and telling the truth."

"And?" said the chairman.

"He somehow possesses extraordinary hand-to-hand combat ability and fast reaction times; we believe he wiped out the Cowboy and his elite unit single-handedly," said Cathy.

"The Cowboy!" The Chairman turned to the CSO. "Why didn't anyone report this to me?"

"We thought we could handle it," mumbled the CSO.

"Obviously not." The chairman turned to Cathy. "Please continue."

"In fact, we arrested him two weeks ago, but Mary O'Brian managed to break into the holding cell and rescue him. It happened just before the operation. We believe that Mary O'Brian put a tracking device inside Nathan Jenkins' clothes," said Cathy.

"This is totally unacceptable." the chairman gazed at the CSO. "You are fired." He then looked around the table, stopping at Cathy. "Have you heard any more about Mary O'Brian or this Nathan Jenkins?"

"No, but we believe they are planning a major attack on OBU, possibly a direct hit on our HQ," said Cathy.

249

The chairman turned to the CSO. "What have you done to protect our HQ?"

The CSO said, "We put more agents on guard at the HQ, but we don't believe they will be able to locate the HQ's position; our security software has never been cracked before."

"I wouldn't bet anything on your words." The chairman turned to the guy with a 'chief information officer' (CIO) sign. "Is it possible to compartmentalize OBU to minimize the risk or move the HQ out of London entirely?"

The CIO said, "It's a very time-consuming task to change the access arrangement between HQ and the rest of OBU and we have to keep the whole system running all the time; otherwise, the costs of any outages are huge. Anyway, we have done our best to minimize the exposure and will continue to do so."

The chairman stared at the CIO. "What's the worst-case scenario if Mary O'Brian succeeds?"

"It'd depend on when it happened; if it happens right now, we would lose OBU in its entirety, but we are very close to completing the compartmentalizing task," said the CIO.

"Can't we guard every inch inside HQ?" asked the chairman.

"If they get inside HQ, with over fifty thousand staff working there at any time, it would be impossible to identify them and they could introduce the virus at any entry point within the HQ. The short answer is that we can't do anything after they gain entry to the HQ," said the CSO.

"Are you telling me there is nothing we can do to secure HQ?" asked the chairman.

"I do have one last card up my sleeve, sir." Cathy told everyone about the details of her plan.

The chairman turned to the CIO. "You use as many resources as required to finish the compartmentalizing task as soon as possible." He then turned to Cathy. "You will be in charge of the security of HQ directly."

"Yes, sir," said Cathy.

**Chapter 35**

The British Museum was one of the most visited hotspots in London, and today's everlasting crowds once more proved that point. As they rubbed shoulders with thousands of overseas visitors in the digital world, Mary whispered to Nathan, "Are you sure this is the right place?" Gary's expression also showed his doubts.

Nathan scanned around and then whispered back to Mary, "Yes, it is from the outside, I just haven't found the entry point yet."

"Is it always this hard to find the entry point?" asked Gary in a quiet voice.

"How would I know? This is also my first time having to look for it." Nathan pushed through the crowds, scanning around. He started to doubt his newly gained ability; had he really seen through the HQ mask or was it just wishful thinking? They had been walking up and down the halls of the enormous museum for a couple of hours now, through the ancient Greece and Roman sections to the Middle East and ancient Egypt area on the ground level, right to the upper level of Europe and Asia, but he hadn't seen anything remotely related to a HQ entry point. When they came down to the ground floor again, they stopped and stood in front of a round building underneath the huge dome. Mary said, "Do you think they suddenly changed the location?"

Gary shook his head. "Unlikely because the implications are too much to manage if they still want OBU in service; it'd take months to organize such a huge change."

"So the only explanation is that they put another layer of masks on top of the normal mask," Nathan said thoughtfully.

"But why can't you see through it?" asked Mary.

Gary thought for a while and said slowly, "We haven't checked any toilets yet."

"Oh no, don't tell me the entry points are inside the toilets?" said Mary.

"There is only one way to find out." Nathan led the way towards the nearest bathroom.

It was an awkward experience for Nathan to look in the female bathrooms via Mary's jumper, but he searched every cubicle. Finally, the efforts paid off; Nathan spotted the entry point in the male toilets on level 2 next to the Korea section.

Mary walked into the toilets quickly, ignoring a few curious glances from other visitors. They all squeezed into the one cubicle. "Gary, it's your turn."

"I can't see anything here except the toilet seat, toilet paper, and cubicle panels," said Gary.

Of course, it was quite a different view to Nathan's eyes. They were no longer inside the toilet cubicle, but in front of a stainless-steel door. He pointed at the scan point. "Gary, scan your entry card here."

"Mate, that's the toilet paper roll," laughed Gary.

"For God's sake, just do it, Gary," said Mary.

Gary took his card and was about to put it on top of the toilet roll; Nathan stopped him.

"What's the matter?" Mary asked.

Nathan closed his eyes, concentrating for a few seconds. He opened his eyes and said, "I have a bad feeling that this is a trap."

"What?" asked both Mary and Gary at the same time.

"Trust me on this; my instincts have been proved right before," Nathan said.

"What should we do then?" Gary looked at Mary.

Nathan spoke before Mary could answer the question. "I am going in, but I want you both to stay out of OBU." He put his hand up to stop Mary's oncoming objections. "If it's not a trap, I am more than capable of gaining entry and loading the virus, but if it is a trap you two would be more burden than help when facing the agents."

Mary put her hand on Nathan's cheek. "I can't let you take the risk alone. I am happy to die with you."

"Mary, I am not going to die; it's just much easier for me to do it alone."

"Nathan is right." Gary passed the security card to Nathan, and also took another card out of his pocket. "This is the virus that we discussed in detail. Are you sure you know how to load it?"

Nathan nodded, then thought about something else. He took his mask off and passed it to Gary. "If by any chance I am captured or killed, without the mask they won't be able to trace my real body, right?"

Gary put Nathan's mask into his own pocket. "They would eventually find your login point, but it would take a while because they would have to go through every single data entry in order to find yours. There are billions of entries every day so it'd take them quite some time, but they would find you eventually."

Tears filled Mary's eyes. "Nathan, please let me go with you…I don't want you to die alone."

Nathan chuckled. "Come on, Mary, it's not certain that I'm going to die. Remember we are going to destroy OBU for Amy and our many other friends who have died for this, and we've still got to save humanity."

Mary put both her arms round Nathan's neck, and kissed him for a very long time. Gary patted Nathan on his back before walking silently out of the cubicle.

Finally, Mary released her lips from Nathan's, but still kept hold of his neck. She looked into his eyes for a long time and then said, "Nathan, I will guard your real body until you are back with me, regardless of what happens to you in OBU. That is a promise."

Nathan waited until Gary confirmed that he and Mary had both left the premises safely via his jumper, and then he took a deep breath. He swiped the security card over the scan spot. Sparks flashed out and the toilet disappeared instantly. He looked around; he was now inside a large hall, the entry hall of the headquarters of OBU Corporation, but he was the only person around.

It was strange, indeed. Nathan paused for a moment, then walked to a lift. The doors opened and Nathan walked in. There was nobody inside the lift; this didn't look good at all. He drew his gun and made sure it was ready to fire.

The lift doors opened smoothly, and Nathan found that he was back to where he started: he now stood inside the museum again; it was the Korea section. Looking back, Nathan saw the door he had just come out of was the toilet door he went through a few minutes ago, but there was not a single visitor to be seen.

"Throw your weapon down and raise both hands above your head."

Nathan dropped his gun to the floor and raised both of his hands slowly.

Nathan turned; his worst nightmare was coming to life in front of his eyes. The Gunslinger, followed by two dozen elite agents, stood about twenty feet away; their guns were all aimed at him.

"I have to admit that this was a very clever trap, and I walked right into it stupidly," Nathan said.

"Don't be too harsh on yourself," laughed the Gunslinger.

"I guess this is a duplicated digital version of the museum laid on top of the HQ, right?" Nathan said.

"Yes, it is," said the Gunslinger.

"I also guess that there is no way out for me, right?" asked Nathan.

"Correct again; even if by some miracle you get out, you would face a hundred soldiers who are ready to shoot you on sight," the Gunslinger said. "Nathan, I almost feel sorry that I have to kill you."

Nathan shrugged. "That's life, isn't it?"

Whilst talking to the Gunslinger, Nathan was desperately trying to figure out a way out of the situation. Sadly, he seemed to have no options at all: he was outgunned and had also been disarmed. Even if he had his gun in his hand, Nathan had no doubt that the Gunslinger was still faster than him. Had he really run out of options?

He had been in this situation when facing the Cowboy; he had managed to shift his heart away from its normal location to survive the Cowboy's bullets, but it was a big gamble. If the Cowboy had shot his head, he would have been long dead. He could be sure that he would not be able to use the same trick again today: the Gunslinger would be fast enough to put a bullet into both his heart and head. After he died, OBU would live and grow and the human race would be wiped out in a couple of decades. He couldn't let that happen.

His mind went back to Master Wuwei. What would the Master do in this situation? Wuwei, as the fundamental principle of Taoism, doesn't fight force with force, rather follows the flow. It was easy to say it in theory but how could he put it in practical terms to help him out of this certain death situation? He needed to think outside of the box.

Taoism believes that opposites are true, such as the greatest white seems black; greatest forward seems backward; the wisest man seems like a fool; but how could he apply this to his situation?

Nathan knew clearly that he could not be faster than the Gunslinger and had no chance of outshooting the dozens of agents as well, but what if he didn't have to. It seemed like an unthinkable idea, but that's Taoism, thinking outside of the box.

As soon as the concept jumped into his mind, Nathan immediately thought of solutions for part of his problem, but not the critical part. His meditation had helped him self-heal and escape certain death with the Cowboy, but it was not good enough to help him survive the Gunslinger's bullets. If he couldn't achieve it by meditation, why should he meditate at all? Just then, as if lightning had struck through his foggy mind, Nathan knew exactly what he had to do.

The Gunslinger waved his arm. "Cuff him and take him to the cell. Nathan, I will spend a long session with you this time and see how much pain you are able to endure before you break down."

Nathan smiled. "Just wait a moment. You know I won't let you arrest me; I would rather die than face your torture again. Besides, you'll kill me in the end anyway, so what's the point of suffering."

The Gunslinger became alarmed; his hand was a fraction closer to his gun, and the rest of the agents were also raising their guns to aim at Nathan.

## Chapter 36

"Please don't overreact; it was merely a statement. I know you want to know how I killed the Cowboy and his entire unit; unfortunately, there is only one way to find out," Nathan said.

The Gunslinger glanced at the agents once. "Do you want to have a duel with me? Why would I agree to that, when I have you under arrest now?"

Nathan's hands were still raised high. "You don't have to accept it at all; you could shoot me dead like this, or kill me during a duel. I know you are too proud to refuse this once-in-a-lifetime experience. Let's face it, how many worthy opponents have you found during your career? If you don't find out how I killed the Cowboy and his entire unit single-handedly today, you will spend the rest of your life wondering about it. Facing death is the ultimate thrill in your life, and this is definitely the most thrilling event you will ever get. It's most likely that you will shoot me, but there will always be a small chance, no matter how small it might be, that I could kill you in the same way I killed the Cowboy. So now you must decide: face the exciting danger of death, or kill me now. You know you can't refuse the challenge. What do you say?"

The expressions on the Gunslinger's face showed that he had a hard time making the decision. The agent beside him said, "Sir, I would strongly recommend against any decision like that."

The Gunslinger didn't respond; he was still thinking.

Nathan said again, "I will only accept the challenge alone. Yes, I want all of your agents out of the building, only you and me facing each other. Like you said, there

259

is no way out of here, so even if by some miracle I win the standoff, I would still be unable to escape, but if you win, which is more likely in this situation, you would be the best shooter alive."

"Sir, he must have some dirty tricks up his sleeve; please don't even consider it," the agent said to the Gunslinger again.

Nathan shook his hands high in the air. "I am right in front of you, empty handed. You can see exactly what I have, no tricks whatsoever."

The Gunslinger seemed to be making up his mind. He took his gun out of his holster and pointed it at Nathan. Just as Nathan wondered if his strategy had failed, the Gunslinger said, "Pick up your gun with your thumb and index finger; slowly put it under your belt."

"Sir, please don't do it," urged the agent beside the Gunslinger.

The Gunslinger ignored him. He spoke loudly to Nathan. "Walk down the stairs slowly; my gun will be on your back the whole time, so don't do anything stupid."

Nathan walked downstairs as required, and the Gunslinger and the agents followed. They walked down to the ground floor and the entrance gate.

"Move away from the gate." The Gunslinger gazed at Nathan while speaking. "You all get out of the building; after you are out, seal the gate. If I am not out within five minutes, please consider me dead and proceed with the next stage of the operation."

"Sir, you don't need to take the risk; I strongly suggest against it," the agent said.

"Yes, I do; it's not only for my own personal pride, but also to help the agency to understand potential threats. If I die today, you will know the reason by analysing the records. I do this to eliminate future threats to OBU," the Gunslinger said.

"Sir, we need authorization from the board for your decision," argued the agent.

The Gunslinger didn't move his gaze away from Nathan. "I have the privilege and authority to make my own decision in the battlefield. Please get out of the building, all of you."

"Sir, please take care," the agent said as he and the rest of the agents went out of the gate. The large gate shut again behind them. The large hall suddenly became very quiet as deadly silence fell over them.

Nathan said, "Before we start, could I please ask you a couple of questions? They are very important to me personally and I want to know the answers so I can die in peace."

The Gunslinger thought about it. "I'll try my best to answer them."

"Did anyone tip off the Cowboy on how to find us in the warehouse?" asked Nathan.

"No, it was purely a coincidence; he found the warehouse by chance."

"How did you know we were in the nightclub when you arrested me?"

"We had a tracking device on Amy Kelly, but she didn't know about it."

"One last question: did Amy inform you about our secret hideout?"

"No, we found it by using the tracking device on her," the Gunslinger said. "Nathan, we figured out what you were doing in the nightclub, and we intentionally let Mary O'Brian rescue you so we could find your secret hideout. Somehow you managed to escape with Mary

O'Brian when we raided the hideout, but we knew you would try to come here, and we were right: you walked right into this trap."

Nathan shook his head, appearing sad and depressed. "Thanks for answering my questions; I can die in peace now. Shall we get the ball rolling?"

Nathan and the Gunslinger stood about fifteen feet apart, staring at each other. They were watching each other's eyes for the signal to act. They both had their hands down by their sides, next to their guns; their facial muscles appeared relaxed, but their concentration was absolute.

The air was so heavy you could have sliced it with a knife.

Then it happened. It happened so fast that you would need a high-speed camera to see exactly what happened. It seemed that both Nathan and the Gunslinger drew their guns, raised them up and fired at exactly the same time, but the results were quite different.

The Gunslinger fell down with an expression of disbelief on his face. Nathan remained standing.

Nathan remembered that Master Wuwei had told him the ultimate meditation is not meditating at all; in practice, it means one could sink into a state of nothingness, the ultimate level of meditation. So if he could accept his whole existence in OBU as merely imagination, how could anything harm him at all? It was enlightenment and yet still a giant leap of faith. Nathan could still clearly see the puzzled and astonished look on the Gunslinger's face when he saw that his bullets hit Nathan but did no damage. The Gunslinger's first bullet hit Nathan's heart and the second hit his head, even before Nathan's bullets had left his gun; the Gunslinger was indeed faster than Nathan. Nathan blinked his eyes, still in disbelief that he had survived the bullets.

Nathan looked around, trying to figure out what to do next, and then it happened: accompanied by an enormous explosion, the whole museum building was blown up and engulfed in a giant ball of fire and smoke.

It was the same meeting room at the unknown location. The OBU chairman asked, "Cathy, do you know that Amy Kelly turned against us? It was her shooting of the agents that enabled Nathan Jenkins and Mary O'Brian to escape."

Cathy sat at the oval table looking quite depressed. "Sir, how do you know the details? I thought Amy Kelly and all the agents died in the hideout shooting."

"Rob, you tell her." The chairman nodded to a guy opposite Cathy.

Rob Sharp, the director of the games department, spoke in a smug voice. "We dug out the information from Amy Kelly's brain."

"Amy Kelly? I thought she was dead," asked Cathy.

"Yes, she is indeed dead, but we managed to retrieve her memories just in time," said the director.

"I thought it was impossible to retrieve someone's memories," asked Cathy.

"Yes and no." Rob Sharp paused, scanning the table, and then said, "It's not possible to retrieve someone's memories when he is alive because the method we use would kill him, but it's okay if the person has already died. Cutting a long story short, we just had to get Amy Kelly hooked into our device before it was too late."

"Based on her memories, it seems that Amy Kelly didn't report much about Nathan Jenkins back to you, supposedly her handler," said the chairman.

"I have to admit that I never doubted Amy Kelly's loyalty," said Cathy.

"You should have," the director said. "It seems that Amy Kelly fell in love with Nathan Jenkins and she betrayed us in order to protect Nathan Jenkins."

"Amy had fallen in love with Nathan? How did I miss that?" Cathy lowered her gaze, mumbling.

"Cathy, you failed in your duty; due to your relationship with Nathan Jenkins, you are officially off this case," said the chairman.

"Off what case? I thought Nathan was killed when the museum blew up?" asked Cathy.

"No, he is not dead yet, but he will be soon enough." The director grinned.

Made in the USA
Middletown, DE
24 May 2021